CARTOON NETWORK

STEVEN UNIVERSE

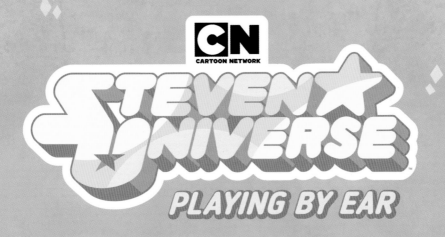

PLAYING BY EAR

kaboom!

WWW.BOOM-STUDIOS.COM

STEVEN UNIVERSE ONGOING Volume Six, February 2020. Published by KaBOOM!, a division of Boom Entertainment, Inc. STEVEN UNIVERSE, CARTOON NETWORK, the logos, and all related characters and elements are trademarks of and © Cartoon Network. A WarnerMedia Company. All rights reserved. (S20) Originally published in single magazine form as STEVEN UNIVERSE ONGOING No. 21-24 © Cartoon Network. A WarnerMedia Company. All rights reserved. (S19) KaBOOM!™ and the KaBOOM! logo are trademarks of Boom Entertainment, Inc., registered in various countries and categories. All characters, events, and institutions depicted herein are fictional. Any similarity between any of the names, characters, persons, events, and/or institutions in this publication to actual names, characters, and persons, whether living or dead, events, and/ or institutions is unintended and purely coincidental. KaBOOM! does not read or accept unsolicited submissions of ideas, stories, or artwork.

BOOM! Studios, 5670 Wilshire Boulevard, Suite 400, Los Angeles, CA 90036-5679. Printed in China. First Printing.

ISBN: 978-1-68415-489-0, eISBN: 978-1-64144-647-1

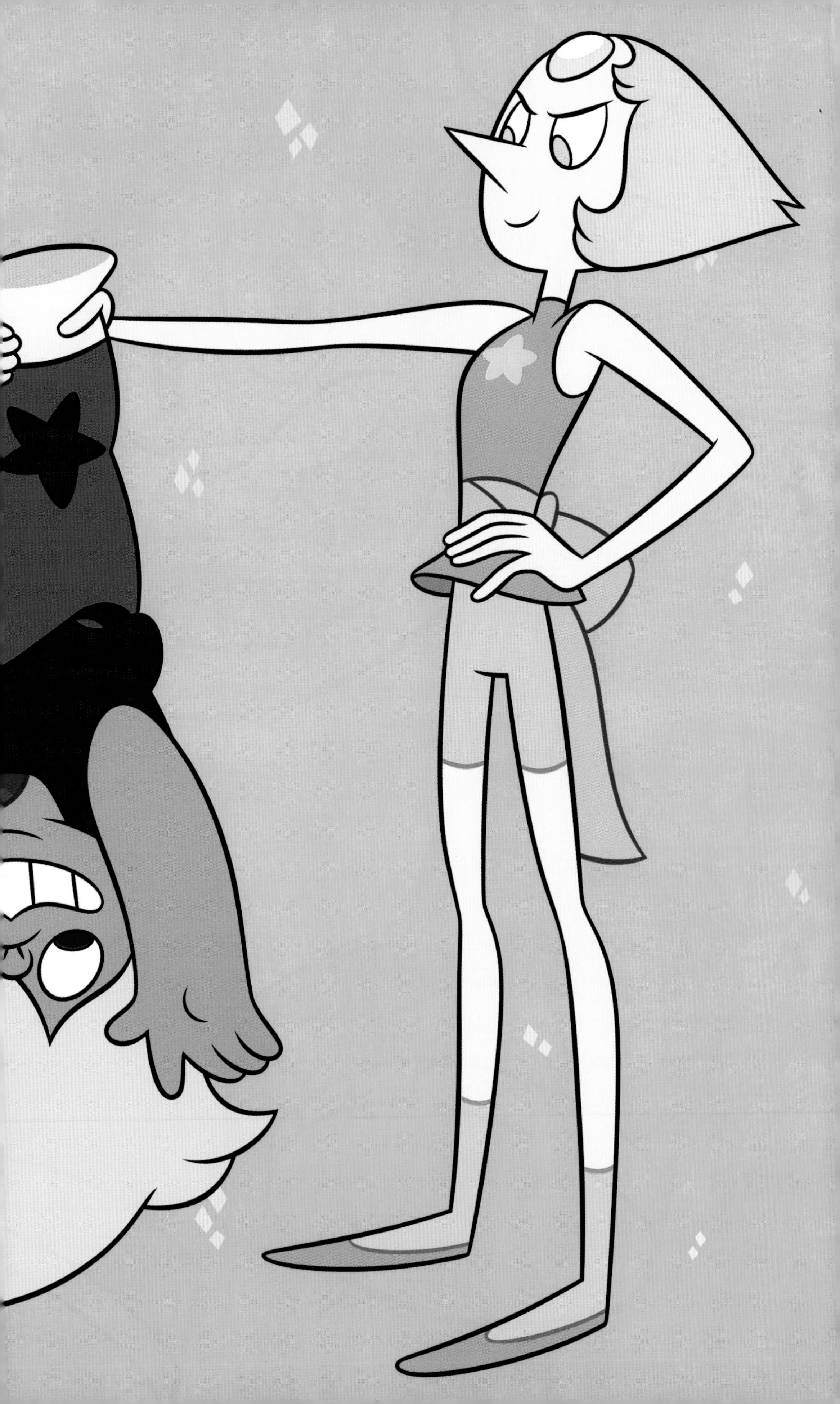

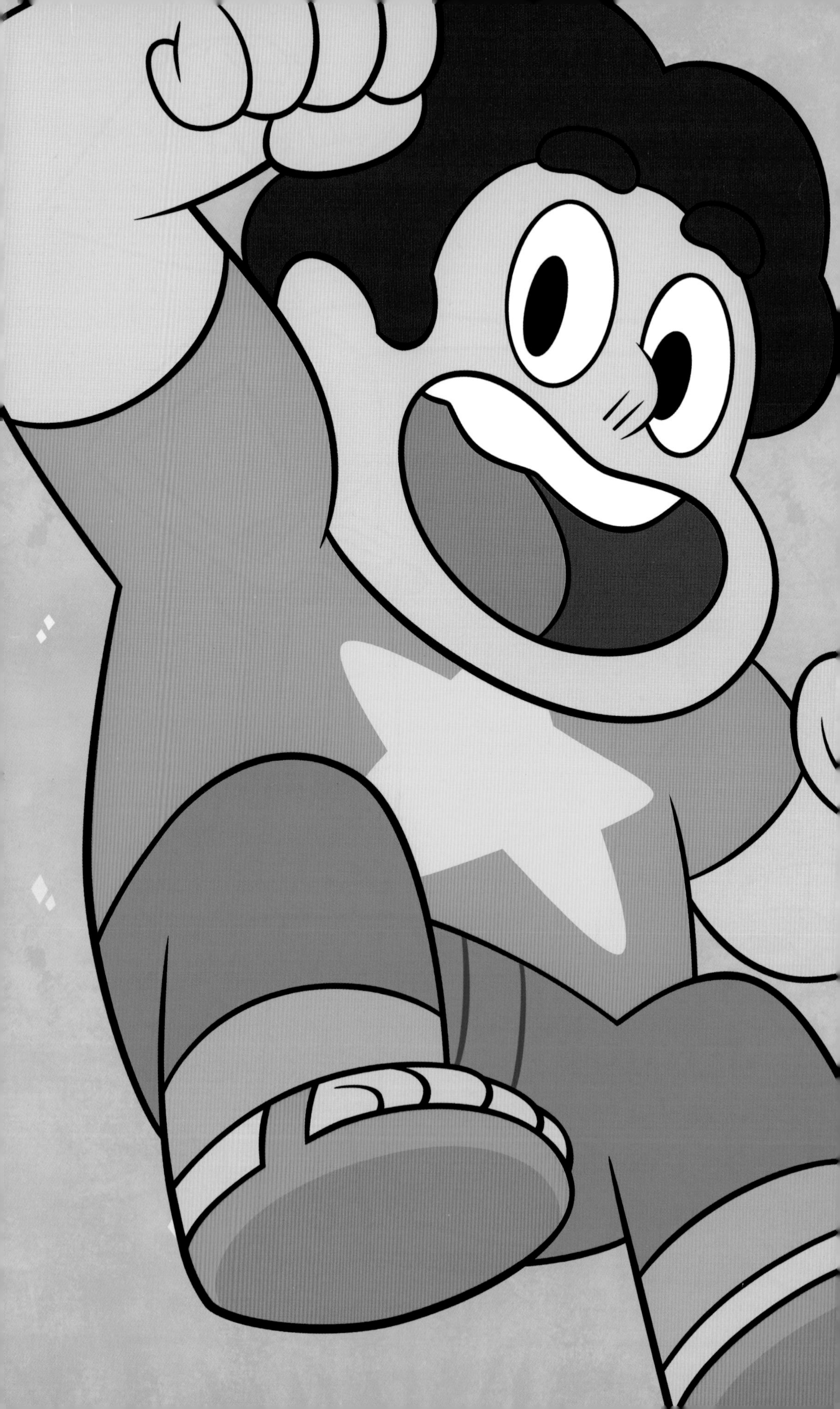

STEVEN UNIVERSE
PLAYING BY EAR

created by
REBECCA SUGAR

written by
GRACE KRAFT

illustrated by
RII ABREGO

colors by
WHITNEY COGAR

letters by
MIKE FIORENTINO

cover by
MISSY PEÑA

series designer
GRACE PARK

series assistant editor
MICHAEL MOCCIO

collection designer
MARIE KRUPINA

editor
MATTHEW LEVINE

Special thanks to
Marisa Marionakis, Janet No, Austin Page,
Conrad Montgomery, Jackie Buscarino and
the wonderful folks at Cartoon Network.

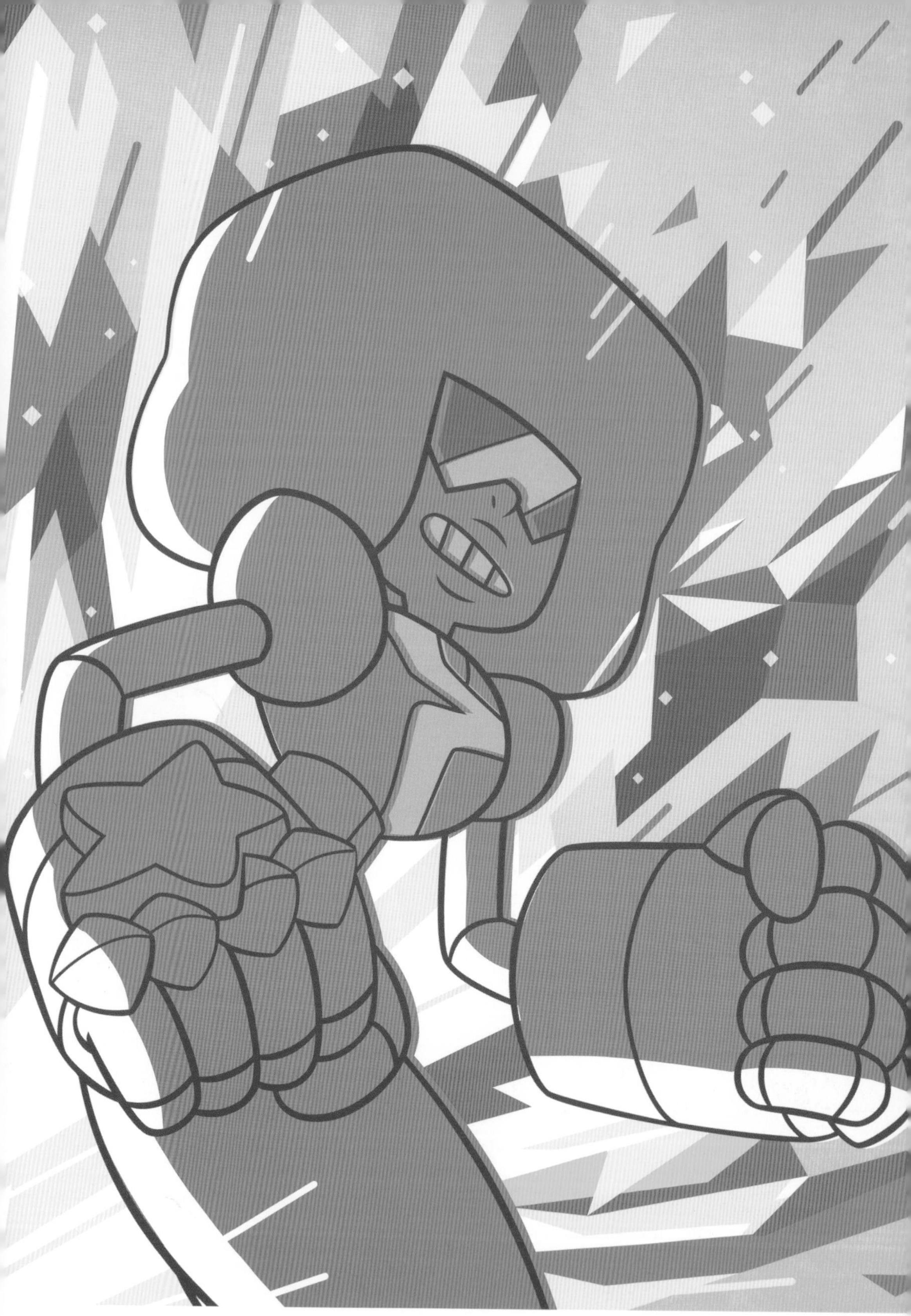

CHAPTER TWENTY-ONE

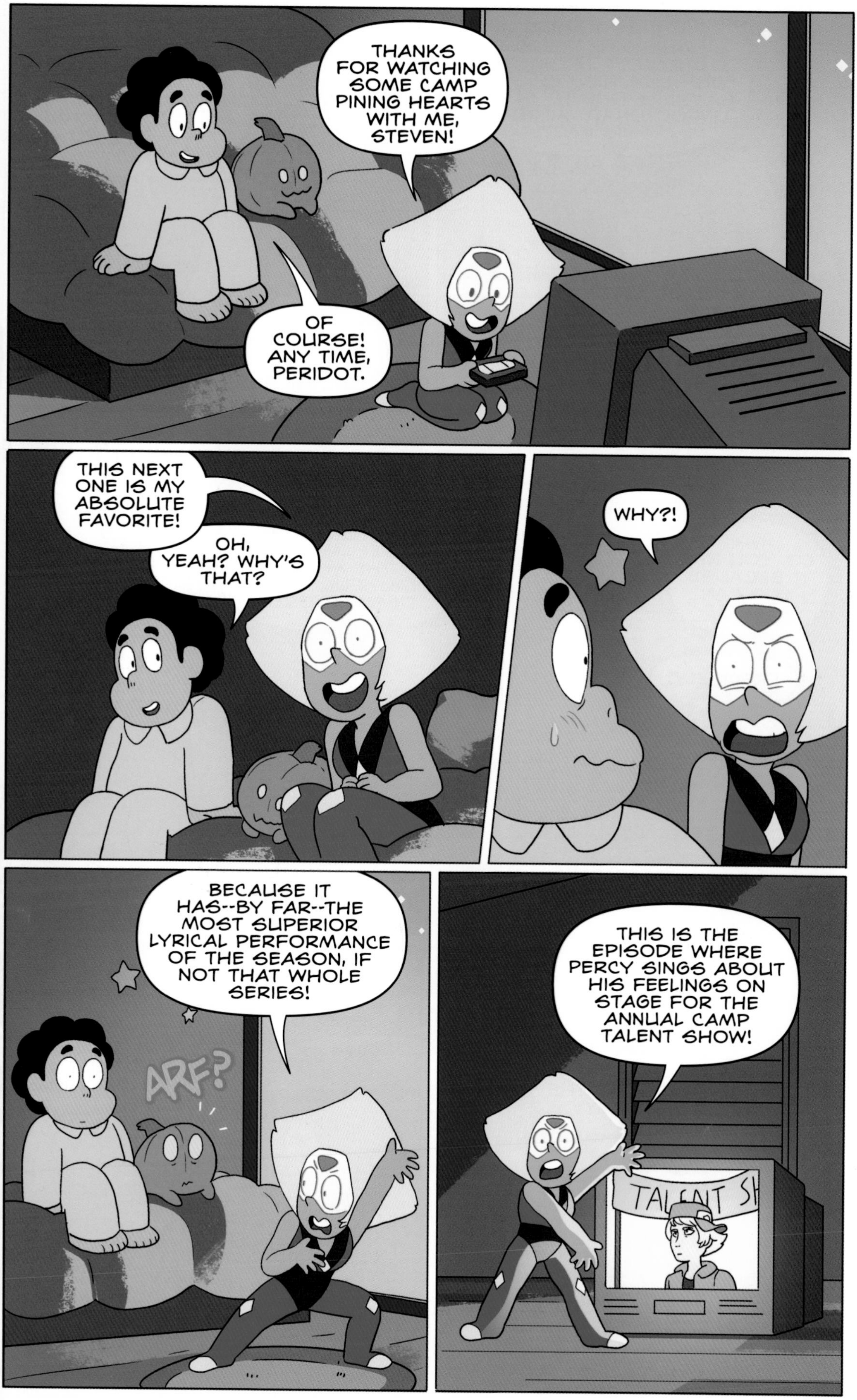
THANKS FOR WATCHING SOME CAMP PINING HEARTS WITH ME, STEVEN!
OF COURSE! ANY TIME, PERIDOT.
THIS NEXT ONE IS MY ABSOLUTE FAVORITE!
OH, YEAH? WHY'S THAT?
WHY?!
BECAUSE IT HAS--BY FAR--THE MOST SUPERIOR LYRICAL PERFORMANCE OF THE SEASON, IF NOT THAT WHOLE SERIES!
ARF?
THIS IS THE EPISODE WHERE PERCY SINGS ABOUT HIS FEELINGS ON STAGE FOR THE ANNUAL CAMP TALENT SHOW!
TALENT SH

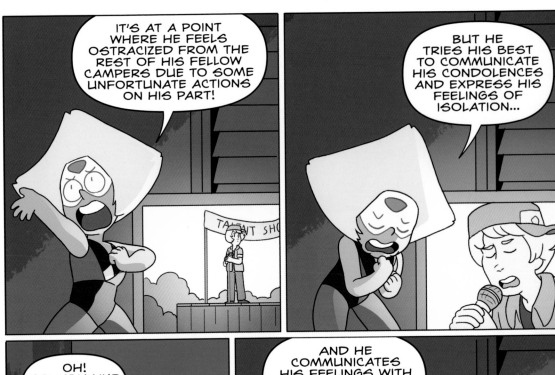

IT'S AT A POINT WHERE HE FEELS OSTRACIZED FROM THE REST OF HIS FELLOW CAMPERS DUE TO SOME UNFORTUNATE ACTIONS ON HIS PART!

TALENT SHO

BUT HE TRIES HIS BEST TO COMMUNICATE HIS CONDOLENCES AND EXPRESS HIS FEELINGS OF ISOLATION...

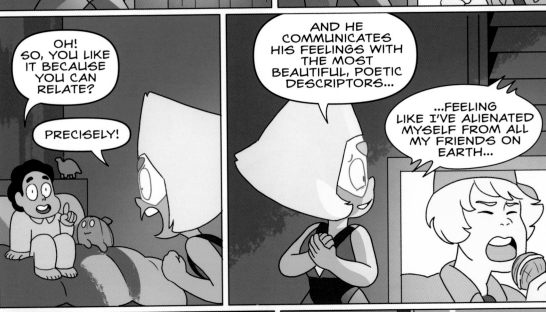

OH! SO, YOU LIKE IT BECAUSE YOU CAN RELATE?

PRECISELY!

AND HE COMMUNICATES HIS FEELINGS WITH THE MOST BEAUTIFUL, POETIC DESCRIPTORS...

...FEELING LIKE I'VE ALIENATED MYSELF FROM ALL MY FRIENDS ON EARTH...

BUT I JUST WANT SOMEONE

TO STAND WITH ME

AND LOOK AT THE SKYYYYY

TOGETHER...

AWW... THAT'S SO SWEET!

I KNOW RIGHT!

OH, IT'S JUST SO PERFECT! SINCERE AND RELATABLE.

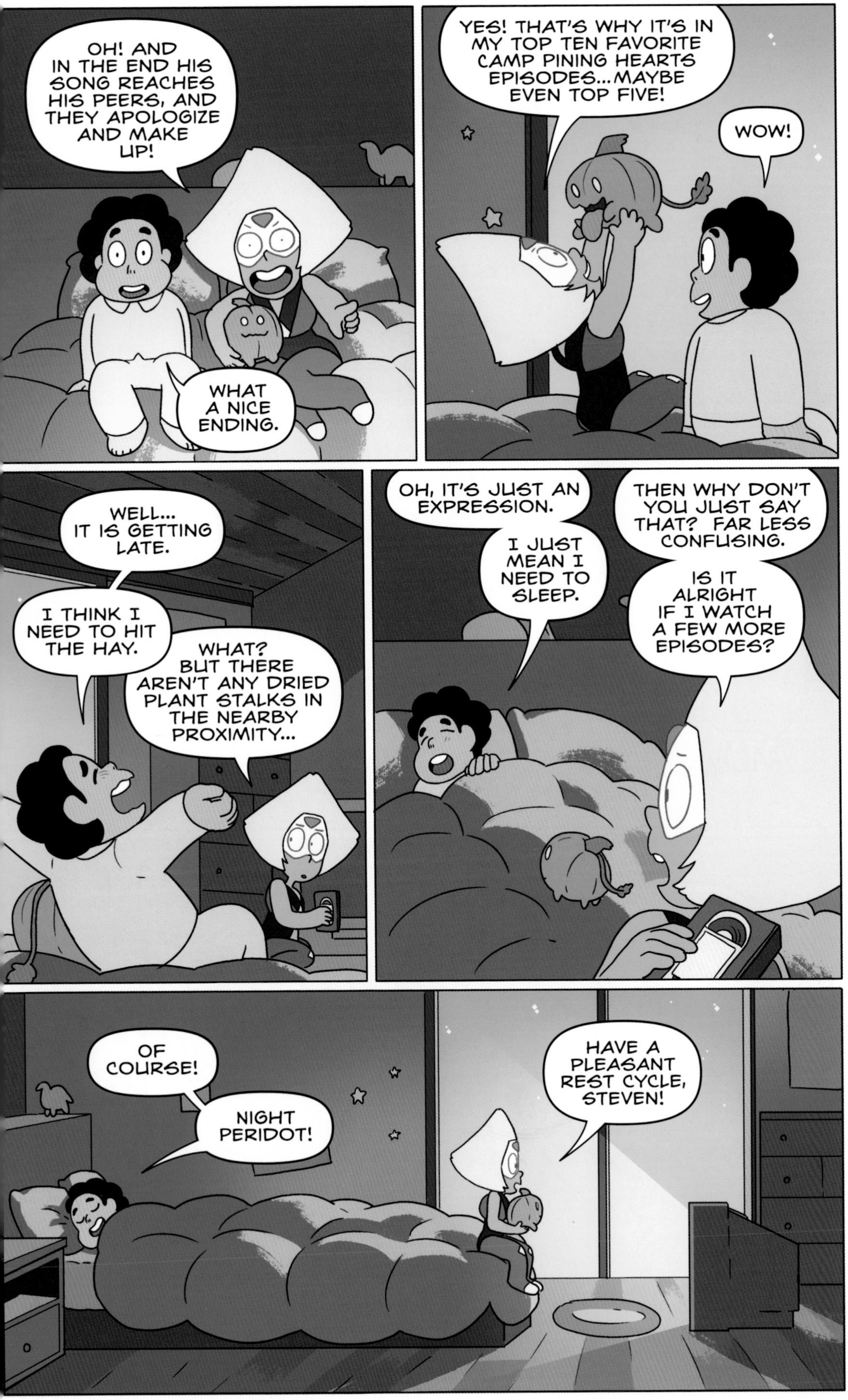
OH! AND IN THE END HIS SONG REACHES HIS PEERS, AND THEY APOLOGIZE AND MAKE UP!
WHAT A NICE ENDING.
YES! THAT'S WHY IT'S IN MY TOP TEN FAVORITE CAMP PINING HEARTS EPISODES...MAYBE EVEN TOP FIVE!
WOW!
WELL... IT IS GETTING LATE.
I THINK I NEED TO HIT THE HAY.
WHAT? BUT THERE AREN'T ANY DRIED PLANT STALKS IN THE NEARBY PROXIMITY...
OH, IT'S JUST AN EXPRESSION.
I JUST MEAN I NEED TO SLEEP.
THEN WHY DON'T YOU JUST SAY THAT? FAR LESS CONFUSING.
IS IT ALRIGHT IF I WATCH A FEW MORE EPISODES?
OF COURSE!
NIGHT PERIDOT!
HAVE A PLEASANT REST CYCLE, STEVEN!

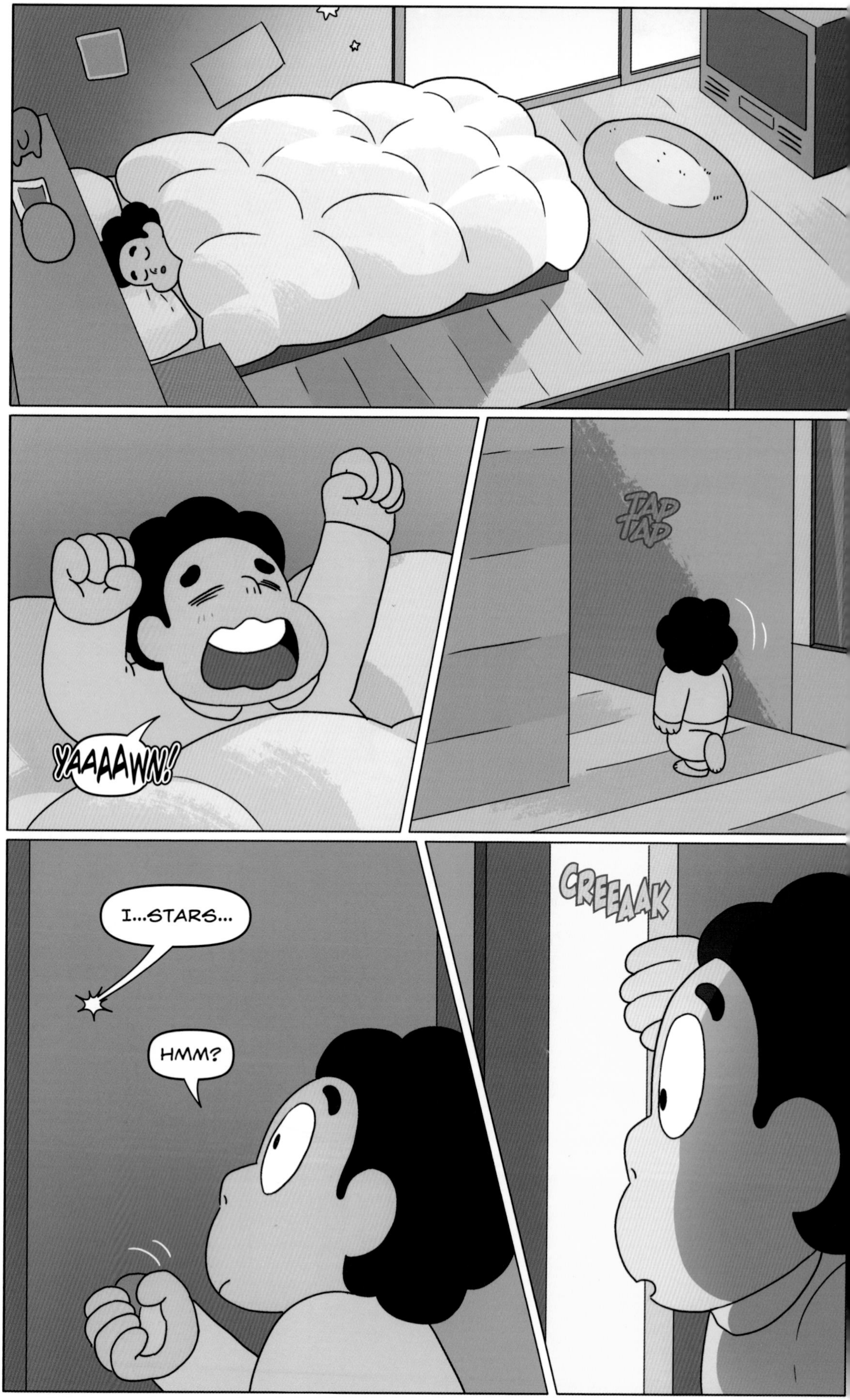
YAAAAWN!
TAP TAP
I...STARS...
HMM?
CREEAAK

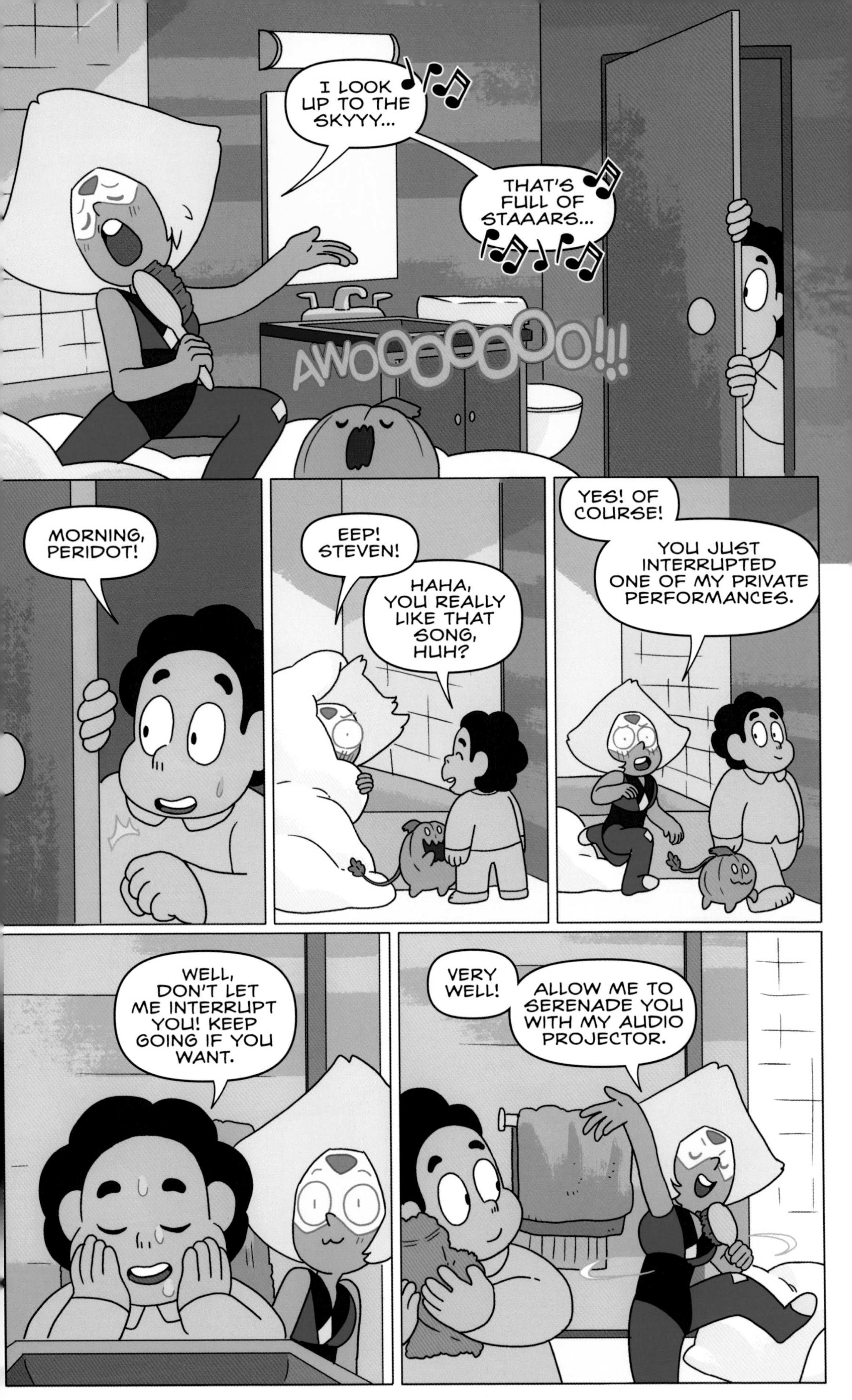
I LOOK UP TO THE SKYYY...
THAT'S FULL OF STAAARS...
AWOOOOOOOO!!!
MORNING, PERIDOT!
EEP! STEVEN!
HAHA, YOU REALLY LIKE THAT SONG, HUH?
YES! OF COURSE!
YOU JUST INTERRUPTED ONE OF MY PRIVATE PERFORMANCES.
WELL, DON'T LET ME INTERRUPT YOU! KEEP GOING IF YOU WANT.
VERY WELL!
ALLOW ME TO SERENADE YOU WITH MY AUDIO PROJECTOR.

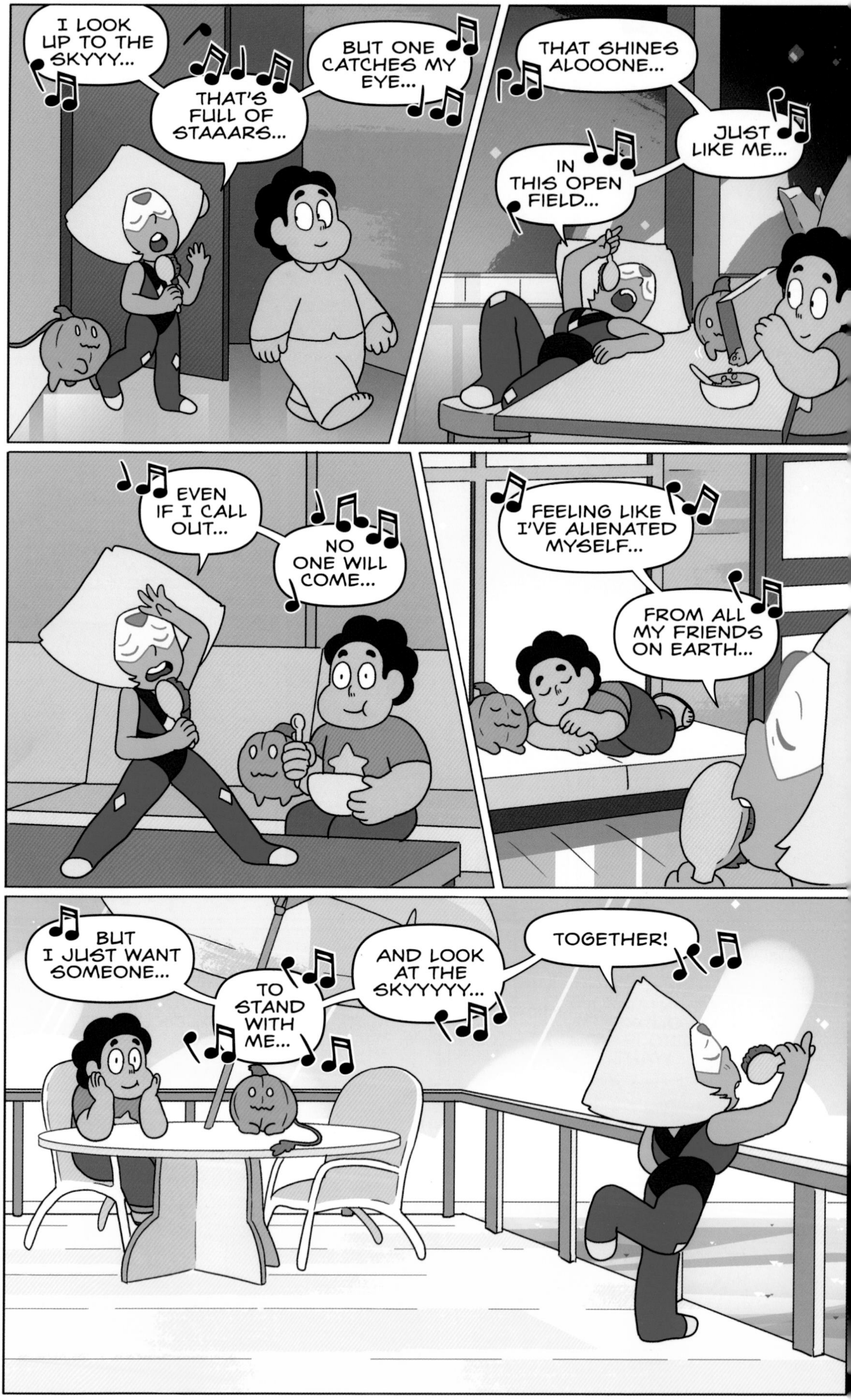

I LOOK UP TO THE SKYYY...
THAT'S FULL OF STAAARS...
BUT ONE CATCHES MY EYE...
THAT SHINES ALOOONE...
IN THIS OPEN FIELD...
JUST LIKE ME...
EVEN IF I CALL OUT...
NO ONE WILL COME...
FEELING LIKE I'VE ALIENATED MYSELF...
FROM ALL MY FRIENDS ON EARTH...
BUT I JUST WANT SOMEONE...
TO STAND WITH ME...
AND LOOK AT THE SKYYYYY...
TOGETHER!

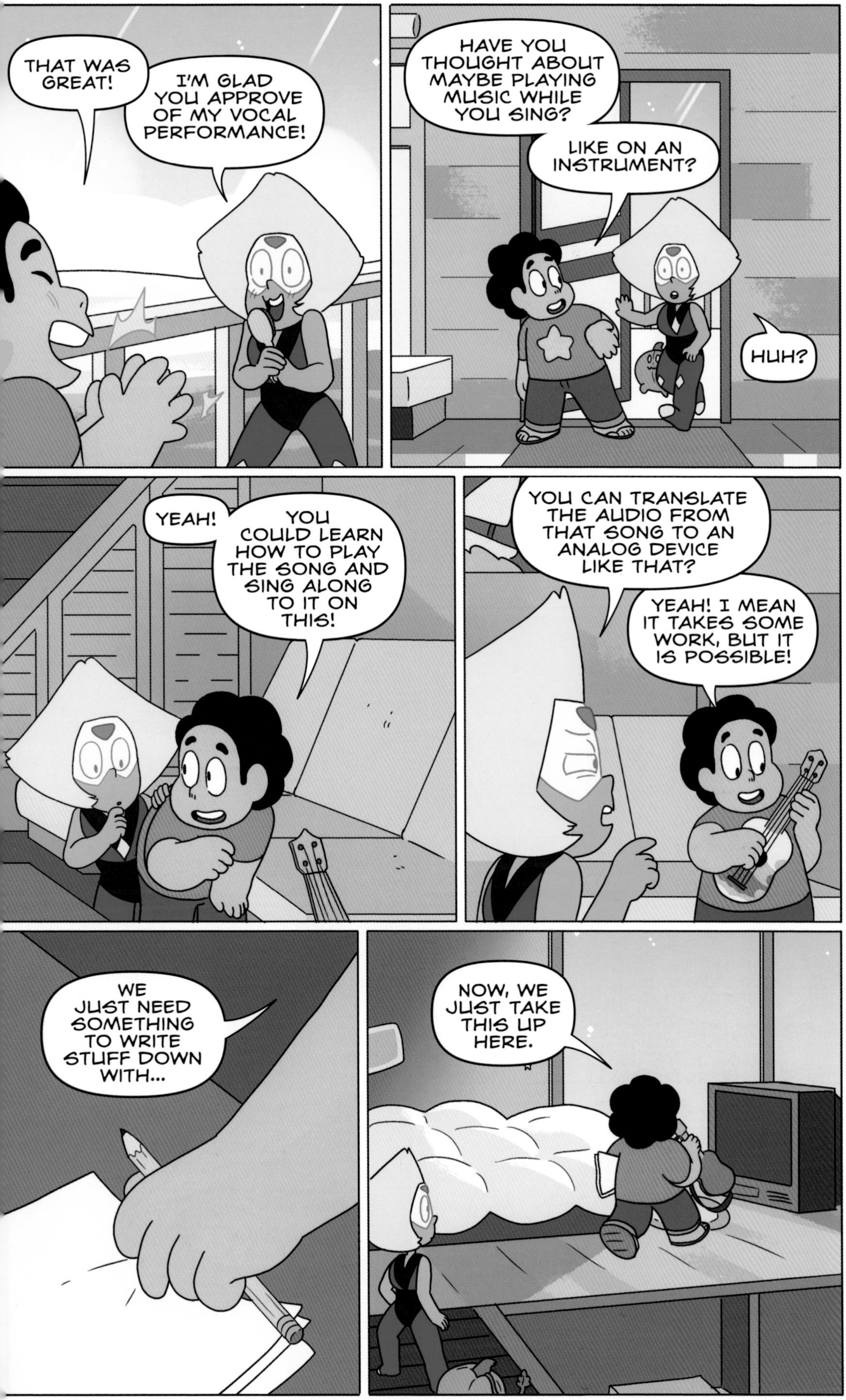
THAT WAS GREAT!
I'M GLAD YOU APPROVE OF MY VOCAL PERFORMANCE!
HAVE YOU THOUGHT ABOUT MAYBE PLAYING MUSIC WHILE YOU SING?
LIKE ON AN INSTRUMENT?
HUH?
YEAH!
YOU COULD LEARN HOW TO PLAY THE SONG AND SING ALONG TO IT ON THIS!
YOU CAN TRANSLATE THE AUDIO FROM THAT SONG TO AN ANALOG DEVICE LIKE THAT?
YEAH! I MEAN IT TAKES SOME WORK, BUT IT IS POSSIBLE!
WE JUST NEED SOMETHING TO WRITE STUFF DOWN WITH...
NOW, WE JUST TAKE THIS UP HERE.

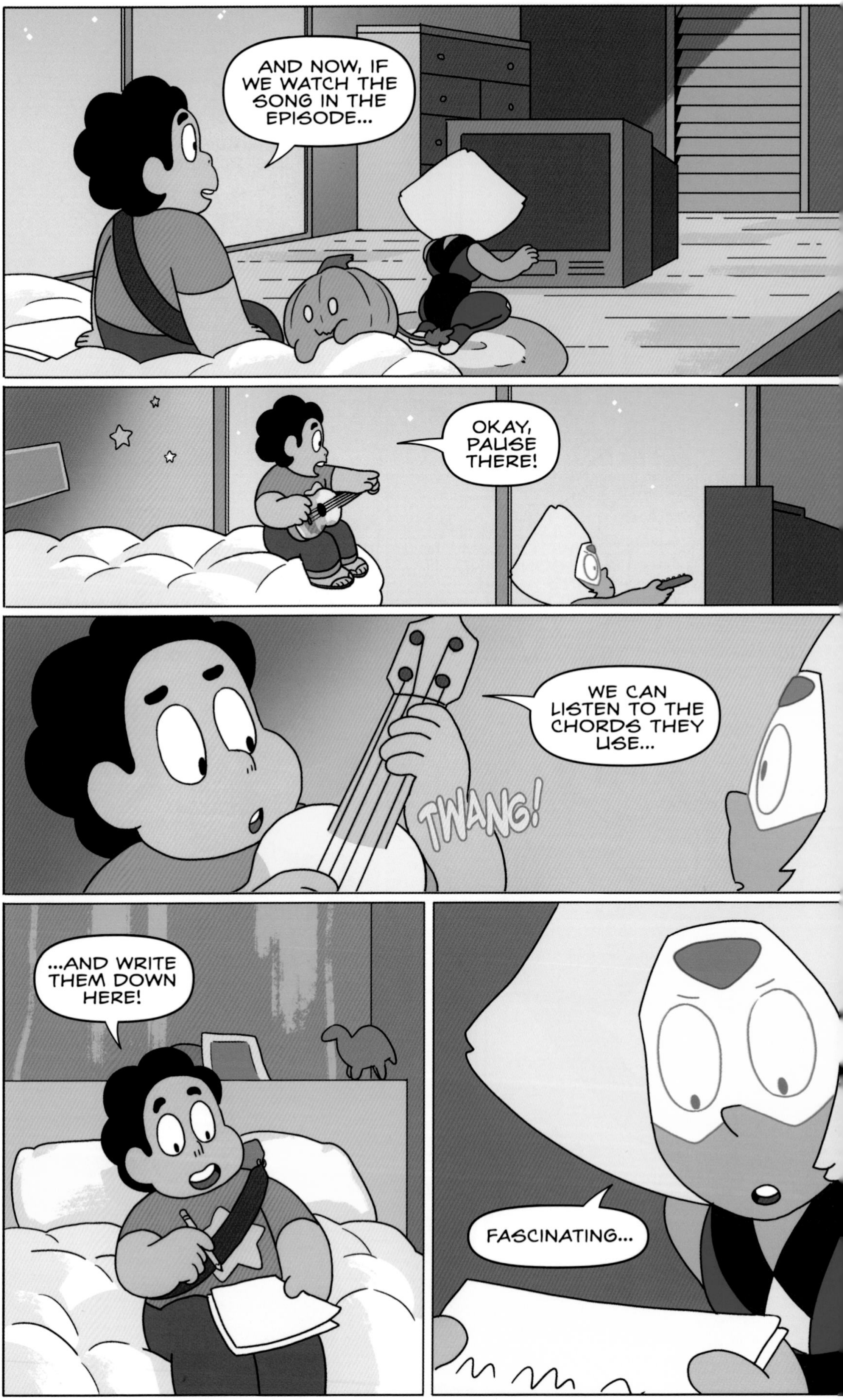
AND NOW, IF WE WATCH THE SONG IN THE EPISODE...
OKAY, PAUSE THERE!
WE CAN LISTEN TO THE CHORDS THEY USE...
TWANG!
...AND WRITE THEM DOWN HERE!
FASCINATING...

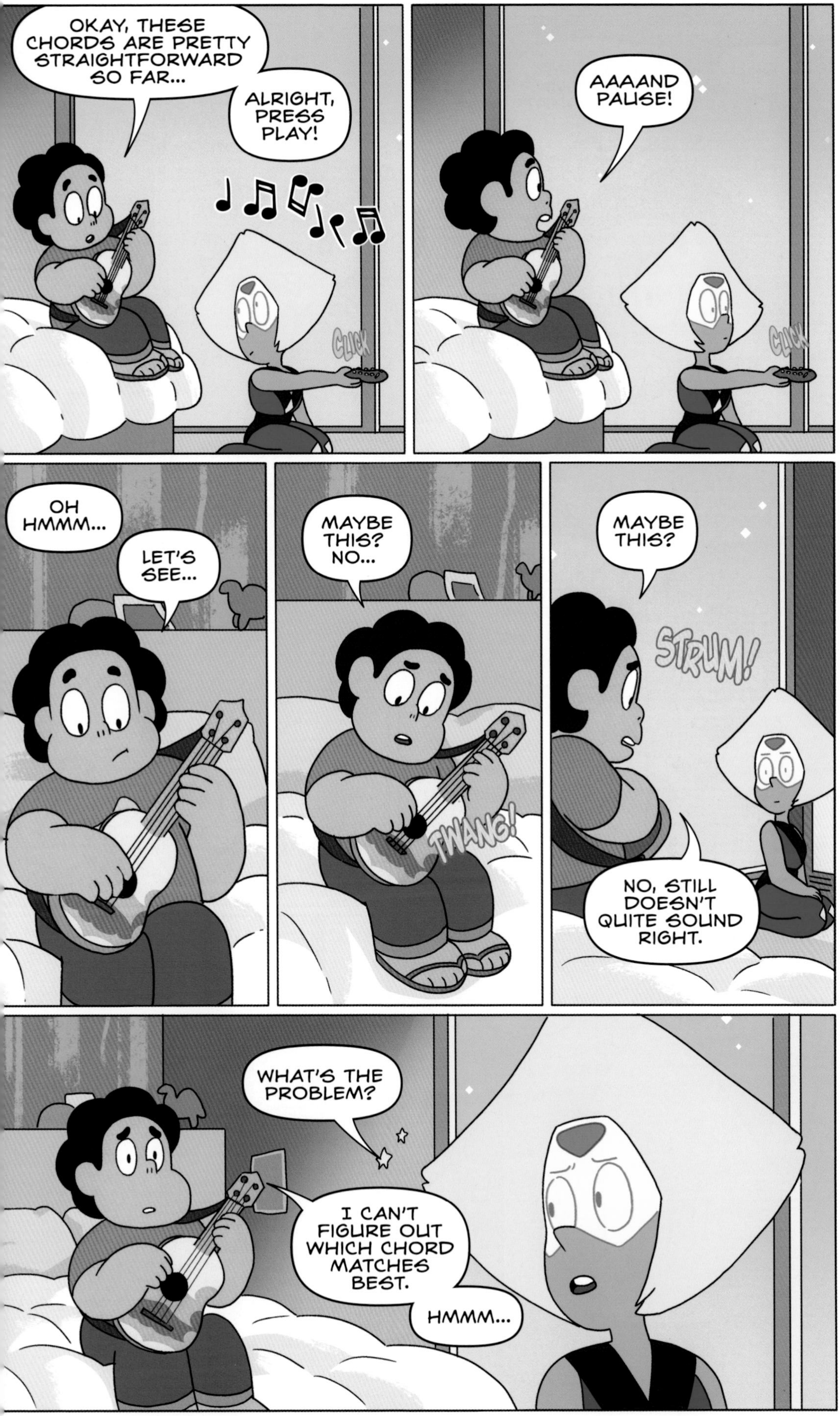
OKAY, THESE CHORDS ARE PRETTY STRAIGHTFORWARD SO FAR...
ALRIGHT, PRESS PLAY!
CLICK
AAAAND PAUSE!
CLICK
OH HMMM...
LET'S SEE...
MAYBE THIS? NO...
TWANG!
MAYBE THIS?
STRUM!
NO, STILL DOESN'T QUITE SOUND RIGHT.
WHAT'S THE PROBLEM?
I CAN'T FIGURE OUT WHICH CHORD MATCHES BEST.
HMMM...

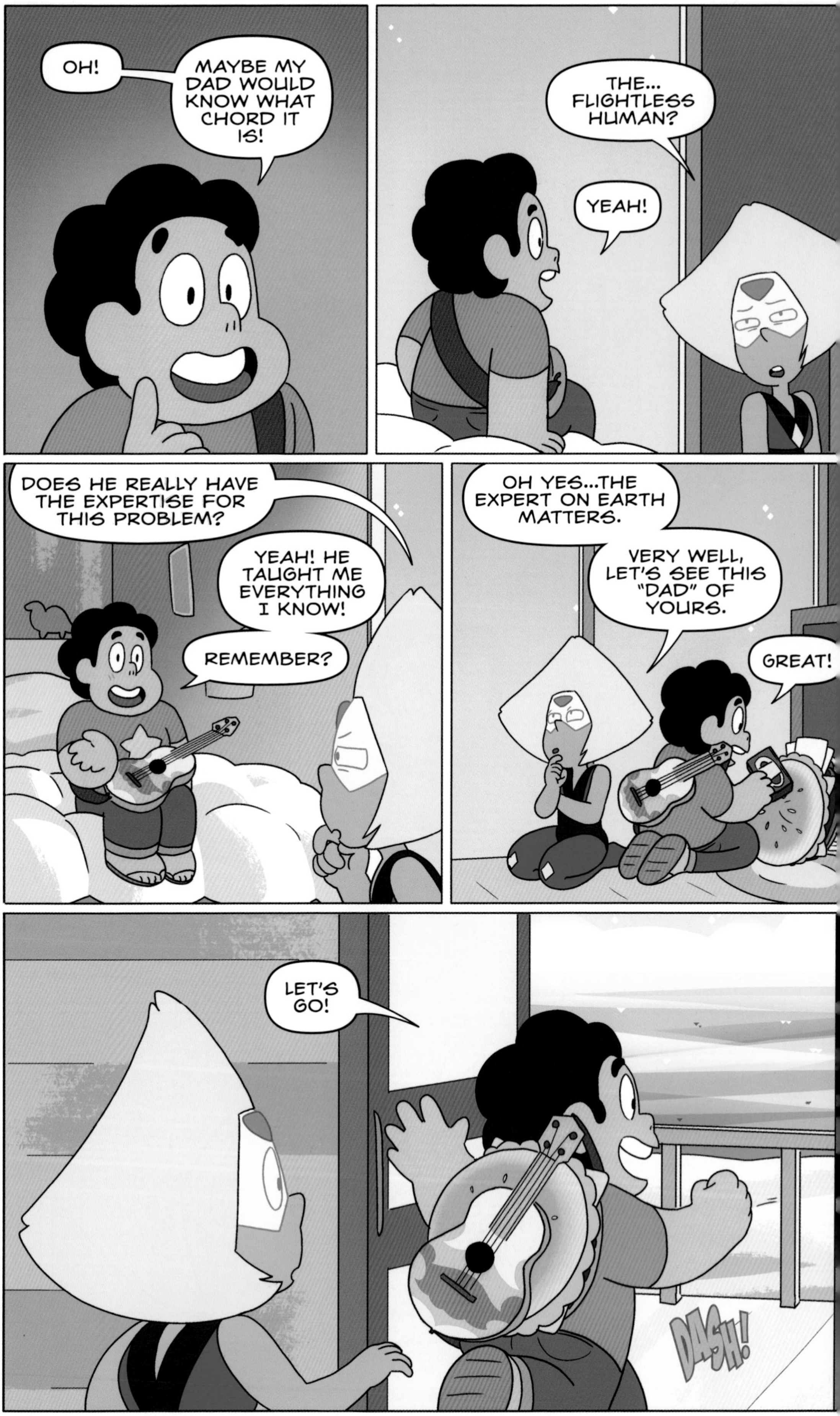
OH!
MAYBE MY DAD WOULD KNOW WHAT CHORD IT IS!
THE... FLIGHTLESS HUMAN?
YEAH!
DOES HE REALLY HAVE THE EXPERTISE FOR THIS PROBLEM?
YEAH! HE TAUGHT ME EVERYTHING I KNOW!
REMEMBER?
OH YES...THE EXPERT ON EARTH MATTERS.
VERY WELL, LET'S SEE THIS "DAD" OF YOURS.
GREAT!
LET'S GO!
DASH!

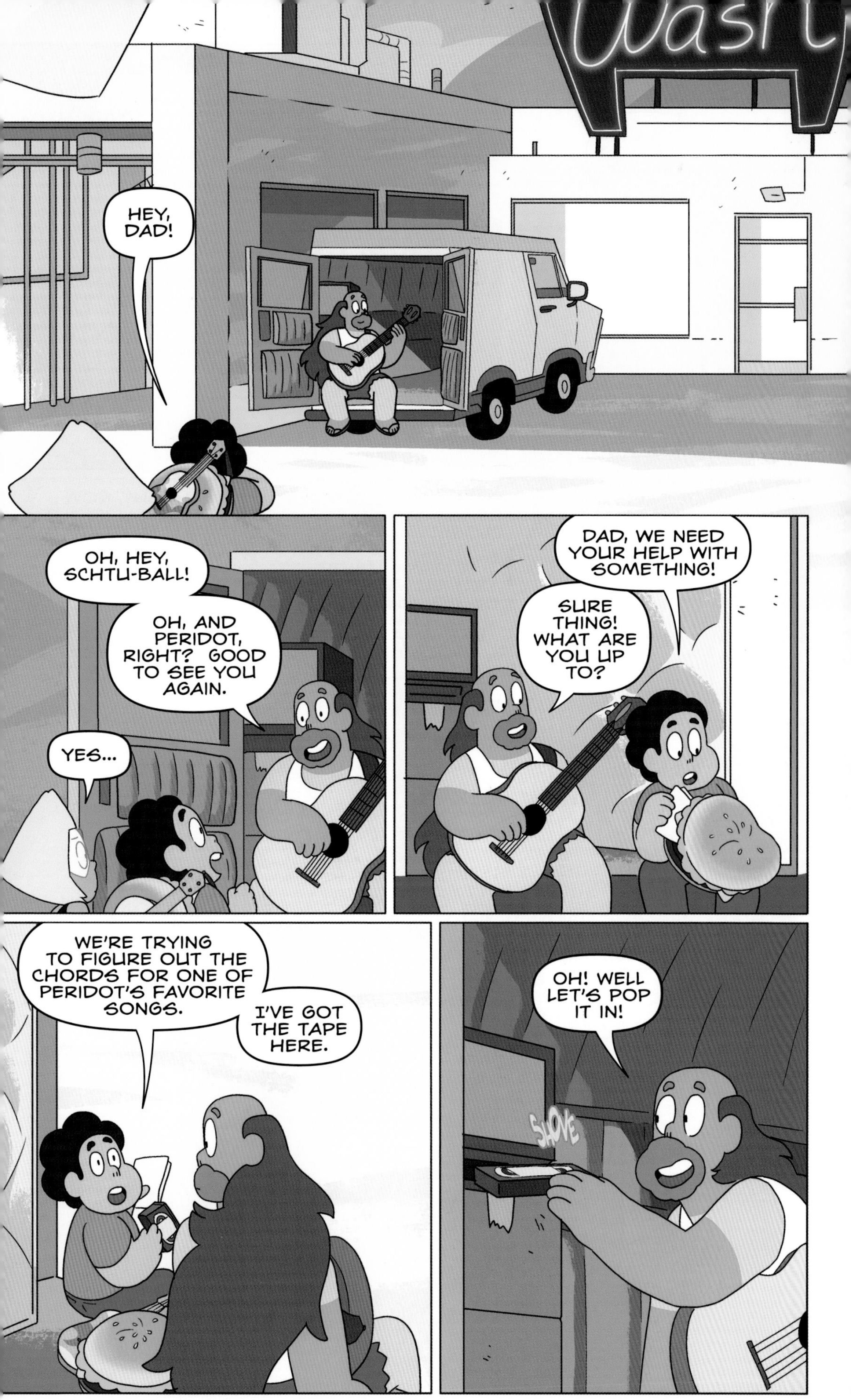
HEY, DAD!
OH, HEY, SCHTU-BALL!
OH, AND PERIDOT, RIGHT? GOOD TO SEE YOU AGAIN.
YES...
DAD, WE NEED YOUR HELP WITH SOMETHING!
SURE THING! WHAT ARE YOU UP TO?
WE'RE TRYING TO FIGURE OUT THE CHORDS FOR ONE OF PERIDOT'S FAVORITE SONGS.
I'VE GOT THE TAPE HERE.
OH! WELL LET'S POP IT IN!
SHOVE

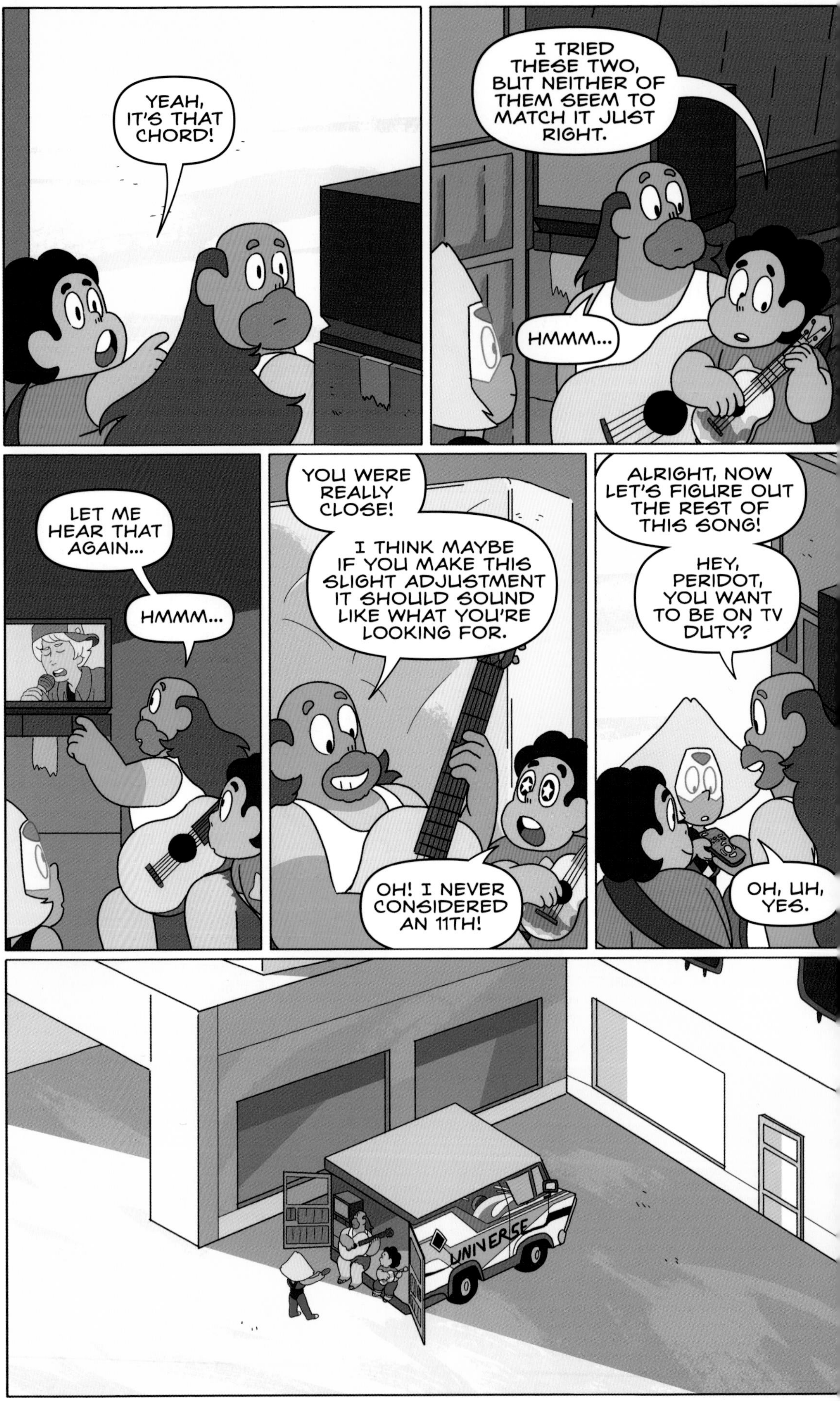
YEAH, IT'S THAT CHORD!
I TRIED THESE TWO, BUT NEITHER OF THEM SEEM TO MATCH IT JUST RIGHT.
HMMM...
LET ME HEAR THAT AGAIN...
HMMM...
YOU WERE REALLY CLOSE!
I THINK MAYBE IF YOU MAKE THIS SLIGHT ADJUSTMENT IT SHOULD SOUND LIKE WHAT YOU'RE LOOKING FOR.
OH! I NEVER CONSIDERED AN 11TH!
ALRIGHT, NOW LET'S FIGURE OUT THE REST OF THIS SONG!
HEY, PERIDOT, YOU WANT TO BE ON TV DUTY?
OH, UH, YES.
UNIVERSE

OKAY! I THINK THAT'S ALL OF IT.

YAY! THANKS SO MUCH FOR YOUR HELP, DAD!

HERE YOU GO, PERIDOT!

YESSS!!

HUG!

SO...WHAT DO I DO WITH THIS NOW?

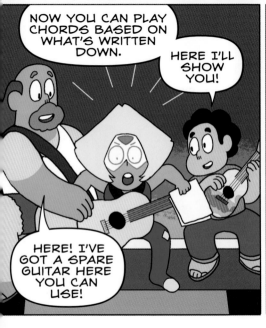

NOW YOU CAN PLAY CHORDS BASED ON WHAT'S WRITTEN DOWN.

HERE I'LL SHOW YOU!

HERE! I'VE GOT A SPARE GUITAR HERE YOU CAN USE!

YOU JUST PUT YOUR HANDS HERE...

AND HERE!

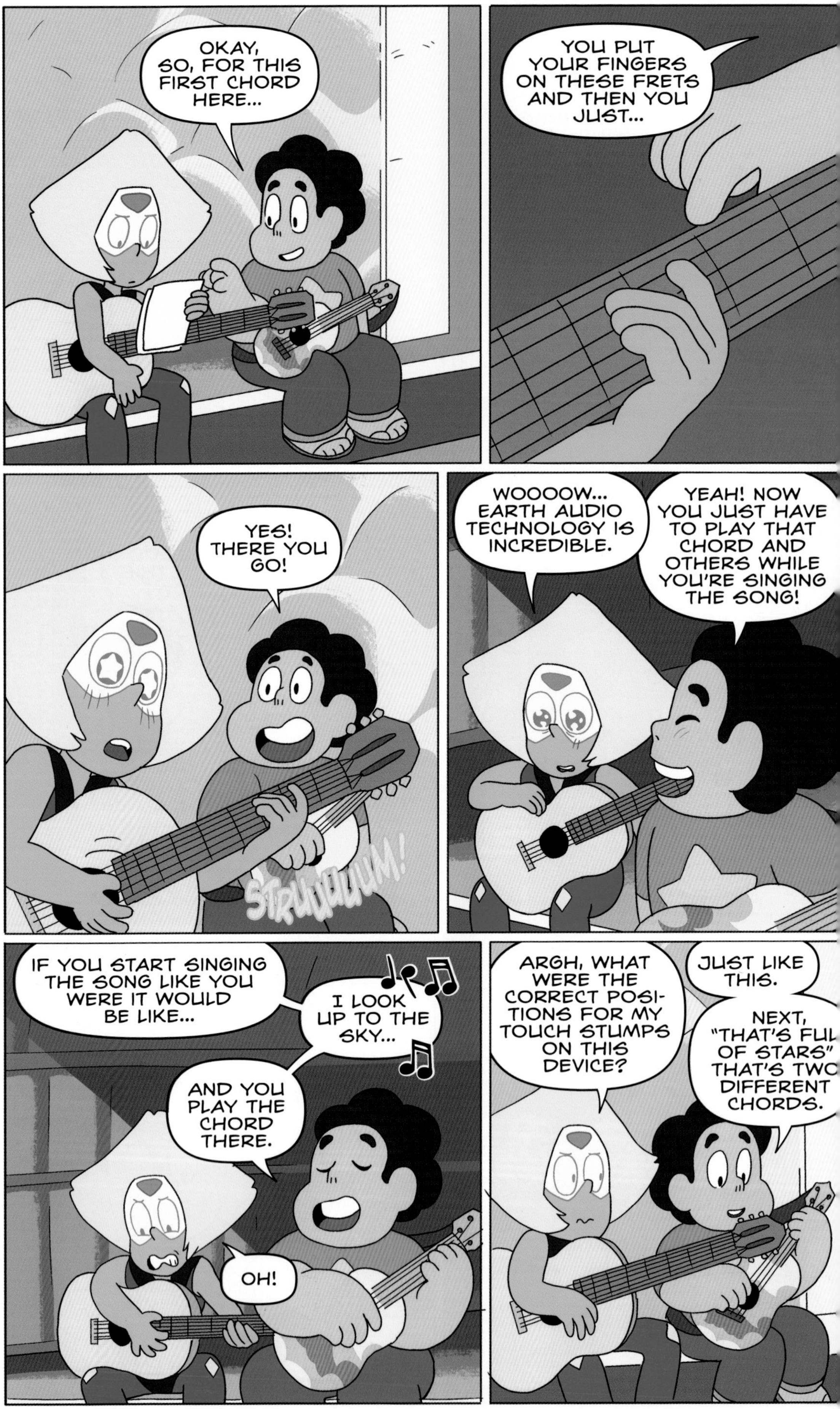
OKAY, SO, FOR THIS FIRST CHORD HERE...
YOU PUT YOUR FINGERS ON THESE FRETS AND THEN YOU JUST...
YES! THERE YOU GO!
STRUUUUUM!
WOOOOW... EARTH AUDIO TECHNOLOGY IS INCREDIBLE.
YEAH! NOW YOU JUST HAVE TO PLAY THAT CHORD AND OTHERS WHILE YOU'RE SINGING THE SONG!
IF YOU START SINGING THE SONG LIKE YOU WERE IT WOULD BE LIKE...
I LOOK UP TO THE SKY...
AND YOU PLAY THE CHORD THERE.
OH!
ARGH, WHAT WERE THE CORRECT POSI-TIONS FOR MY TOUCH STUMPS ON THIS DEVICE?
JUST LIKE THIS.
NEXT, "THAT'S FUL OF STARS" THAT'S TWO DIFFERENT CHORDS.

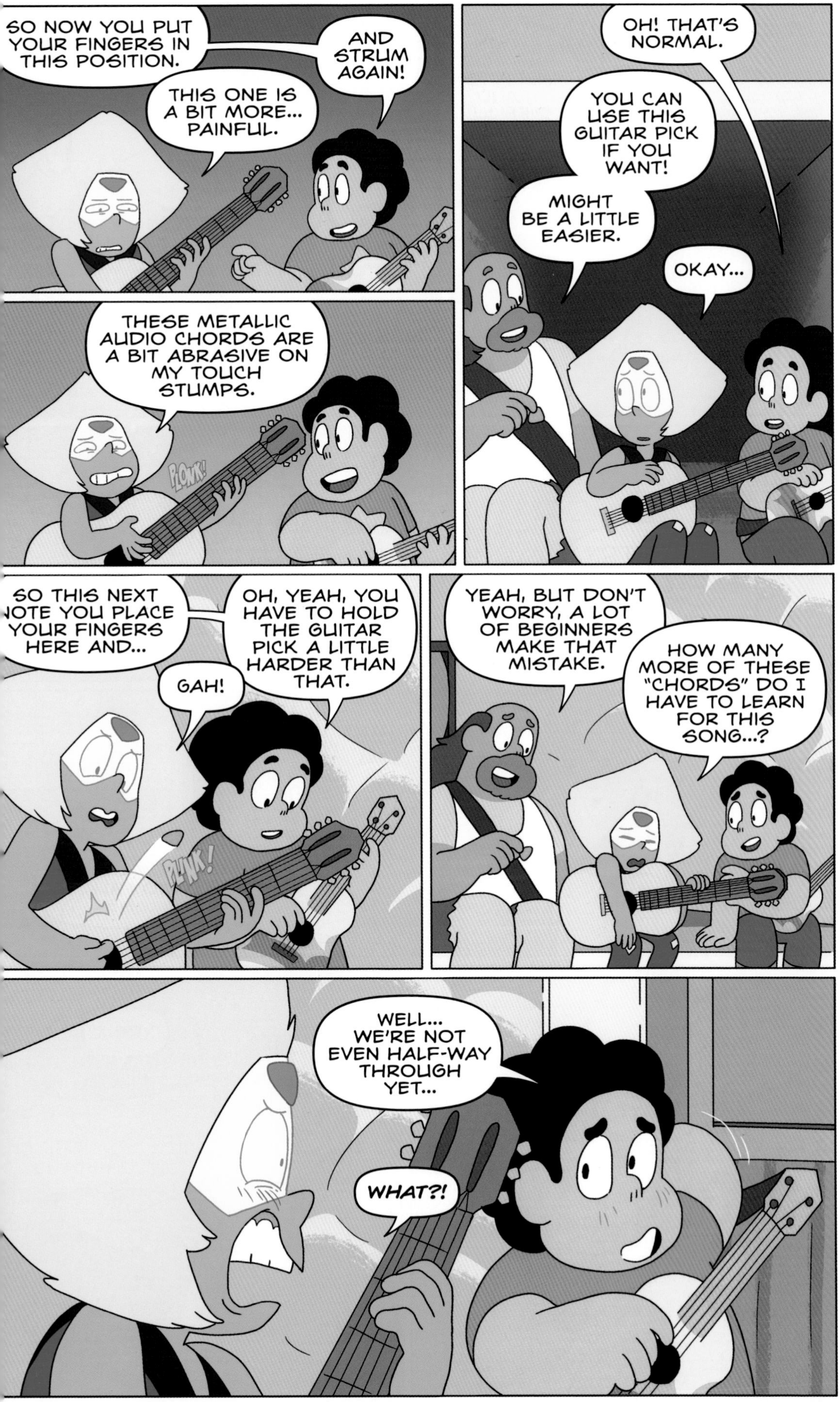
SO NOW YOU PUT YOUR FINGERS IN THIS POSITION.
AND STRUM AGAIN!
THIS ONE IS A BIT MORE... PAINFUL.
OH! THAT'S NORMAL.
YOU CAN USE THIS GUITAR PICK IF YOU WANT!
MIGHT BE A LITTLE EASIER.
OKAY...
THESE METALLIC AUDIO CHORDS ARE A BIT ABRASIVE ON MY TOUCH STUMPS.
PLONK!
SO THIS NEXT NOTE YOU PLACE YOUR FINGERS HERE AND...
OH, YEAH, YOU HAVE TO HOLD THE GUITAR PICK A LITTLE HARDER THAN THAT.
GAH!
PLINK!
YEAH, BUT DON'T WORRY, A LOT OF BEGINNERS MAKE THAT MISTAKE.
HOW MANY MORE OF THESE "CHORDS" DO I HAVE TO LEARN FOR THIS SONG...?
WELL... WE'RE NOT EVEN HALF-WAY THROUGH YET...
WHAT?!

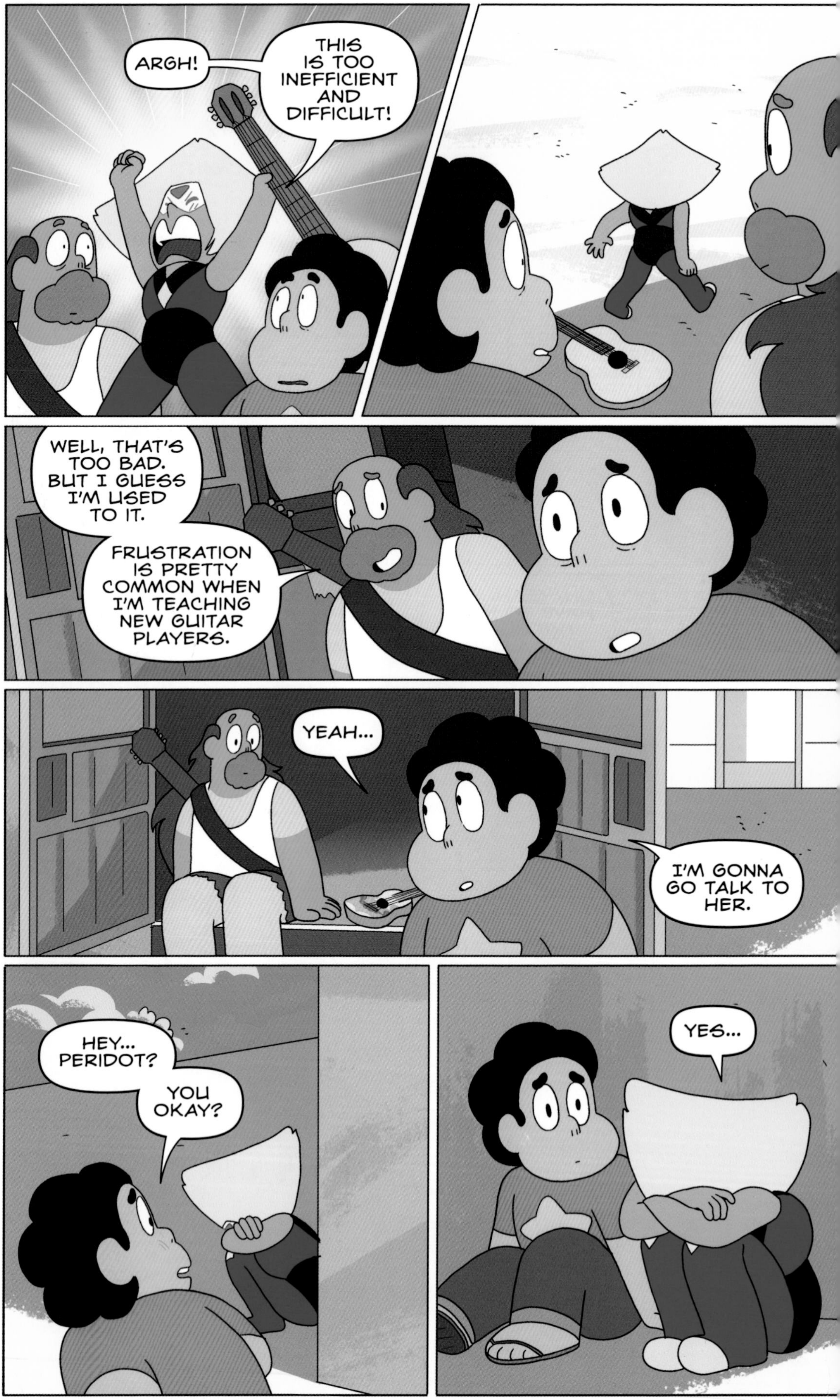
ARGH!
THIS IS TOO INEFFICIENT AND DIFFICULT!
WELL, THAT'S TOO BAD. BUT I GUESS I'M USED TO IT.
FRUSTRATION IS PRETTY COMMON WHEN I'M TEACHING NEW GUITAR PLAYERS.
YEAH...
I'M GONNA GO TALK TO HER.
HEY... PERIDOT?
YOU OKAY?
YES...

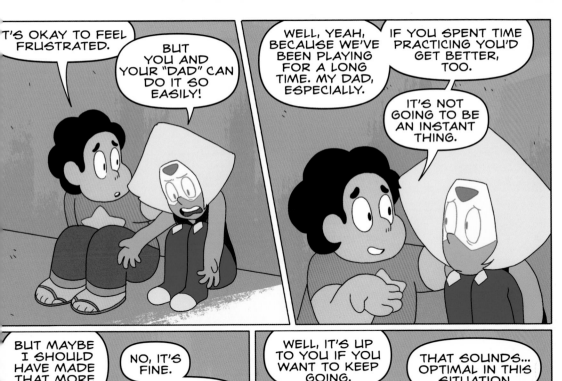

T'S OKAY TO FEEL FRUSTRATED.

BUT YOU AND YOUR "DAD" CAN DO IT SO EASILY!

WELL, YEAH, BECAUSE WE'VE BEEN PLAYING FOR A LONG TIME. MY DAD, ESPECIALLY.

IF YOU SPENT TIME PRACTICING YOU'D GET BETTER, TOO.

IT'S NOT GOING TO BE AN INSTANT THING.

BUT MAYBE I SHOULD HAVE MADE THAT MORE CLEAR...

NO, IT'S FINE.

I SHOULD HAVE EXPECTED THAT.

IT'S STILL JUST... ANNOYING.

WELL, IT'S UP TO YOU IF YOU WANT TO KEEP GOING.

THAT SOUNDS... OPTIMAL IN THIS SITUATION.

BUT FOR NOW, MAYBE WE SHOULD TAKE A BREAK.

WE'RE GONNA HEAD HOME, DAD!

ALRIGHT! SEE YOU AROUND, BUDDY!

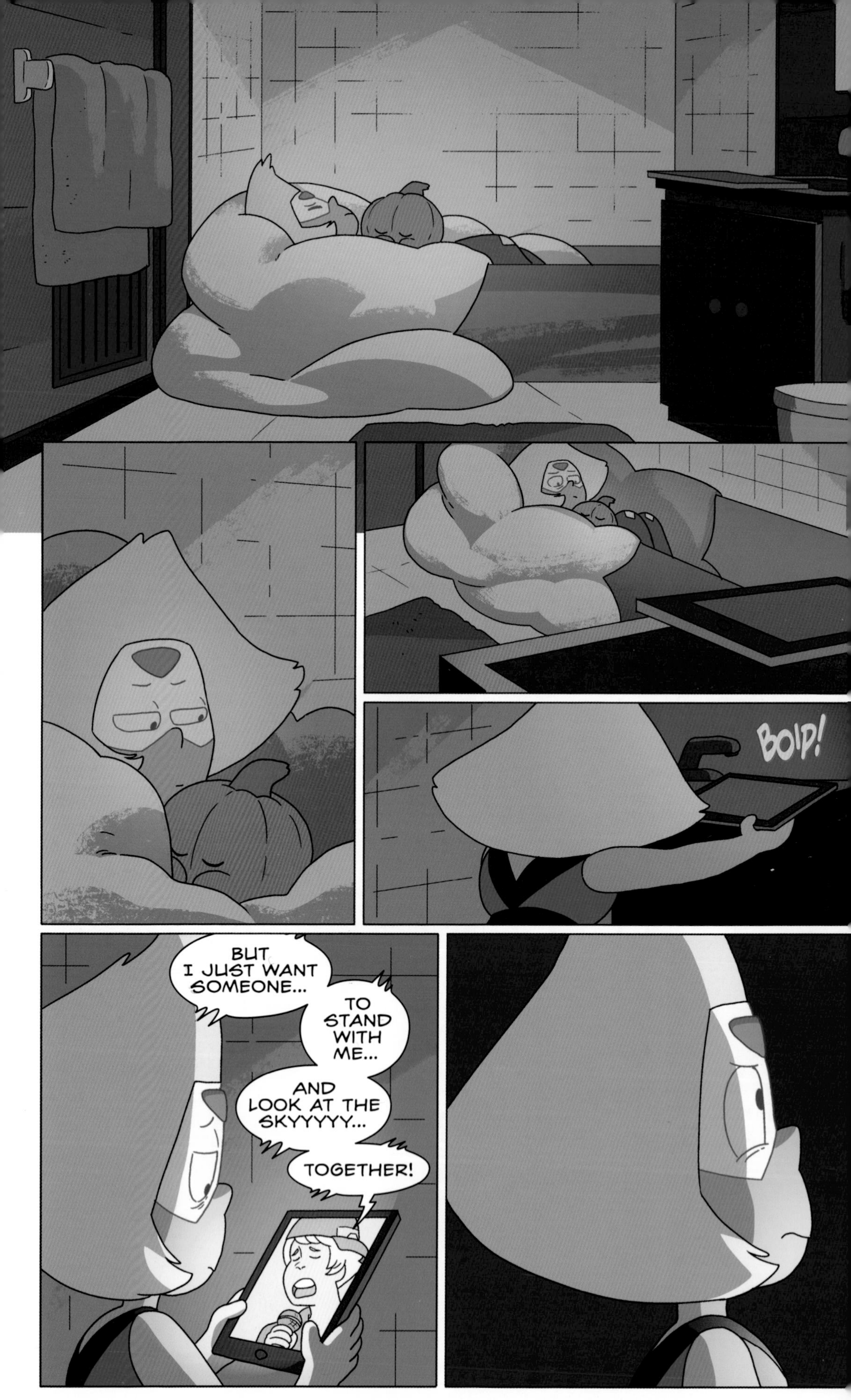
BOIP!
BUT I JUST WANT SOMEONE...
TO STAND WITH ME...
AND LOOK AT THE SKYYYYY...
TOGETHER!

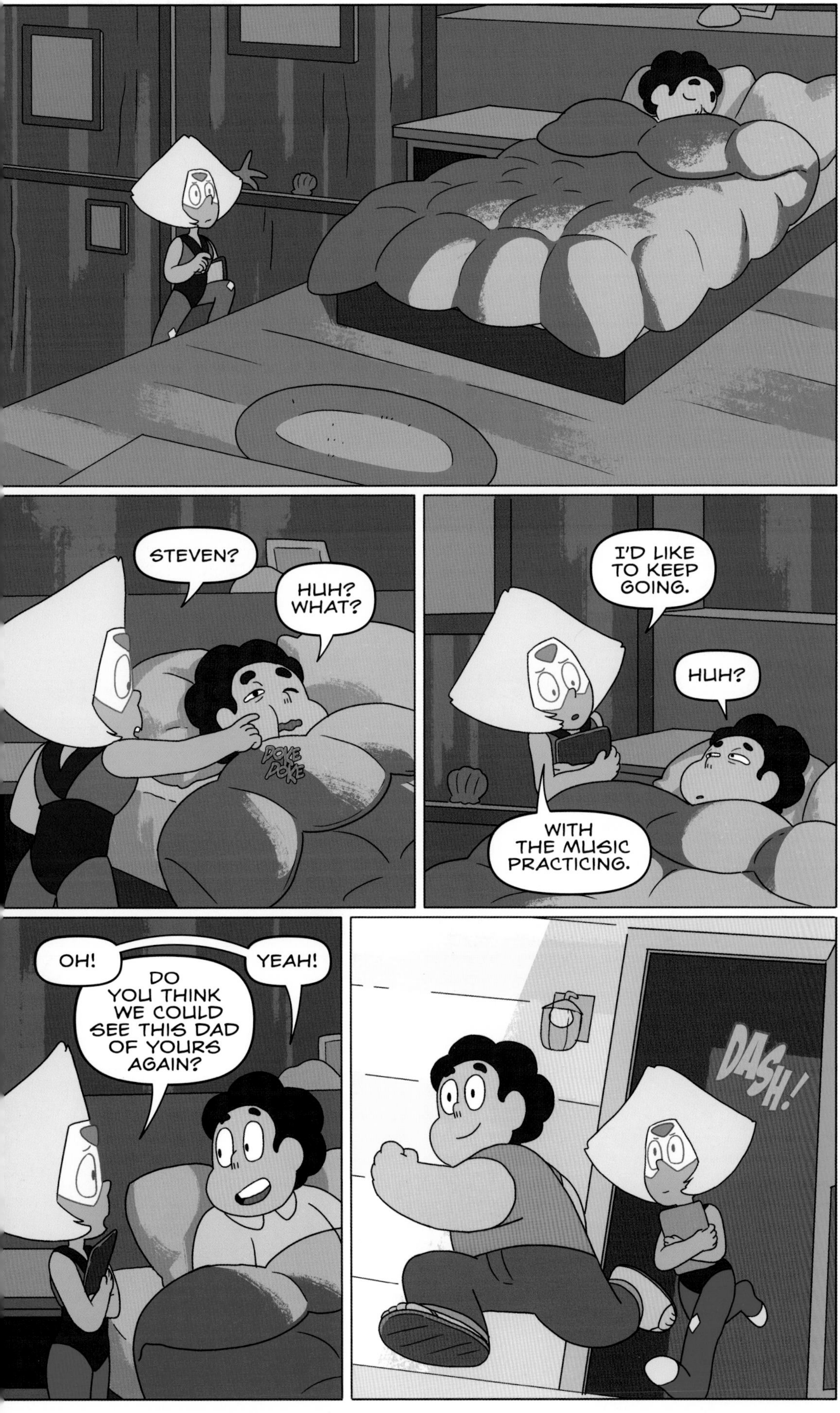
STEVEN?
HUH? WHAT?
POKE POKE
I'D LIKE TO KEEP GOING.
HUH?
WITH THE MUSIC PRACTICING.
OH!
DO YOU THINK WE COULD SEE THIS DAD OF YOURS AGAIN?
YEAH!
DASH!

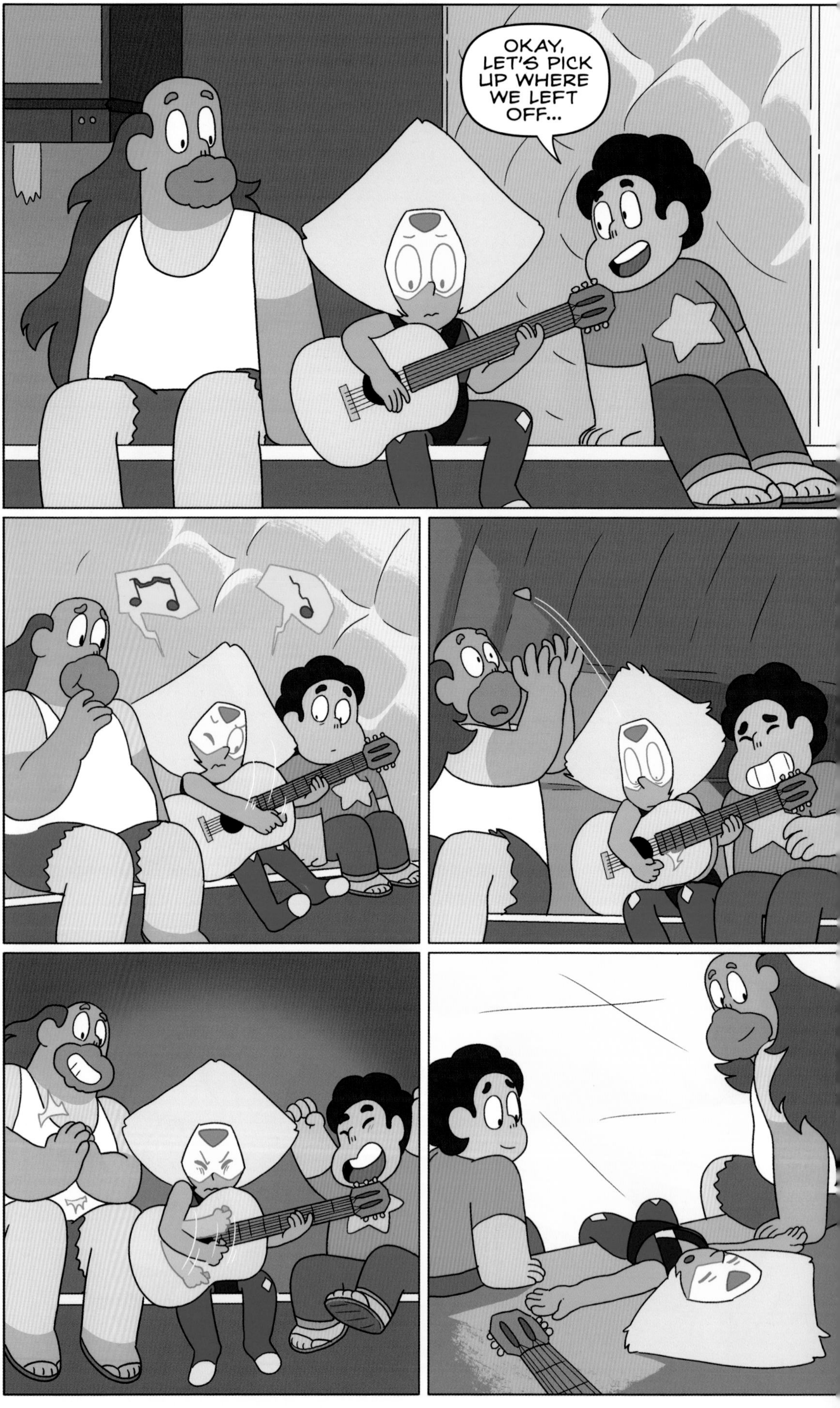
OKAY, LET'S PICK UP WHERE WE LEFT OFF...

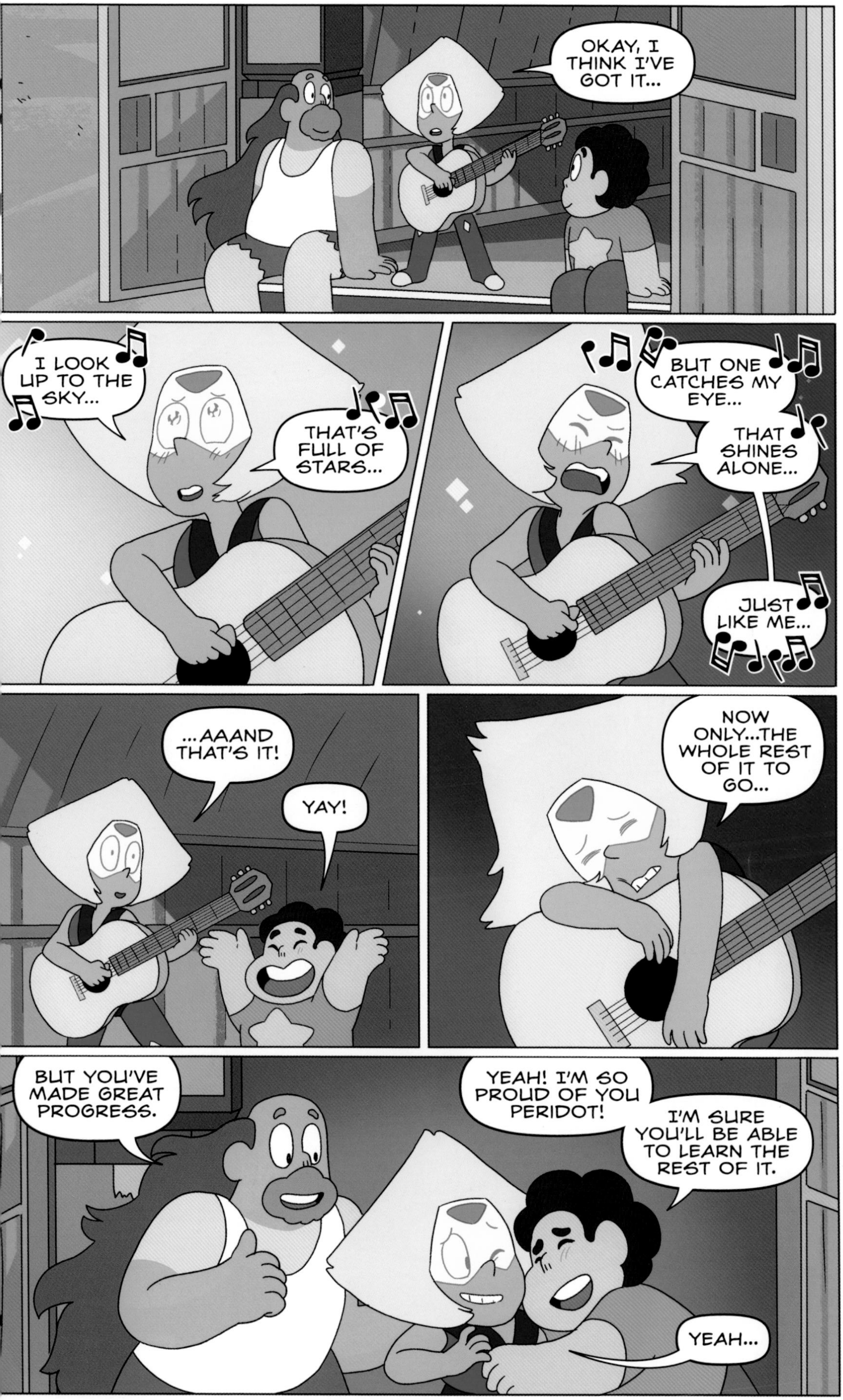
OKAY, I THINK I'VE GOT IT...
I LOOK UP TO THE SKY...
THAT'S FULL OF STARS...
BUT ONE CATCHES MY EYE...
THAT SHINES ALONE...
JUST LIKE ME...
...AAAND THAT'S IT!
YAY!
NOW ONLY...THE WHOLE REST OF IT TO GO...
BUT YOU'VE MADE GREAT PROGRESS.
YEAH! I'M SO PROUD OF YOU PERIDOT!
I'M SURE YOU'LL BE ABLE TO LEARN THE REST OF IT.
YEAH...

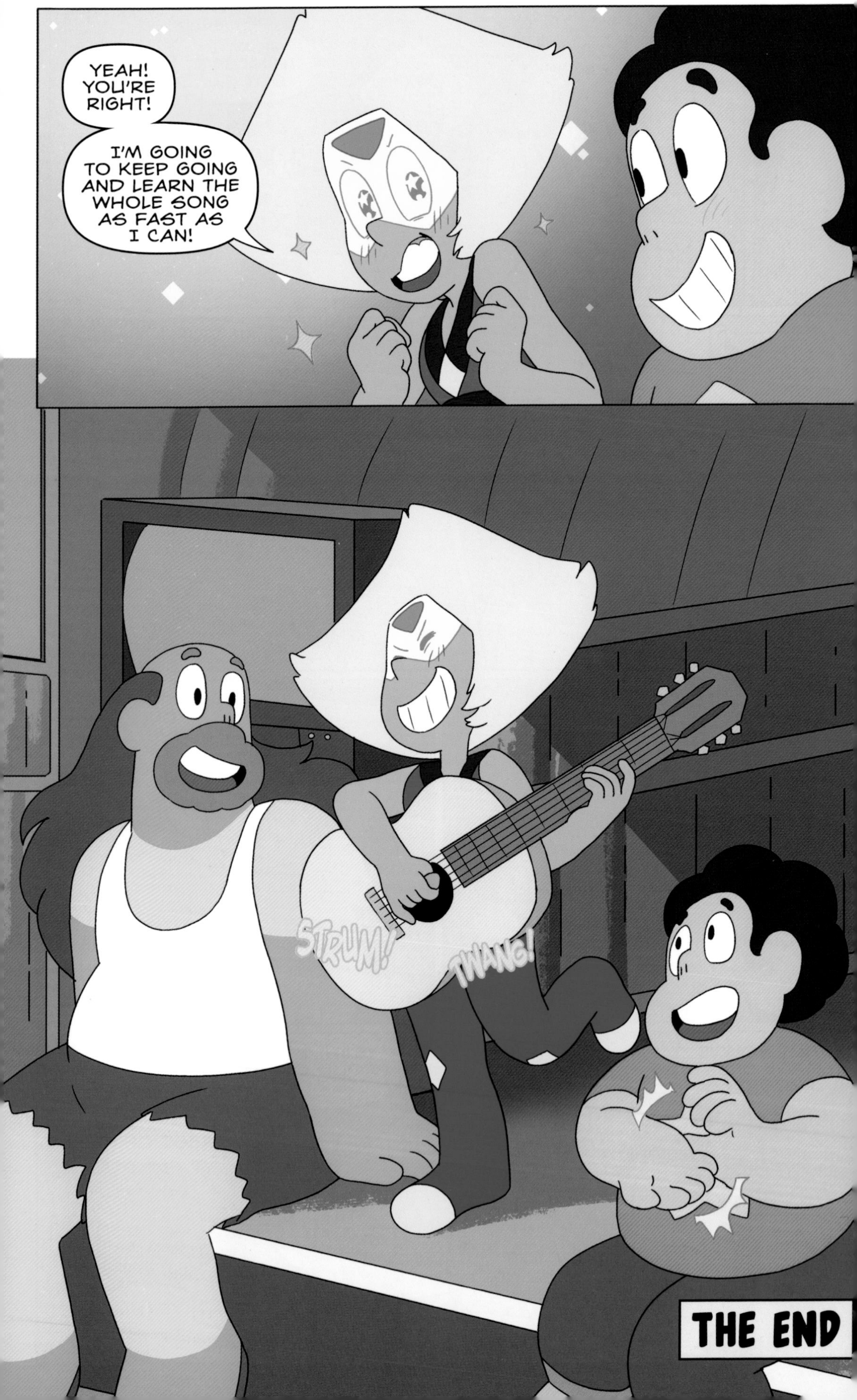
YEAH! YOU'RE RIGHT!
I'M GOING TO KEEP GOING AND LEARN THE WHOLE SONG AS FAST AS I CAN!
STRUM!
TWANG!
THE END

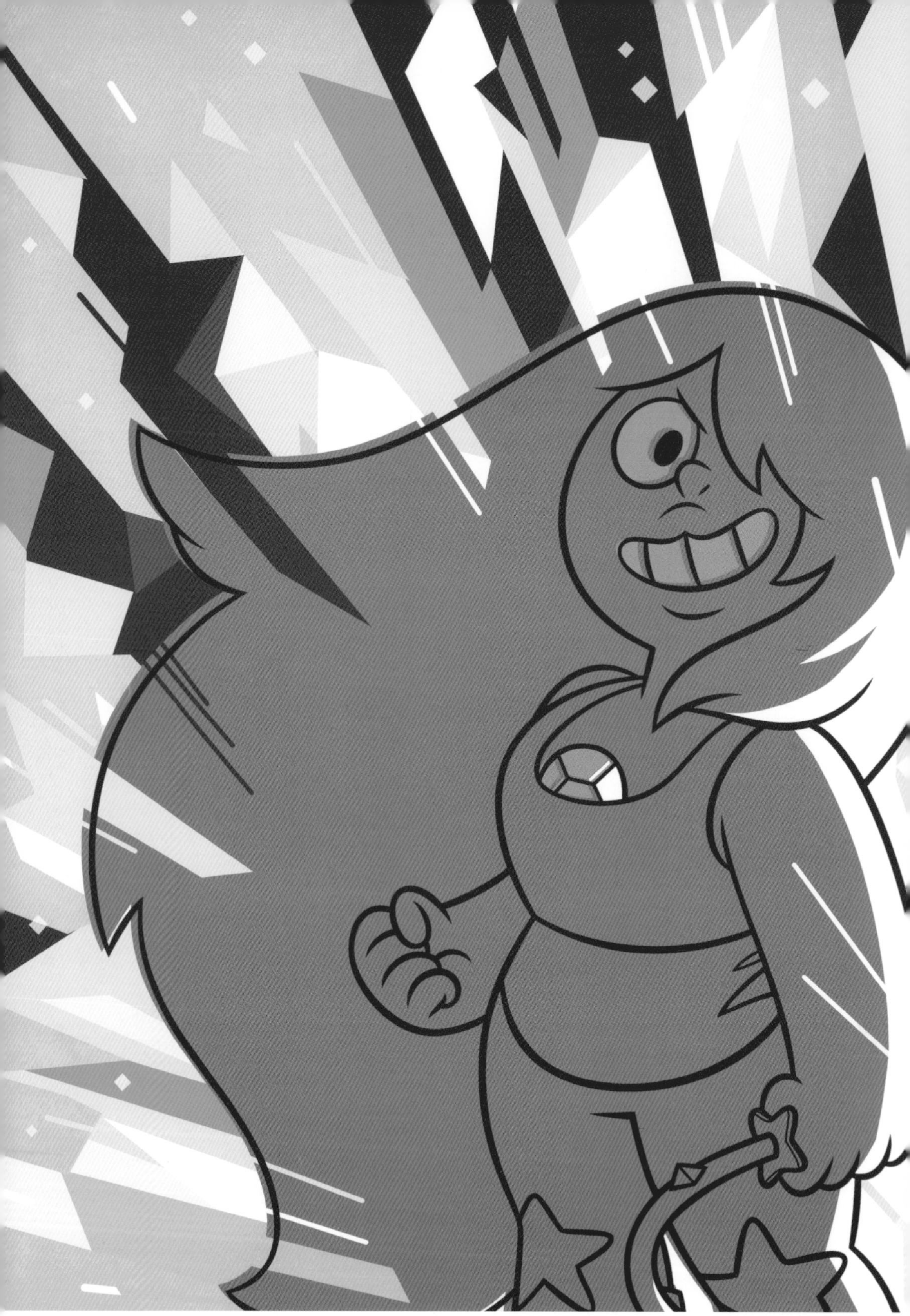

CHAPTER TWENTY-TWO

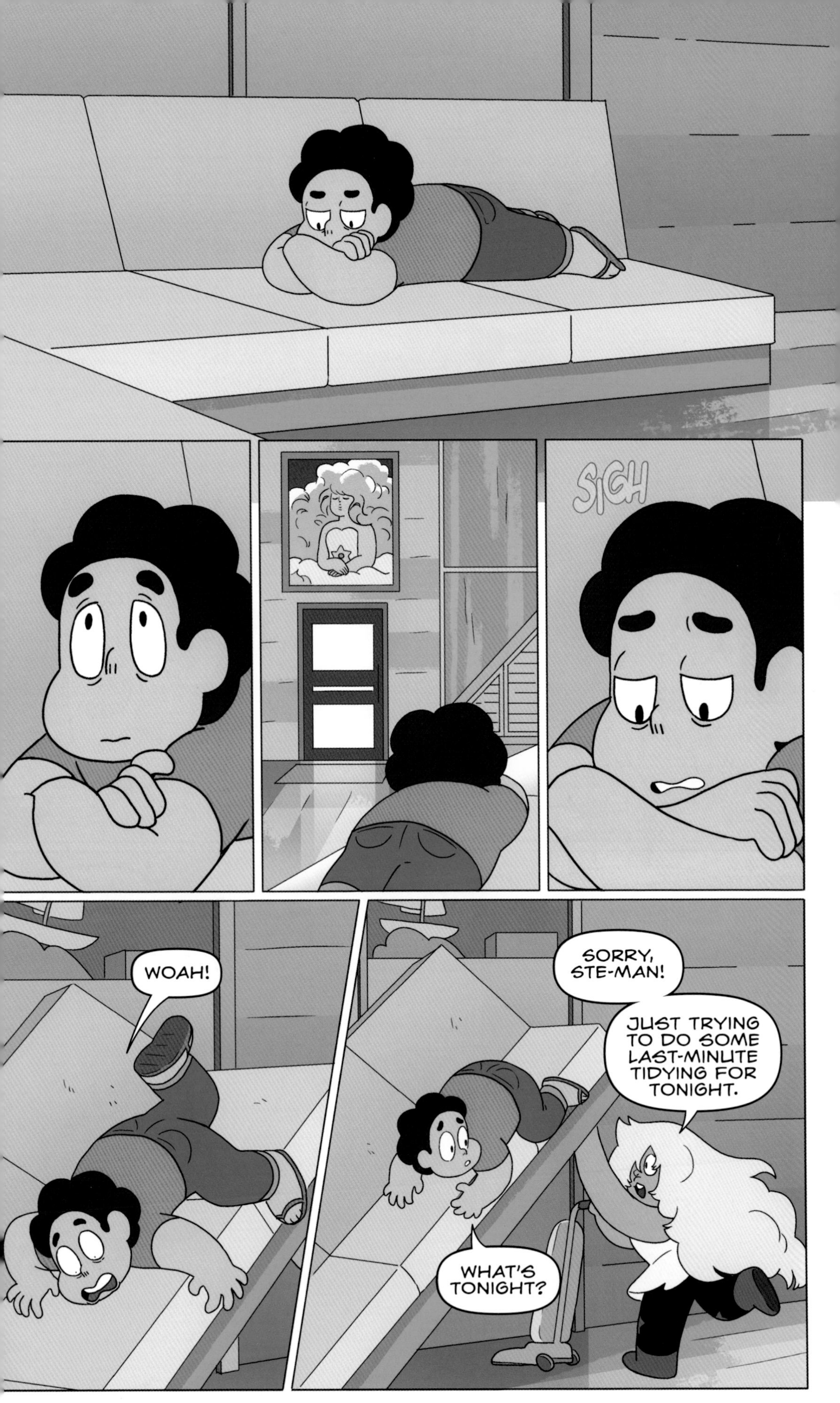
SIGH
WOAH!
SORRY, STE-MAN!
JUST TRYING TO DO SOME LAST-MINUTE TIDYING FOR TONIGHT.
WHAT'S TONIGHT?

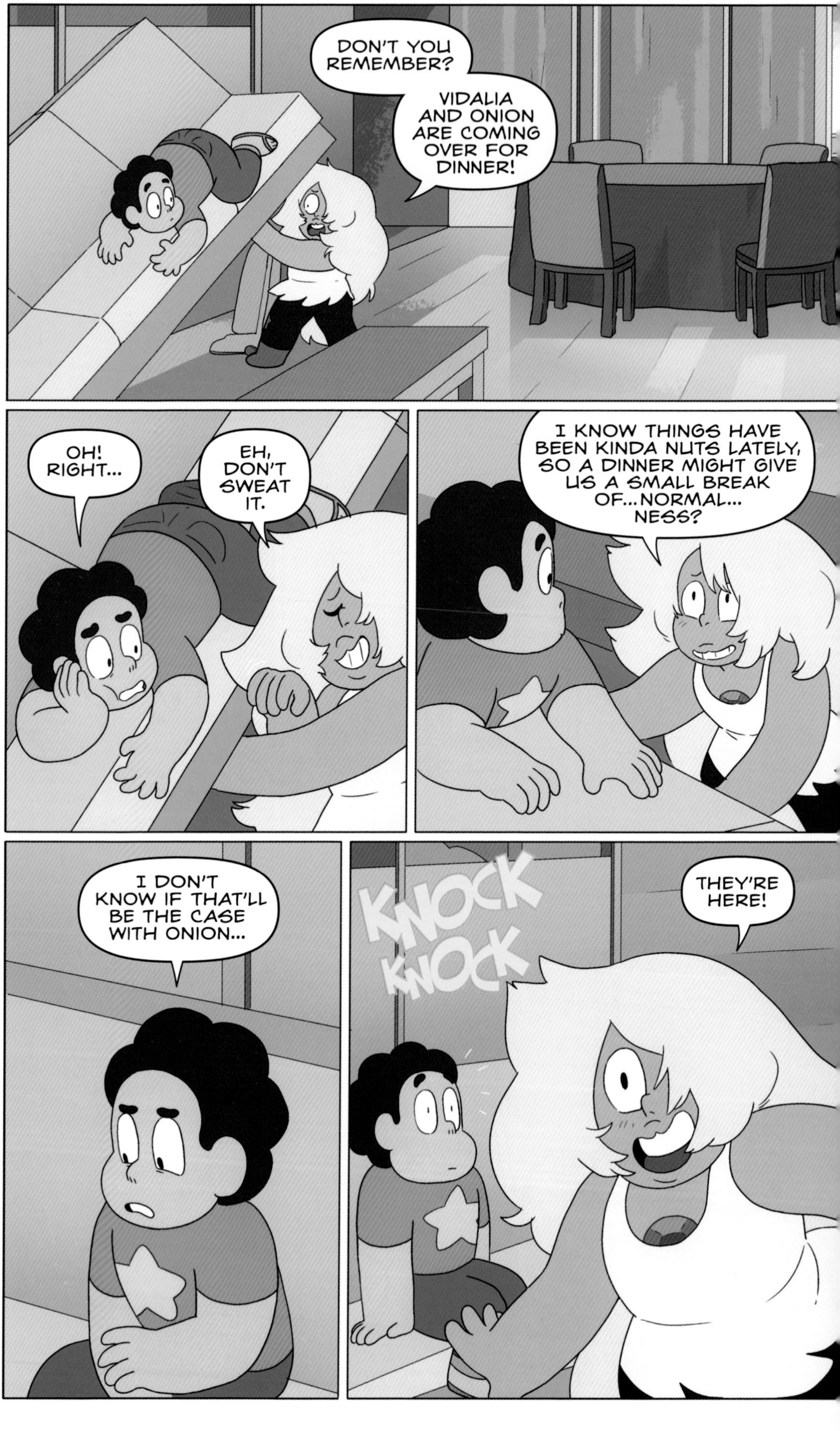
DON'T YOU REMEMBER?
VIDALIA AND ONION ARE COMING OVER FOR DINNER!
OH! RIGHT...
EH, DON'T SWEAT IT.
I KNOW THINGS HAVE BEEN KINDA NUTS LATELY, SO A DINNER MIGHT GIVE US A SMALL BREAK OF...NORMAL... NESS?
I DON'T KNOW IF THAT'LL BE THE CASE WITH ONION...
KNOCK KNOCK
THEY'RE HERE!

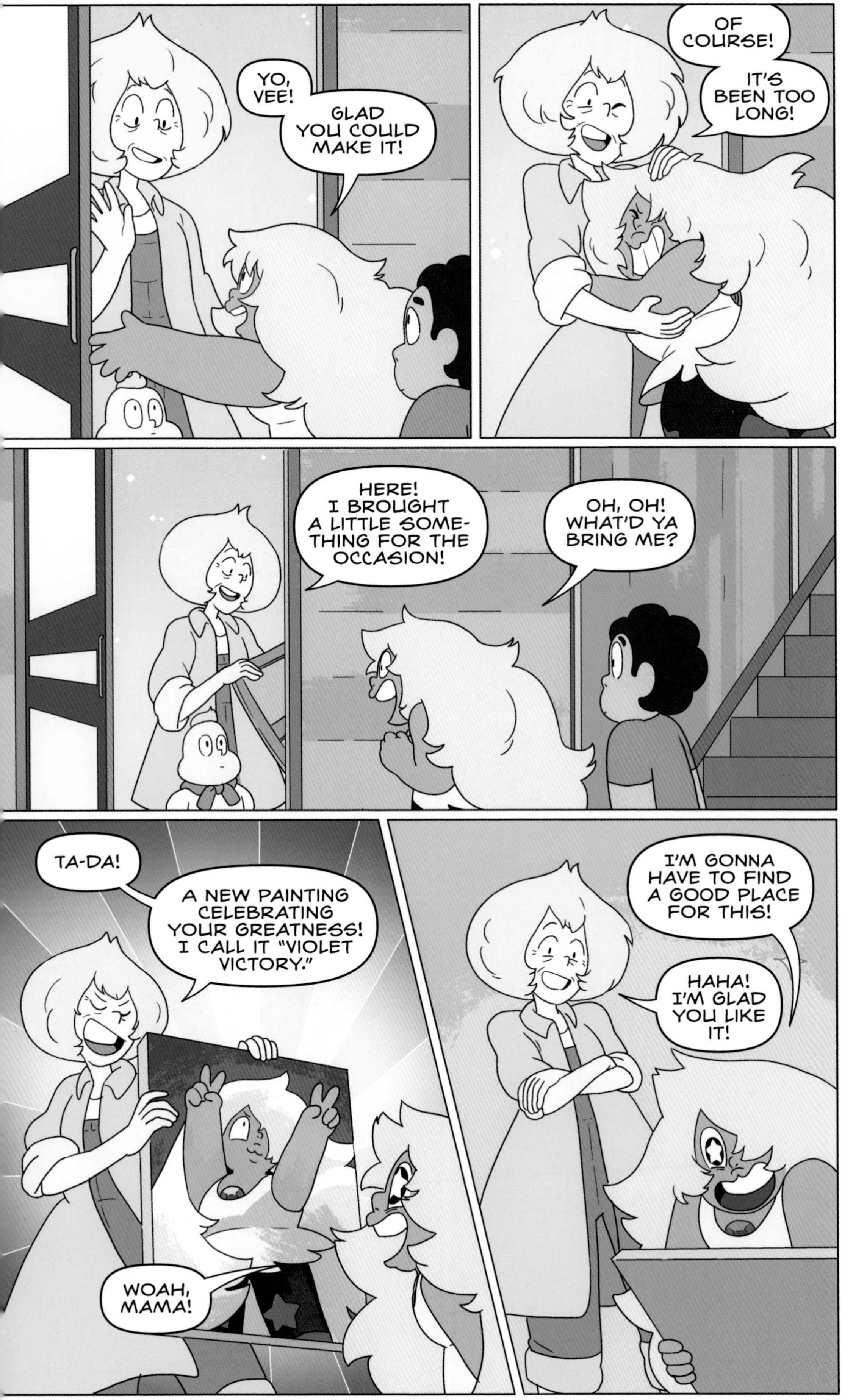
YO, VEE!
GLAD YOU COULD MAKE IT!
OF COURSE!
IT'S BEEN TOO LONG!
HERE! I BROUGHT A LITTLE SOME-THING FOR THE OCCASION!
OH, OH! WHAT'D YA BRING ME?
TA-DA!
A NEW PAINTING CELEBRATING YOUR GREATNESS! I CALL IT "VIOLET VICTORY."
WOAH, MAMA!
I'M GONNA HAVE TO FIND A GOOD PLACE FOR THIS!
HAHA! I'M GLAD YOU LIKE IT!

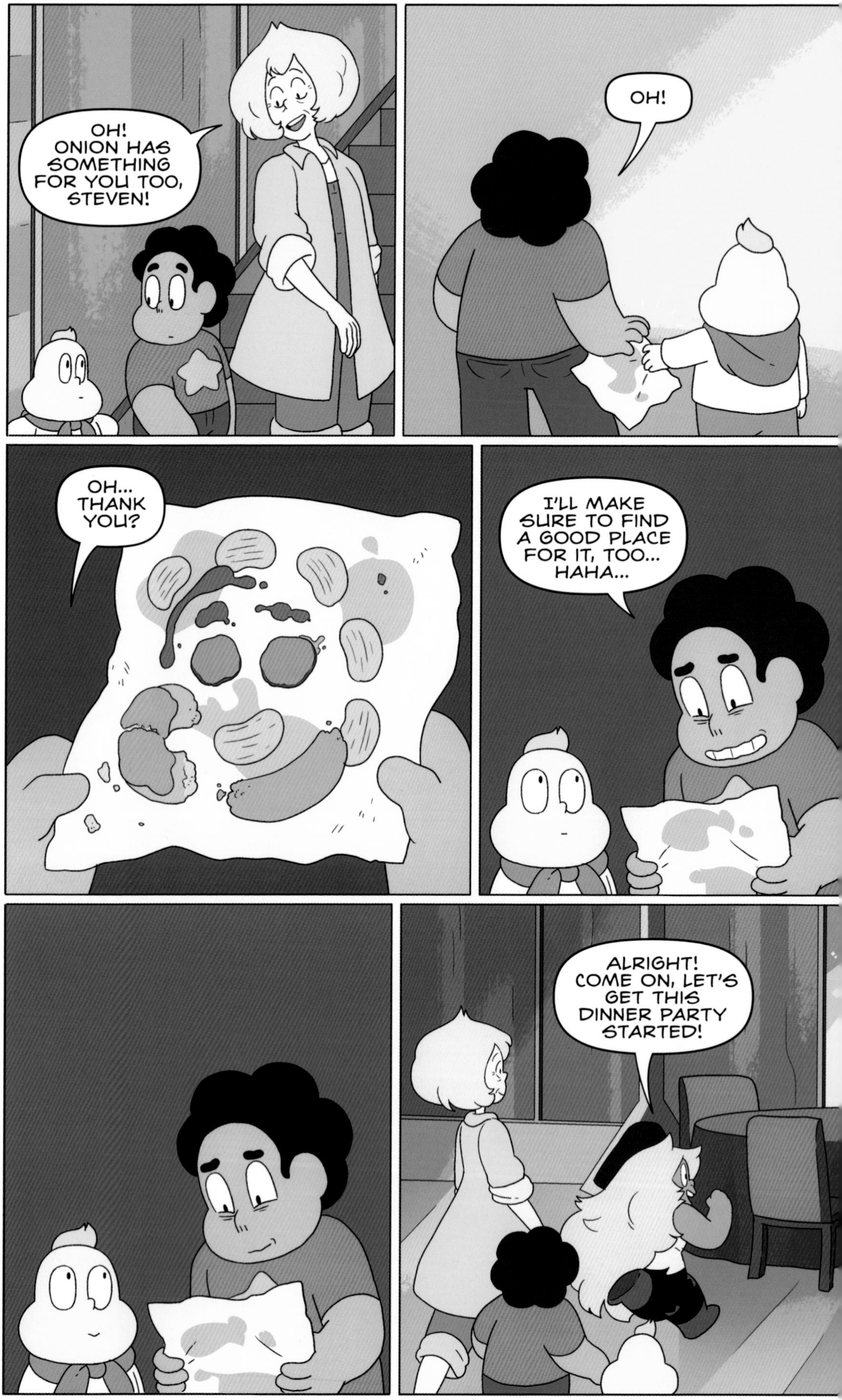
OH! ONION HAS SOMETHING FOR YOU TOO, STEVEN!
OH!
OH... THANK YOU?
I'LL MAKE SURE TO FIND A GOOD PLACE FOR IT, TOO... HAHA...
ALRIGHT! COME ON, LET'S GET THIS DINNER PARTY STARTED!

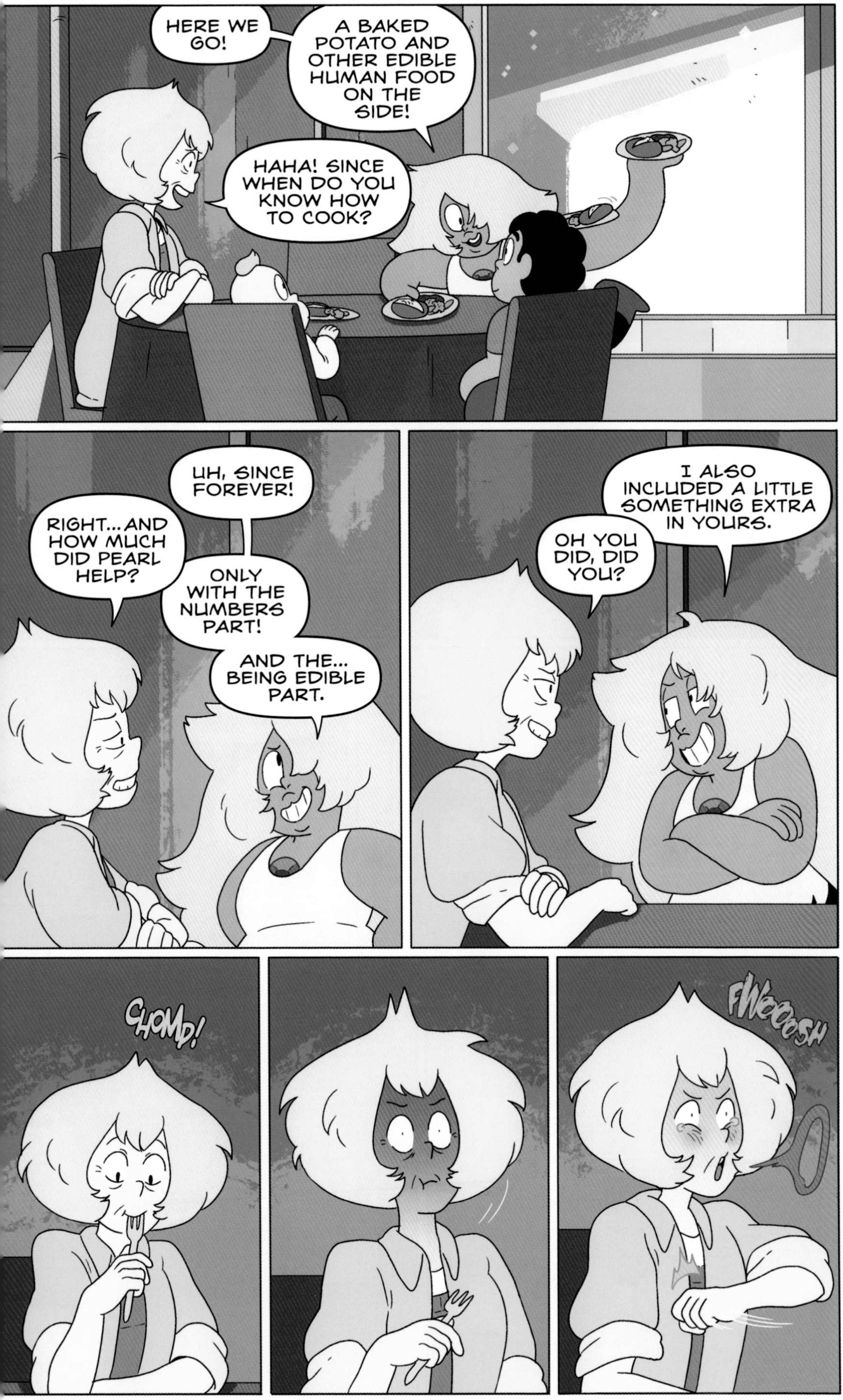
HERE WE GO!
A BAKED POTATO AND OTHER EDIBLE HUMAN FOOD ON THE SIDE!
HAHA! SINCE WHEN DO YOU KNOW HOW TO COOK?
UH, SINCE FOREVER!
RIGHT...AND HOW MUCH DID PEARL HELP?
ONLY WITH THE NUMBERS PART!
AND THE... BEING EDIBLE PART.
I ALSO INCLUDED A LITTLE SOMETHING EXTRA IN YOURS.
OH YOU DID, DID YOU?
CHOMP!
FWOOOSH

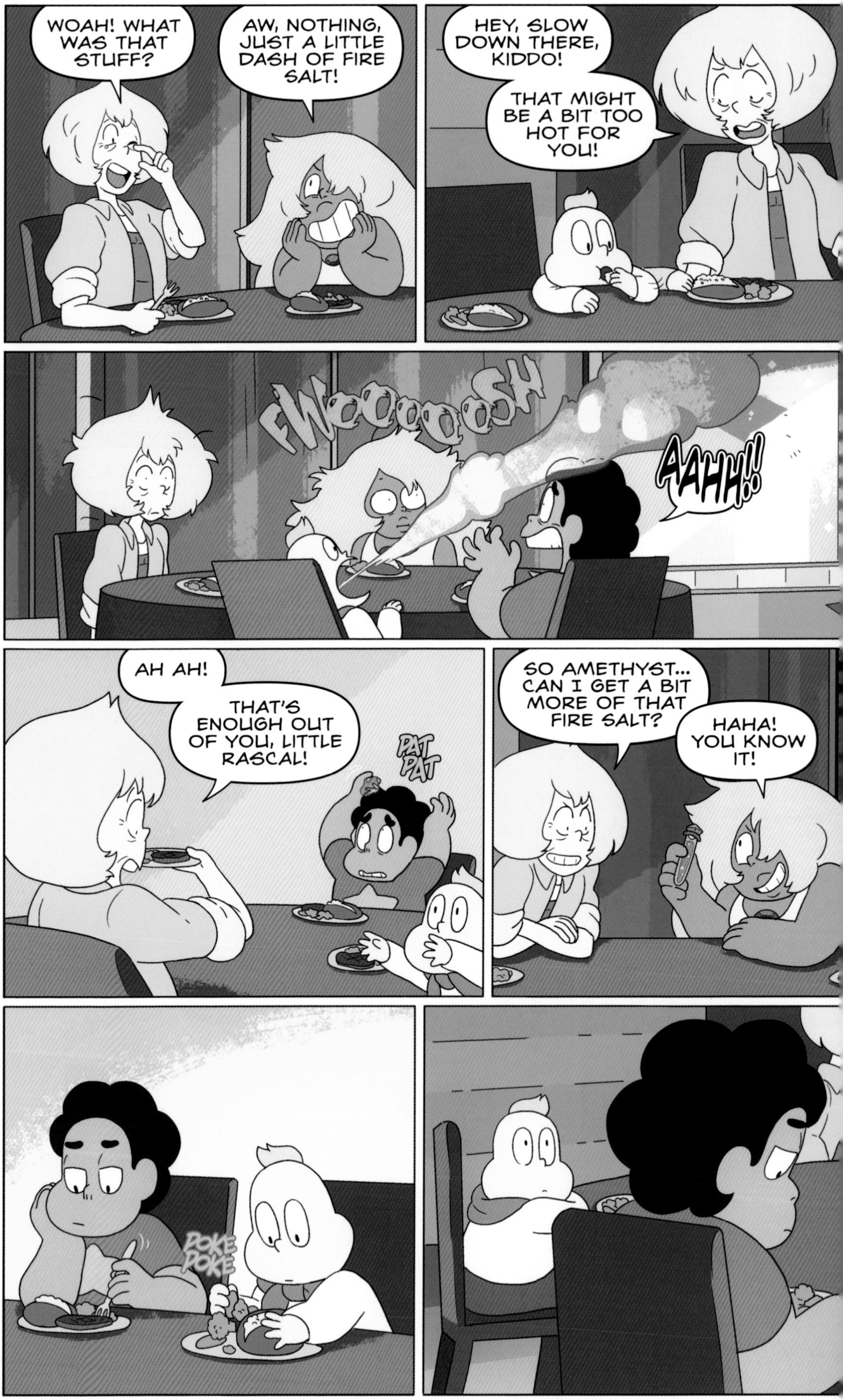
WOAH! WHAT WAS THAT STUFF?
AW, NOTHING, JUST A LITTLE DASH OF FIRE SALT!
HEY, SLOW DOWN THERE, KIDDO!
THAT MIGHT BE A BIT TOO HOT FOR YOU!
FWOOOOOSH
AAHH!!
AH AH!
THAT'S ENOUGH OUT OF YOU, LITTLE RASCAL!
PAT PAT
SO AMETHYST... CAN I GET A BIT MORE OF THAT FIRE SALT?
HAHA! YOU KNOW IT!
POKE POKE

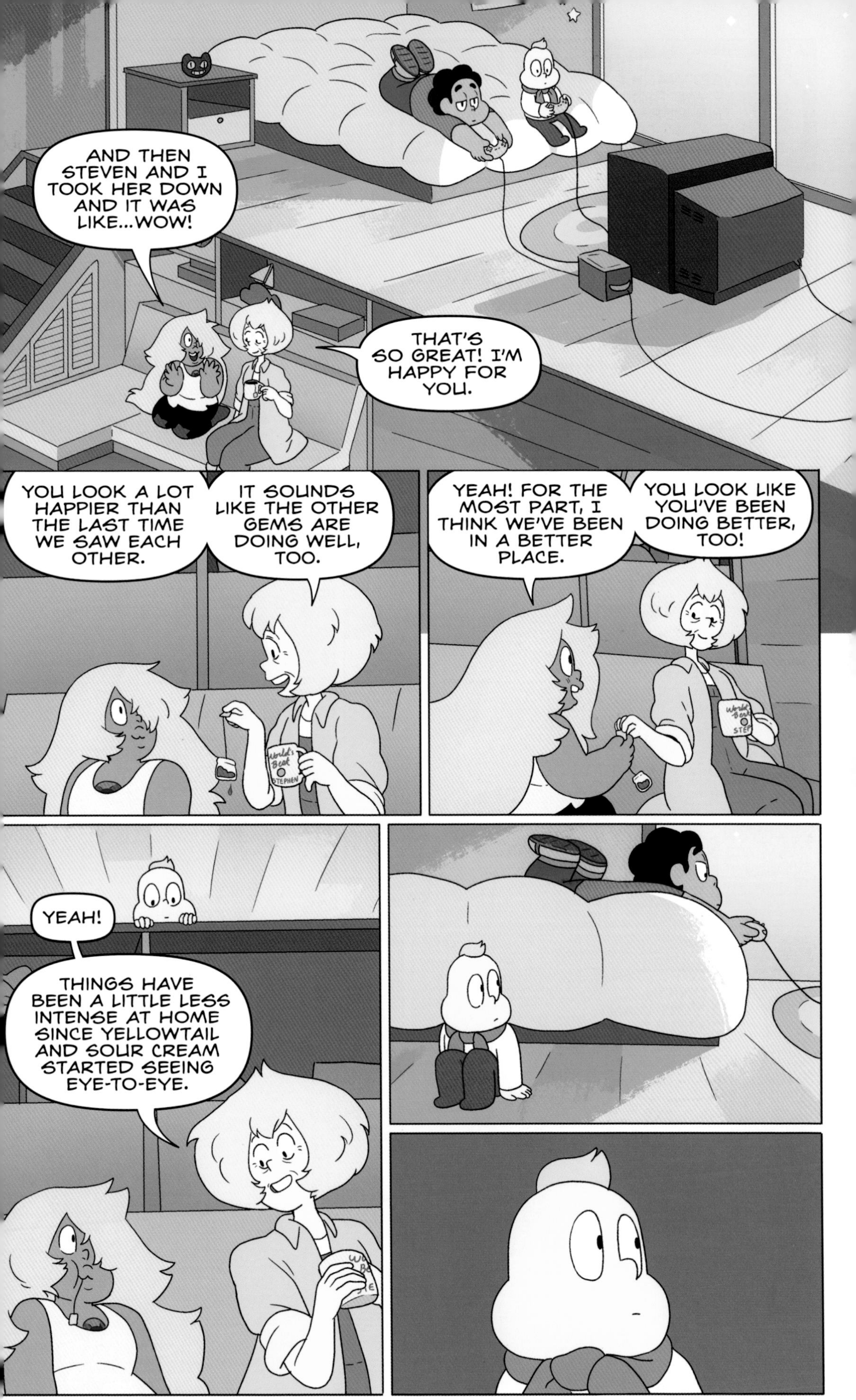
AND THEN STEVEN AND I TOOK HER DOWN AND IT WAS LIKE...WOW!
THAT'S SO GREAT! I'M HAPPY FOR YOU.
YOU LOOK A LOT HAPPIER THAN THE LAST TIME WE SAW EACH OTHER.
IT SOUNDS LIKE THE OTHER GEMS ARE DOING WELL, TOO.
World's Best STEPHEN
YEAH! FOR THE MOST PART, I THINK WE'VE BEEN IN A BETTER PLACE.
YOU LOOK LIKE YOU'VE BEEN DOING BETTER, TOO!
YEAH!
THINGS HAVE BEEN A LITTLE LESS INTENSE AT HOME SINCE YELLOWTAIL AND SOUR CREAM STARTED SEEING EYE-TO-EYE.

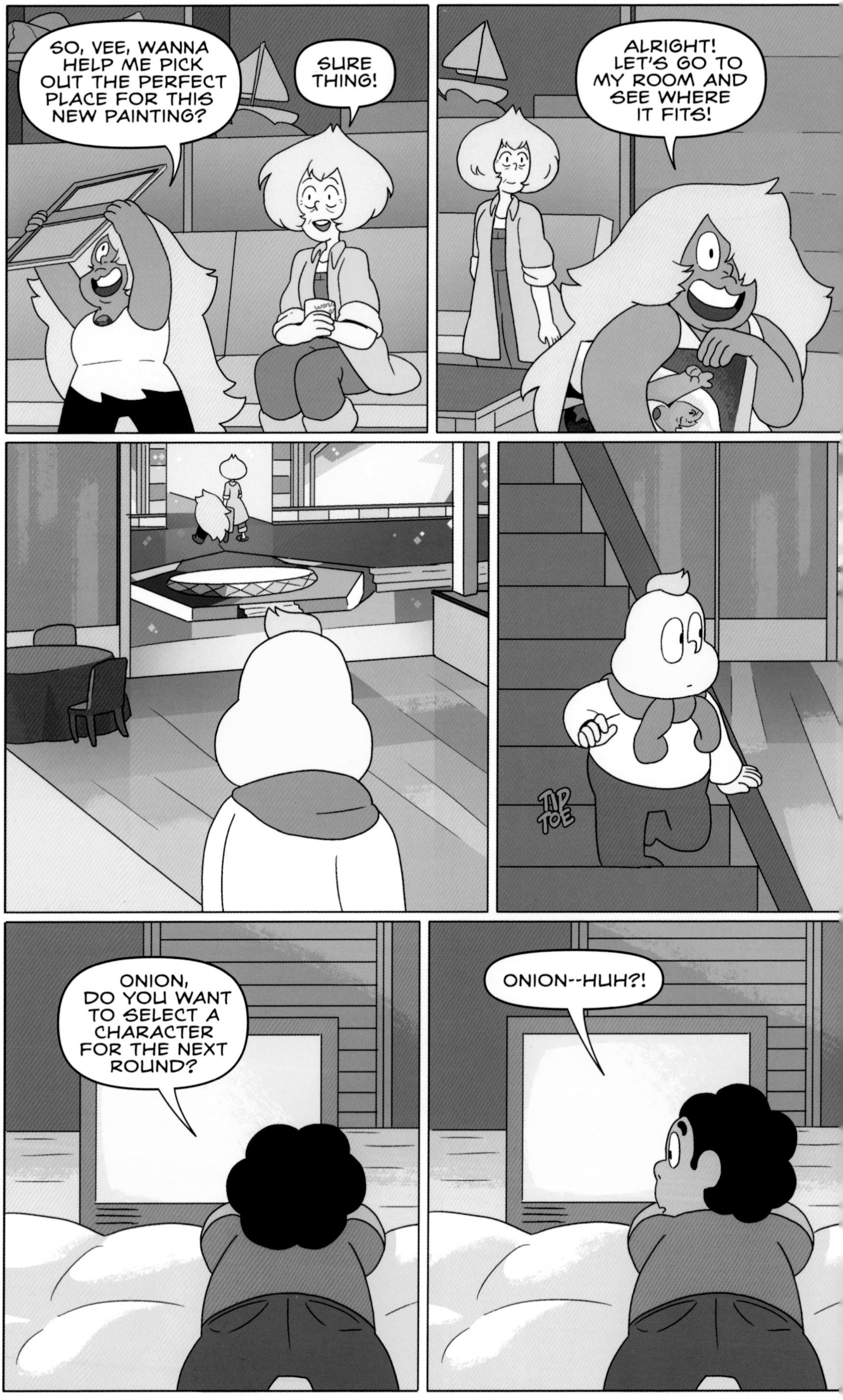
SO, VEE, WANNA HELP ME PICK OUT THE PERFECT PLACE FOR THIS NEW PAINTING?
SURE THING!
ALRIGHT! LET'S GO TO MY ROOM AND SEE WHERE IT FITS!
TIP TOE
ONION, DO YOU WANT TO SELECT A CHARACTER FOR THE NEXT ROUND?
ONION--HUH?!

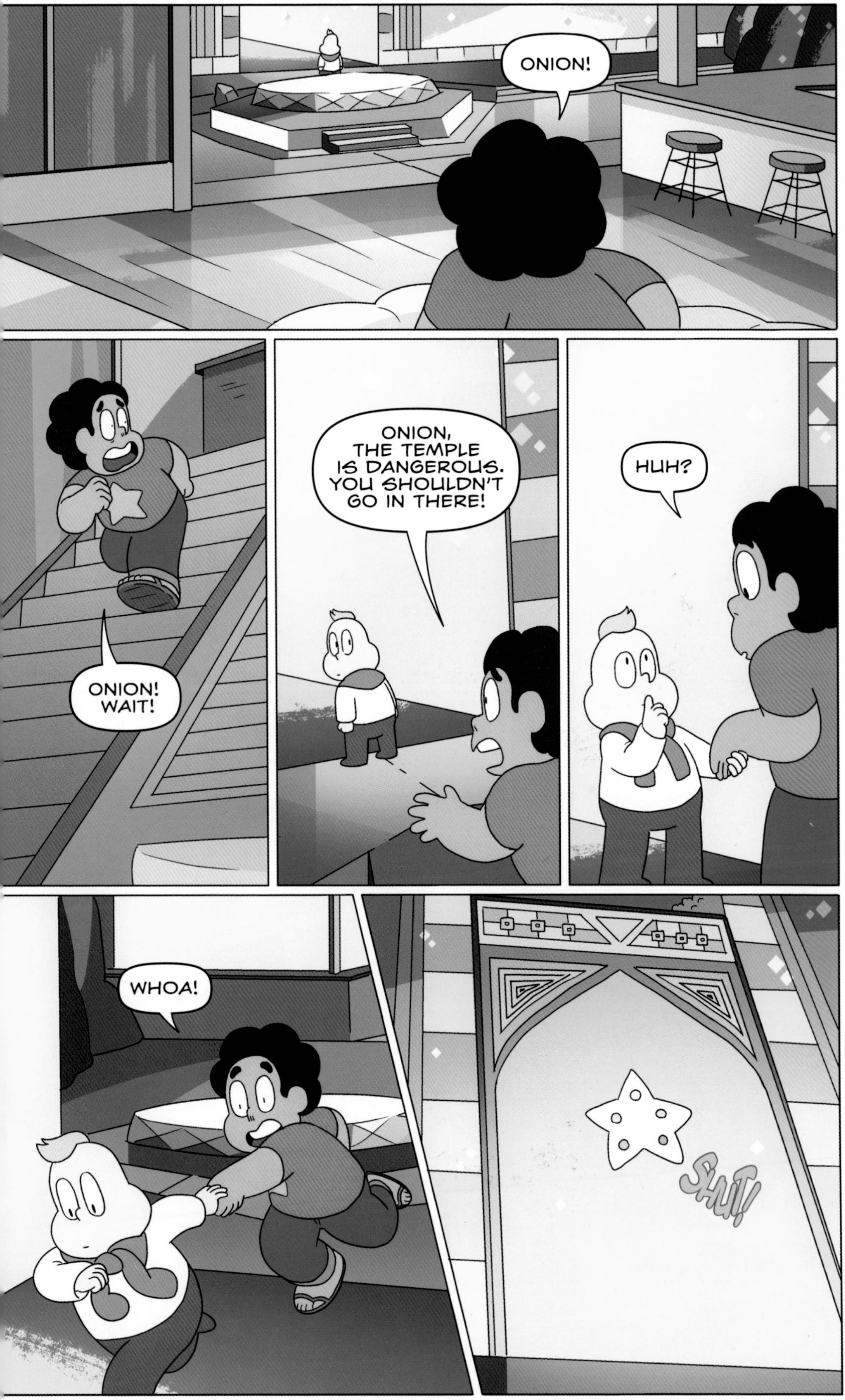
ONION!
ONION! WAIT!
ONION, THE TEMPLE IS DANGEROUS. YOU SHOULDN'T GO IN THERE!
HUH?
WHOA!
SHUT!

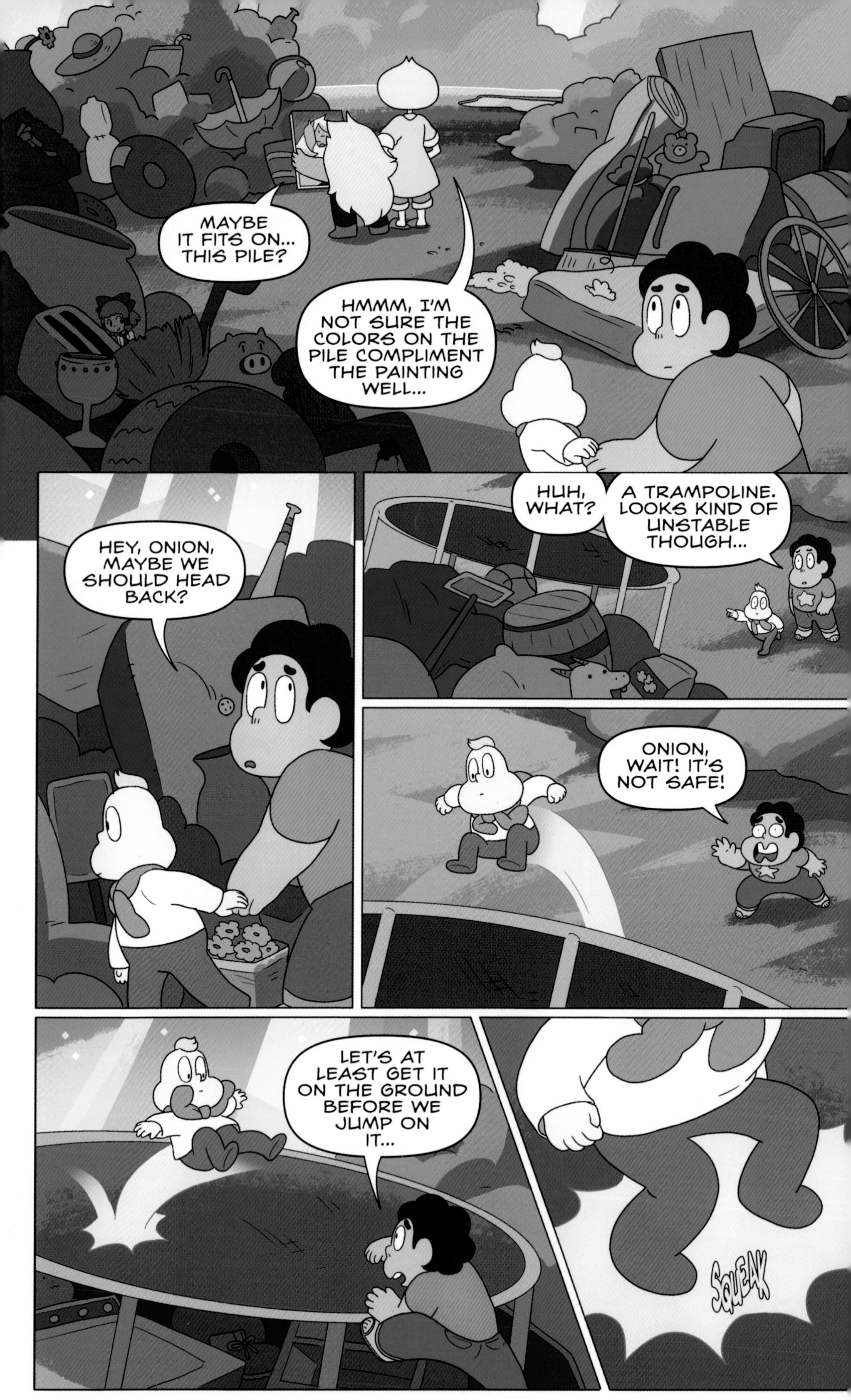
MAYBE IT FITS ON... THIS PILE?
HMMM, I'M NOT SURE THE COLORS ON THE PILE COMPLIMENT THE PAINTING WELL...
HEY, ONION, MAYBE WE SHOULD HEAD BACK?
HUH, WHAT?
A TRAMPOLINE. LOOKS KIND OF UNSTABLE THOUGH...
ONION, WAIT! IT'S NOT SAFE!
LET'S AT LEAST GET IT ON THE GROUND BEFORE WE JUMP ON IT...
SQUEAK

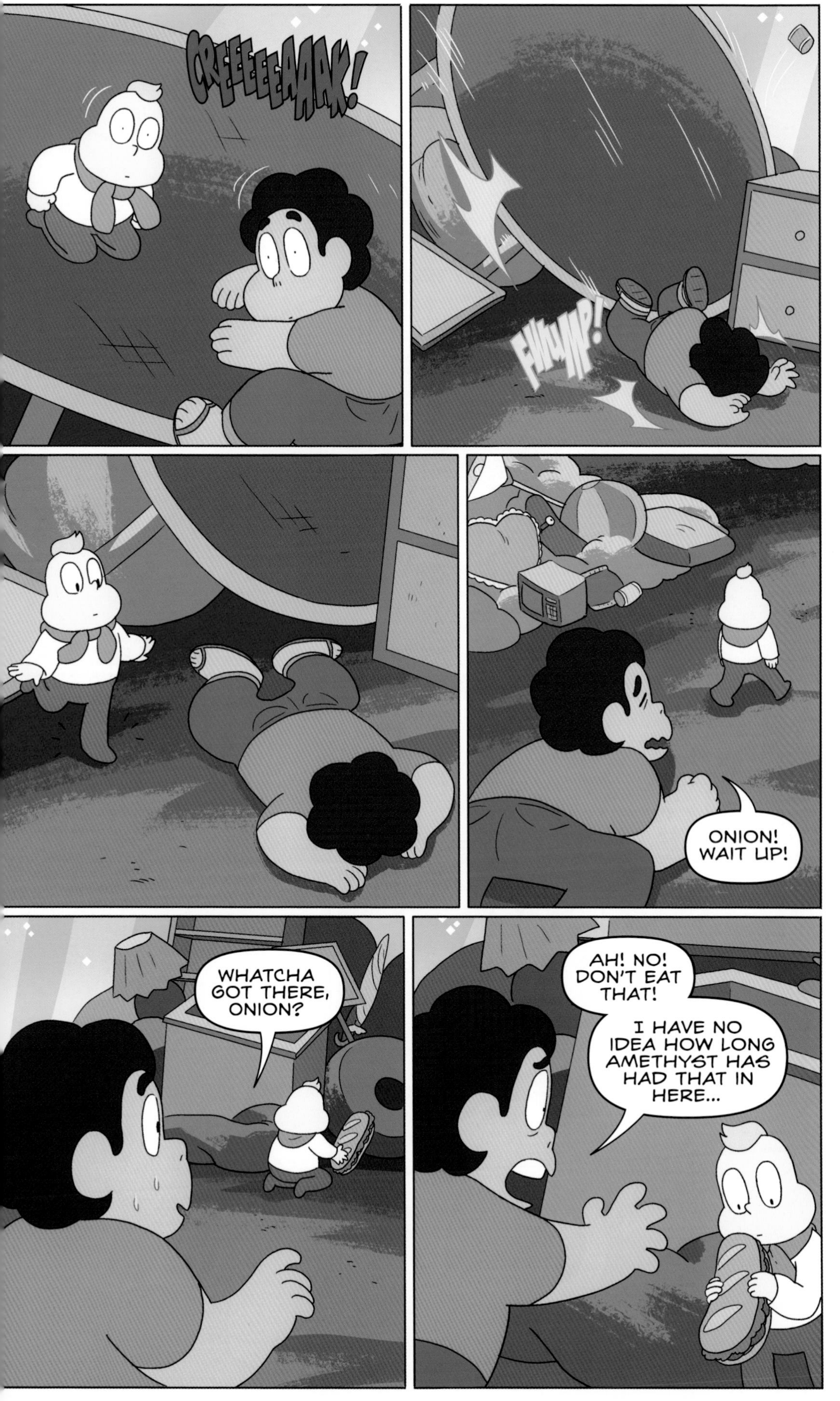

CREEEEEAAAK!
FWUMP!
ONION! WAIT UP!
WHATCHA GOT THERE, ONION?
AH! NO! DON'T EAT THAT!
I HAVE NO IDEA HOW LONG AMETHYST HAS HAD THAT IN HERE...

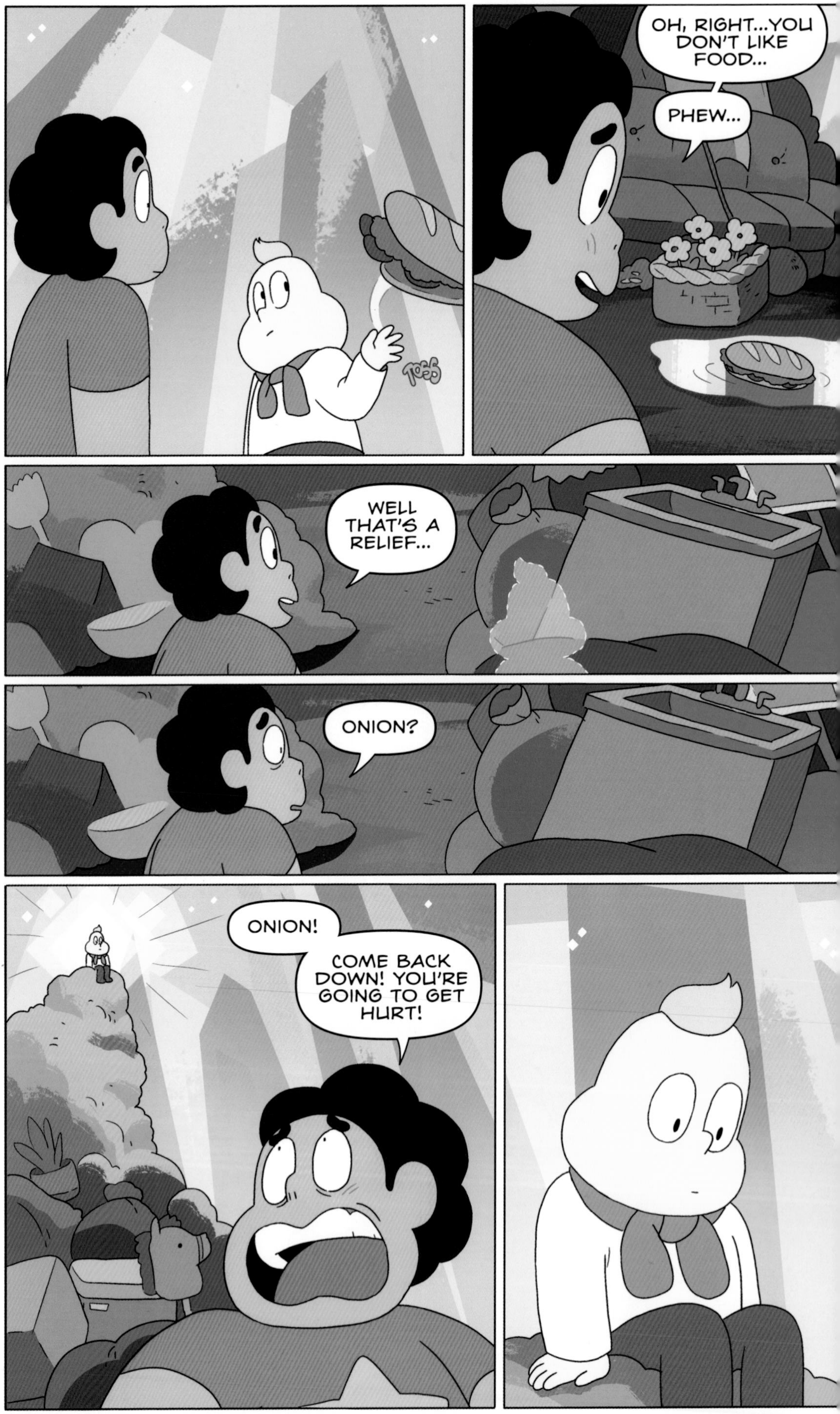
OH, RIGHT...YOU DON'T LIKE FOOD...
PHEW...
WELL THAT'S A RELIEF...
ONION?
ONION!
COME BACK DOWN! YOU'RE GOING TO GET HURT!

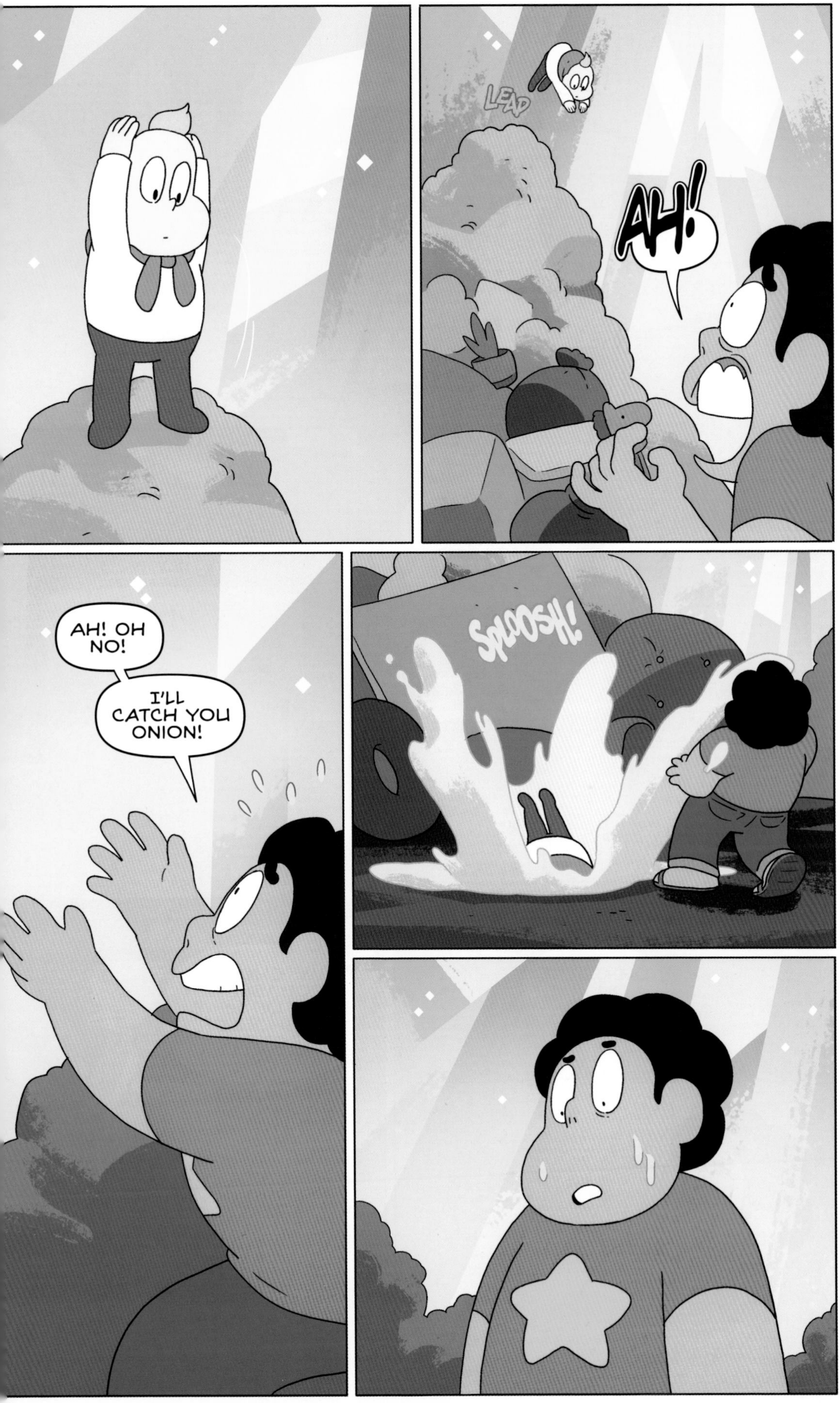
LEAP
AH!
AH! OH NO!
I'LL CATCH YOU ONION!
SPLOOSH!

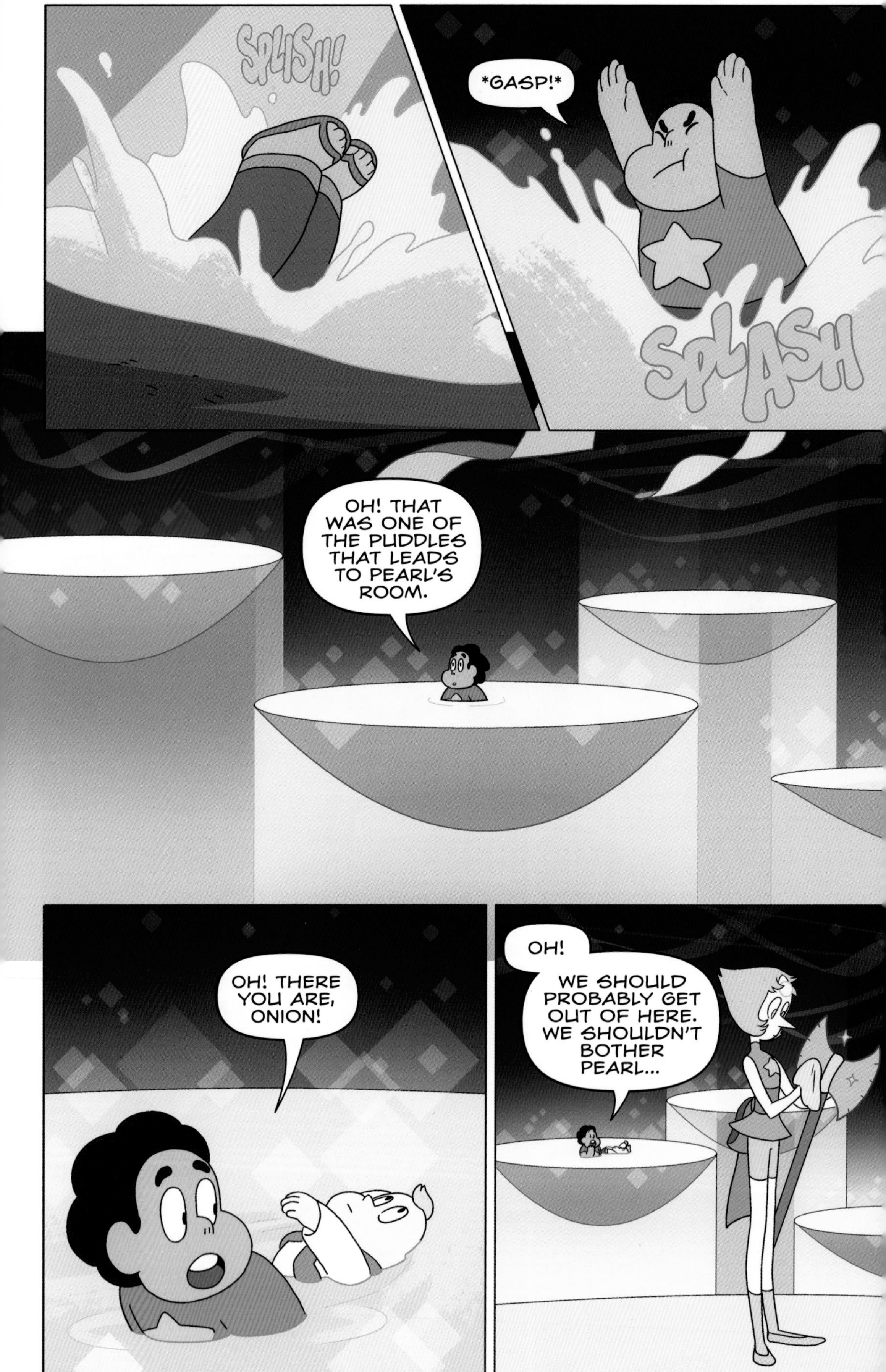
SPLISH!
GASP!
SPLASH
OH! THAT WAS ONE OF THE PUDDLES THAT LEADS TO PEARL'S ROOM.
OH! THERE YOU ARE, ONION!
OH!
WE SHOULD PROBABLY GET OUT OF HERE. WE SHOULDN'T BOTHER PEARL...

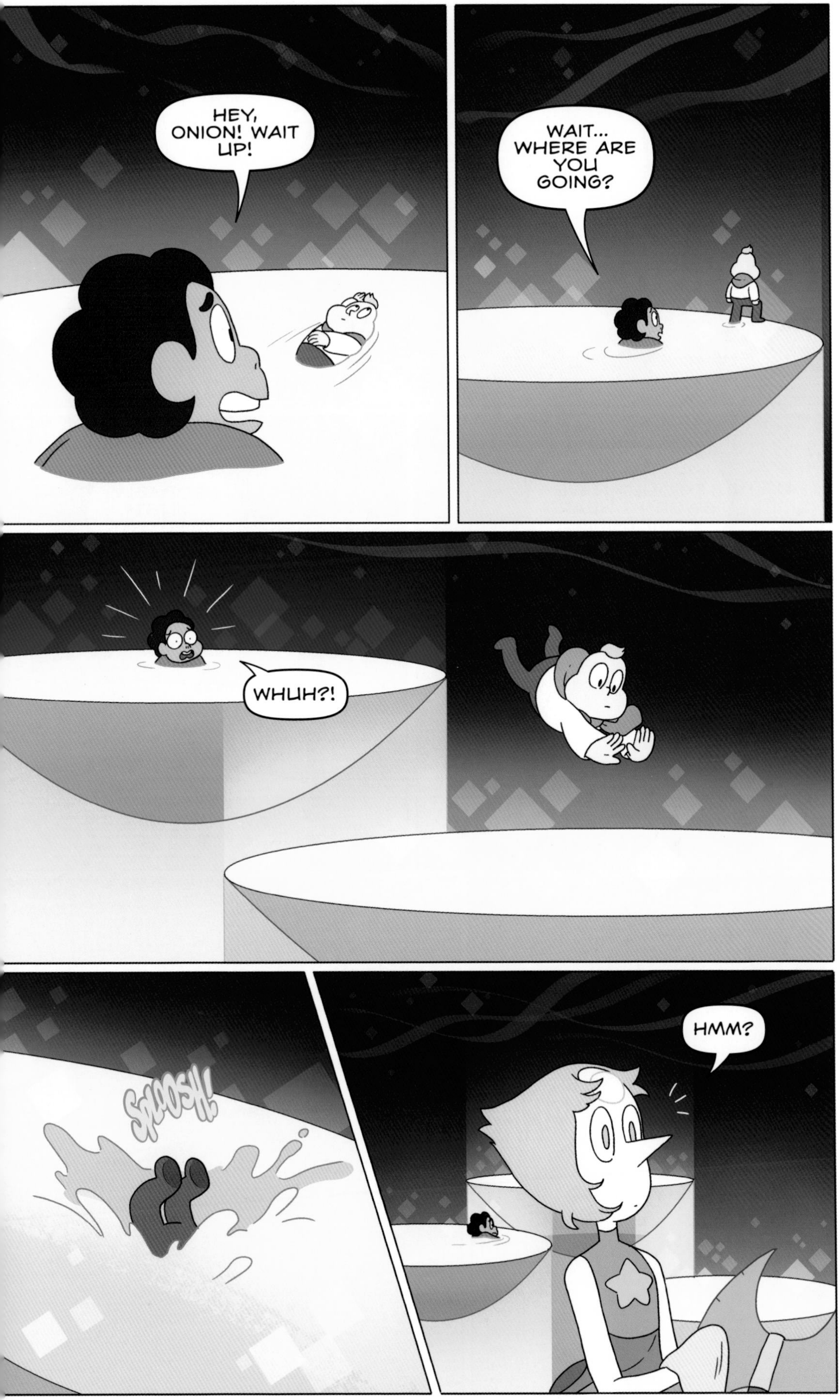
HEY, ONION! WAIT UP!
WAIT... WHERE ARE YOU GOING?
WHUH?!
SPLOOSH!
HMM?

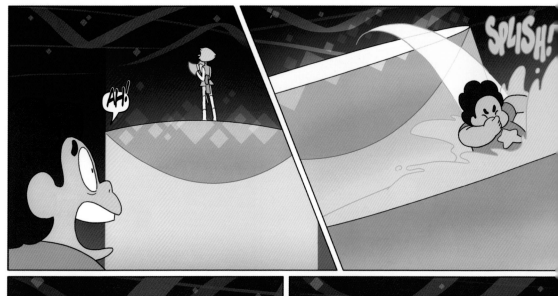

AH!

SPLISH!

HM...
I COULD HAVE
SWORN I HEARD
SOMETHING...

PROBABLY
JUST
AMETHYST.

AGAIN.

AAHH!!

OOF!

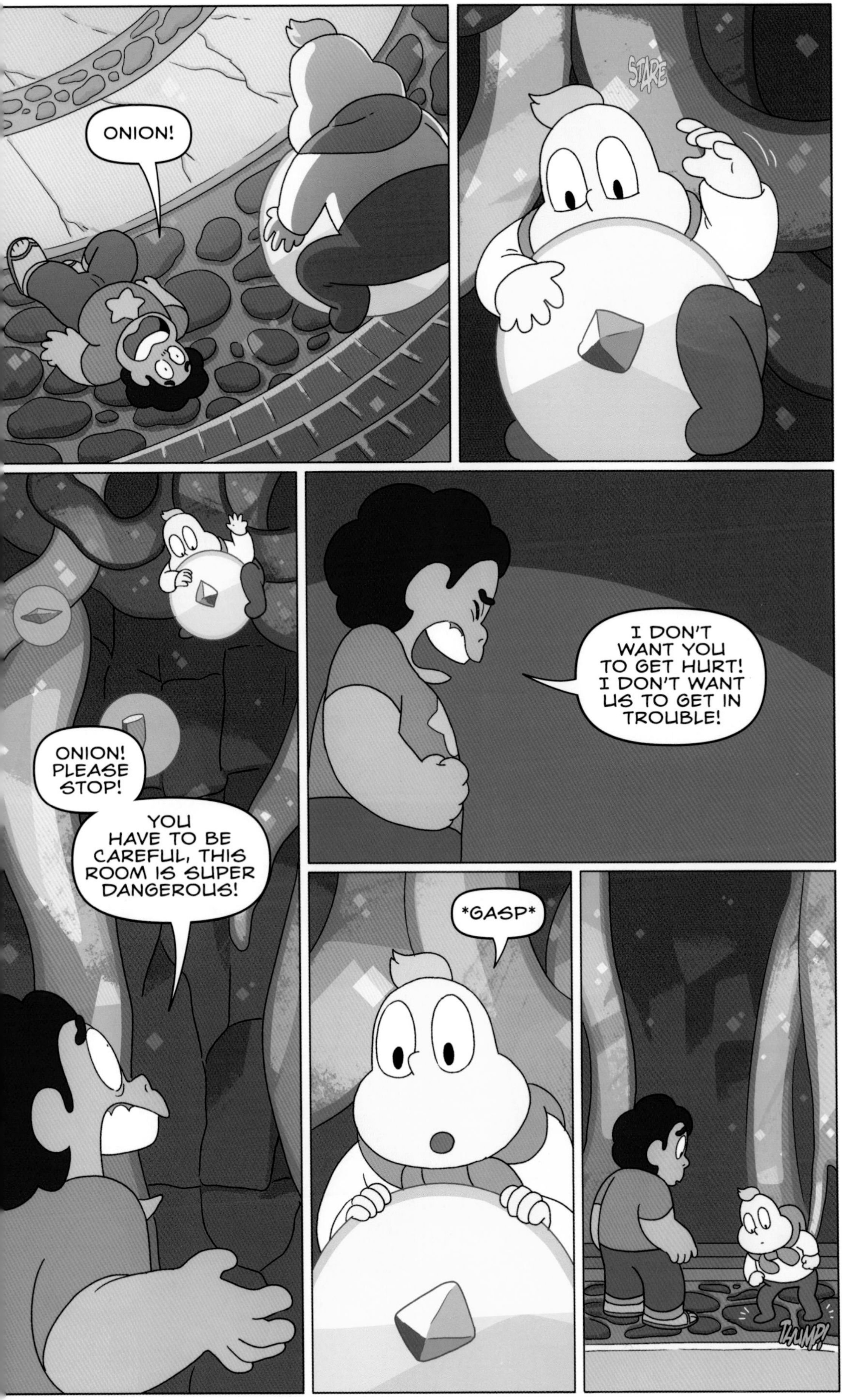
ONION!
STARE
ONION! PLEASE STOP!
YOU HAVE TO BE CAREFUL, THIS ROOM IS SUPER DANGEROUS!
I DON'T WANT YOU TO GET HURT! I DON'T WANT US TO GET IN TROUBLE!
GASP
THUMP!

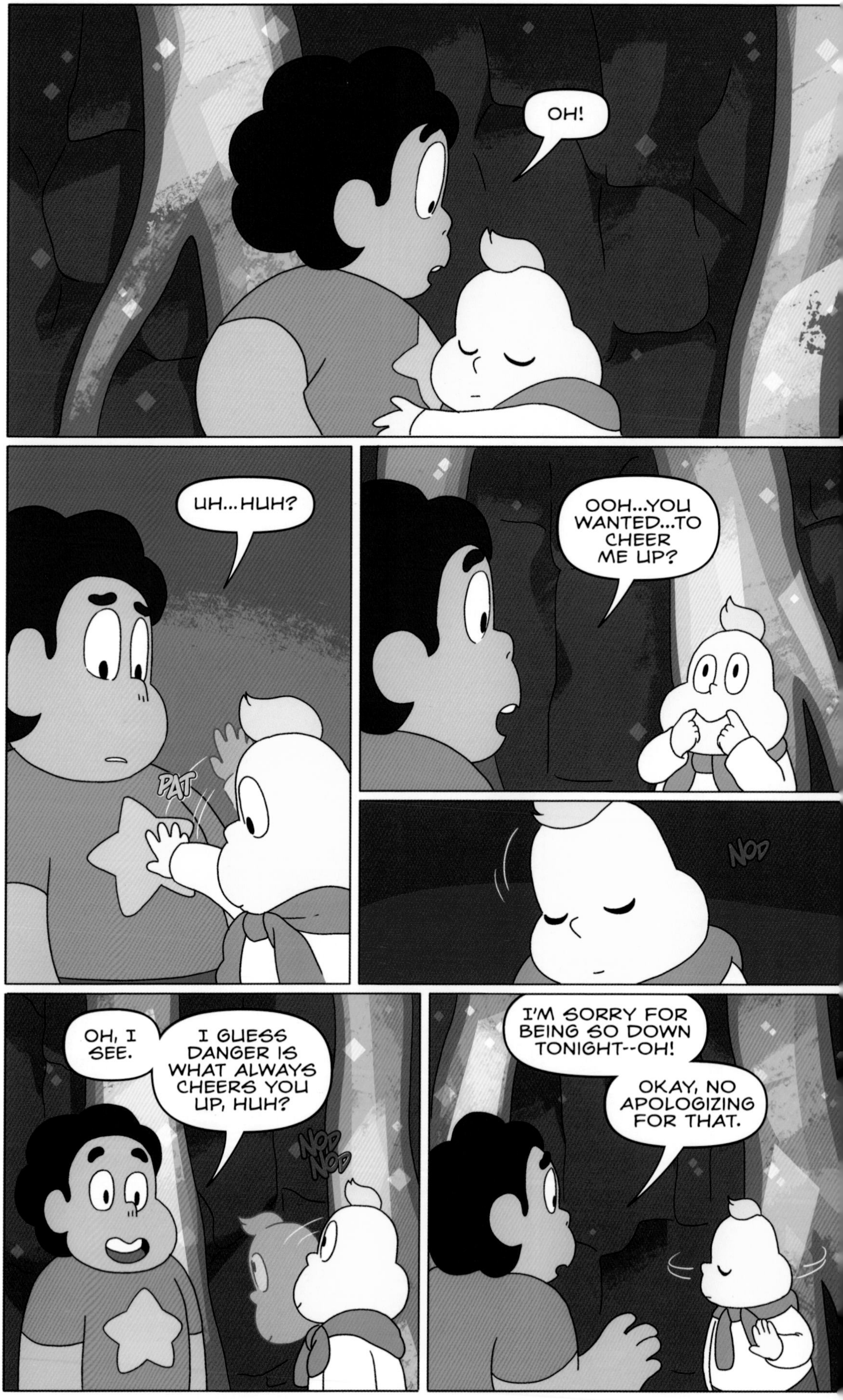
OH!
UH...HUH?
PAT
OOH...YOU WANTED...TO CHEER ME UP?
NOD
OH, I SEE.
I GUESS DANGER IS WHAT ALWAYS CHEERS YOU UP, HUH?
NOD NOD
I'M SORRY FOR BEING SO DOWN TONIGHT--OH!
OKAY, NO APOLOGIZING FOR THAT.

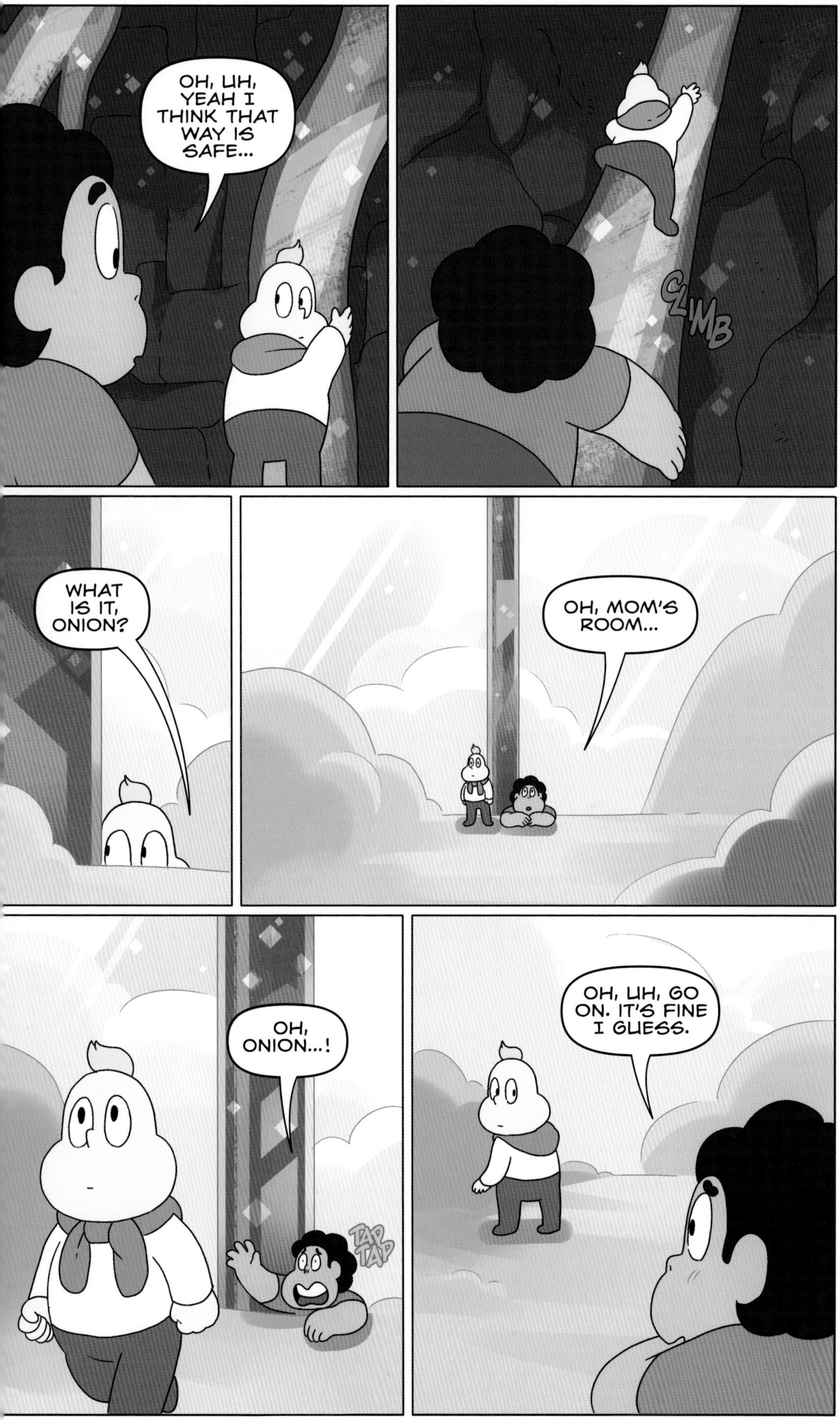
OH, UH, YEAH I THINK THAT WAY IS SAFE...
CLIMB
WHAT IS IT, ONION?
OH, MOM'S ROOM...
OH, ONION...!
TAP TAP
OH, UH, GO ON. IT'S FINE I GUESS.

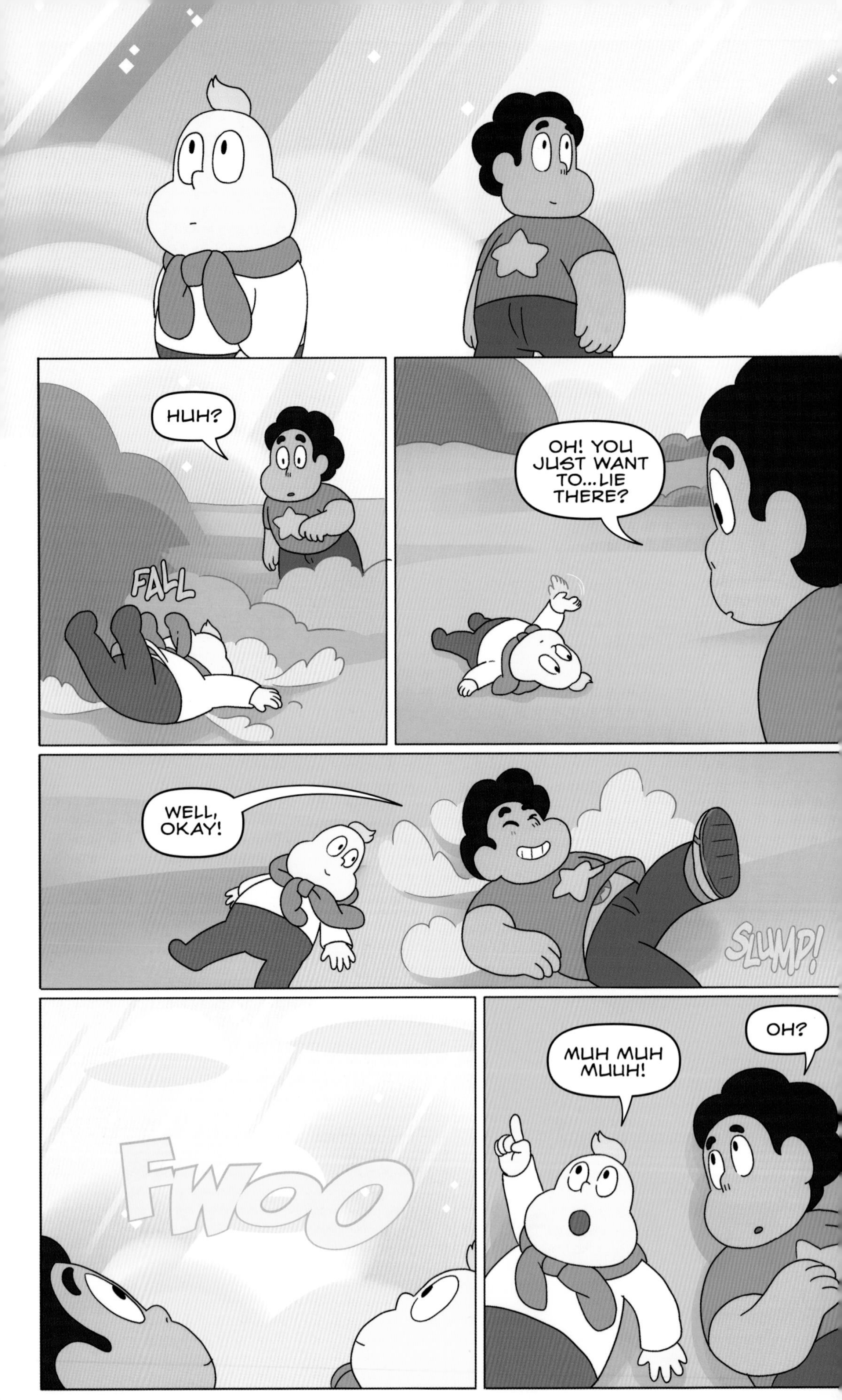
HUH?
FALL
OH! YOU JUST WANT TO...LIE THERE?
WELL, OKAY!
SLUMP!
FWOO
MUH MUH MUUH!
OH?

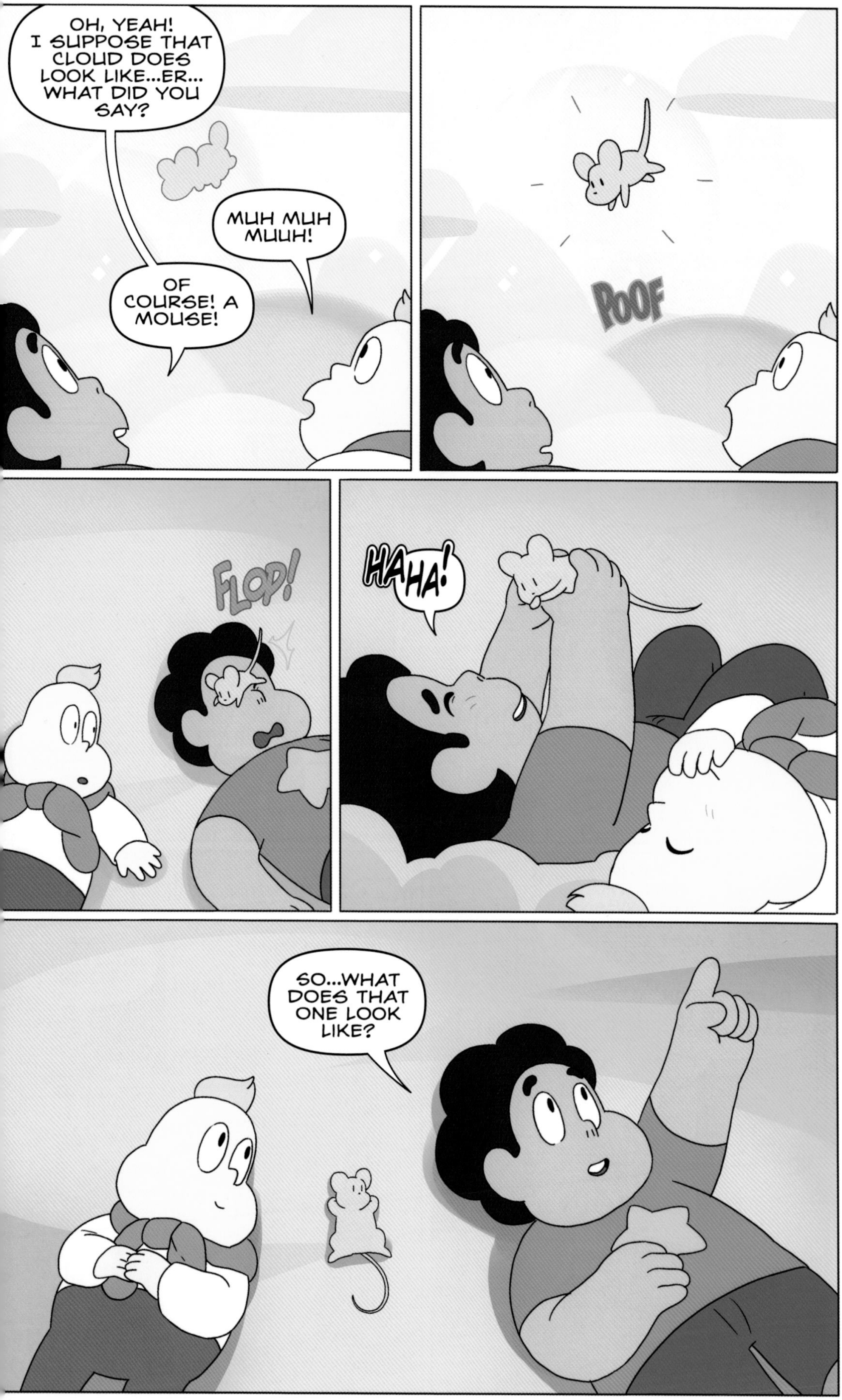
OH, YEAH! I SUPPOSE THAT CLOUD DOES LOOK LIKE...ER... WHAT DID YOU SAY?
MUH MUH MUUH!
OF COURSE! A MOUSE!
POOF
FLOP!
HAHA!
SO...WHAT DOES THAT ONE LOOK LIKE?

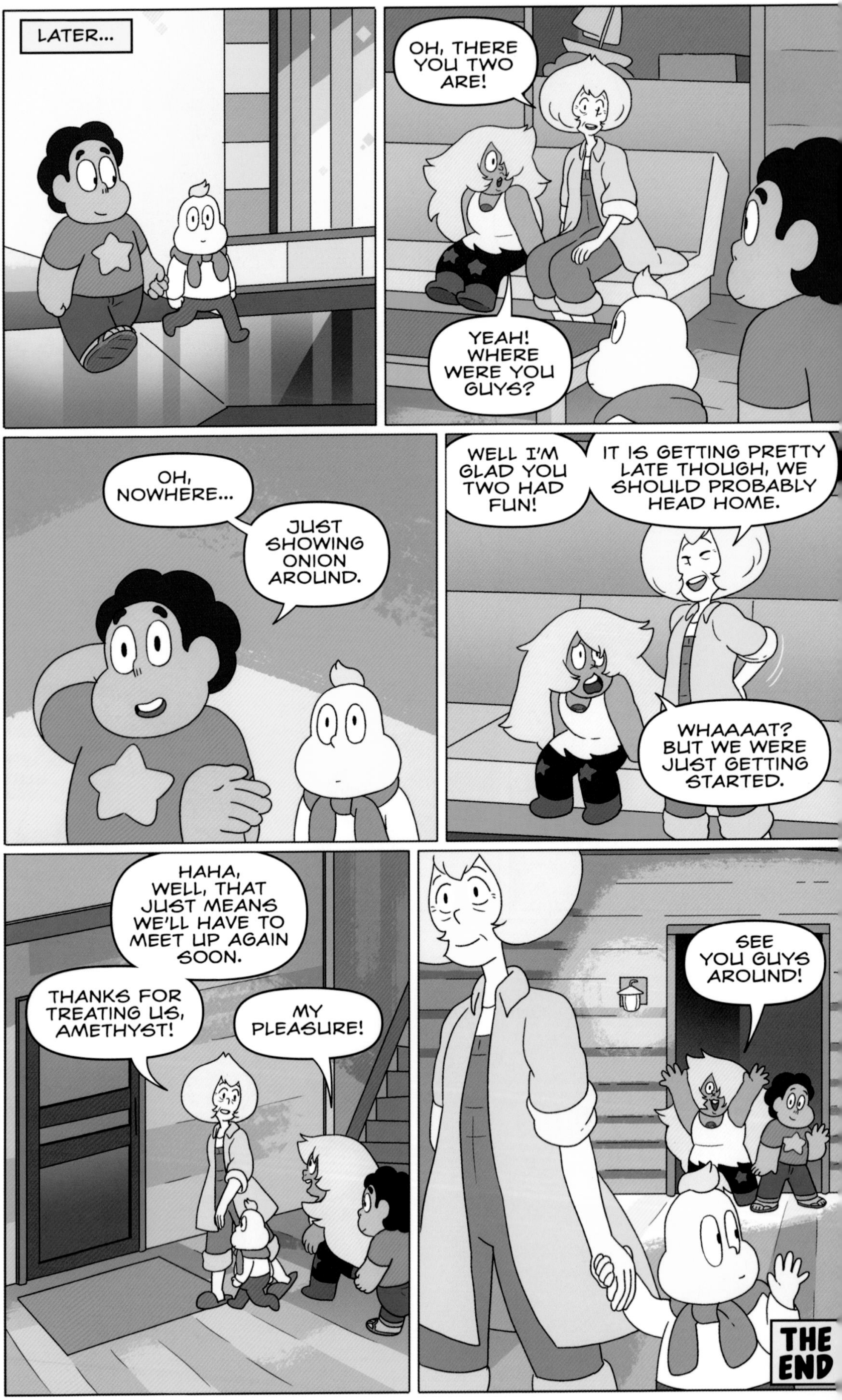

LATER...
OH, THERE YOU TWO ARE!
YEAH! WHERE WERE YOU GUYS?
OH, NOWHERE...
JUST SHOWING ONION AROUND.
WELL I'M GLAD YOU TWO HAD FUN!
IT IS GETTING PRETTY LATE THOUGH, WE SHOULD PROBABLY HEAD HOME.
WHAAAAT? BUT WE WERE JUST GETTING STARTED.
HAHA, WELL, THAT JUST MEANS WE'LL HAVE TO MEET UP AGAIN SOON.
THANKS FOR TREATING US, AMETHYST!
MY PLEASURE!
SEE YOU GUYS AROUND!
THE END

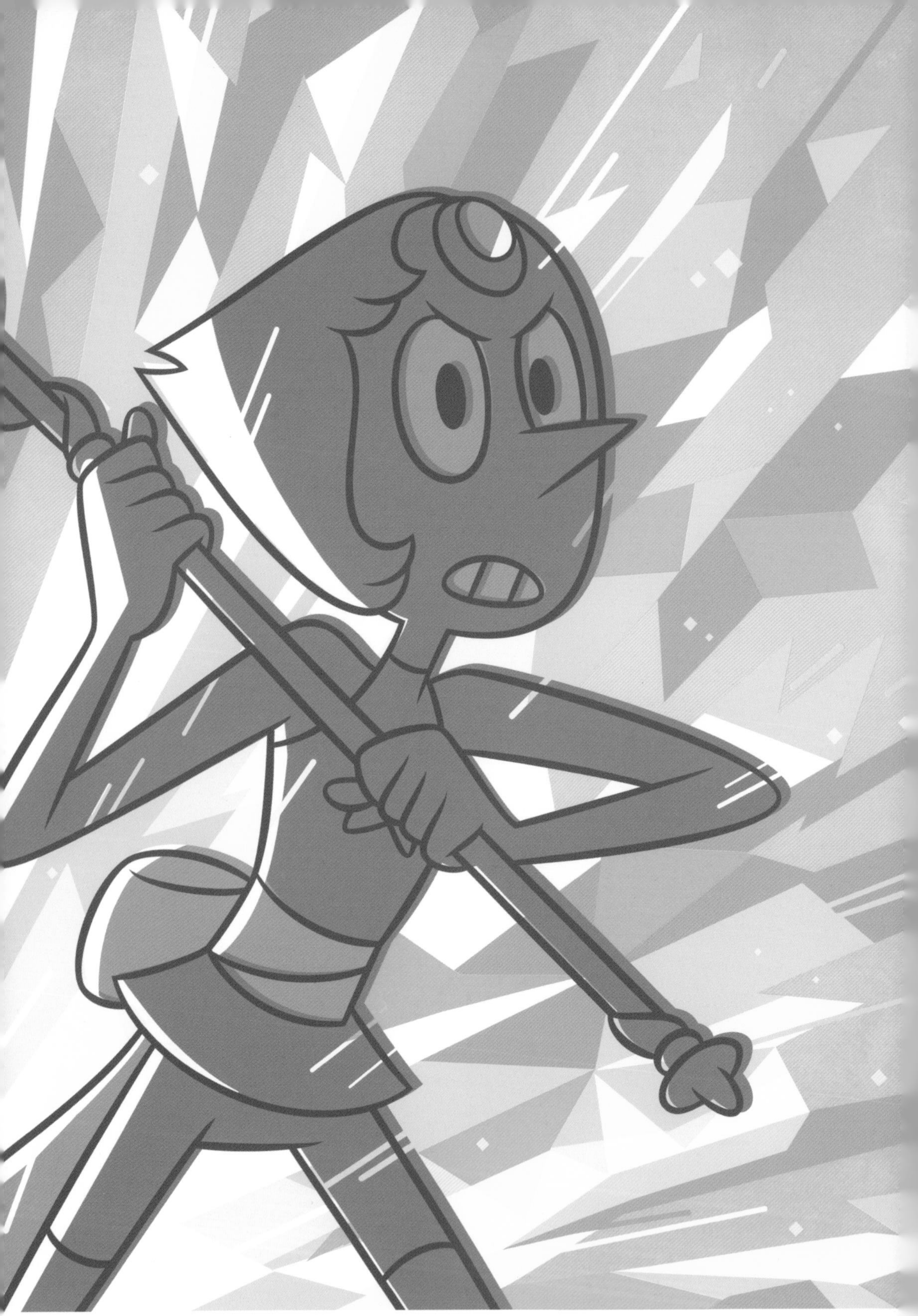

CHAPTER TWENTY-THREE

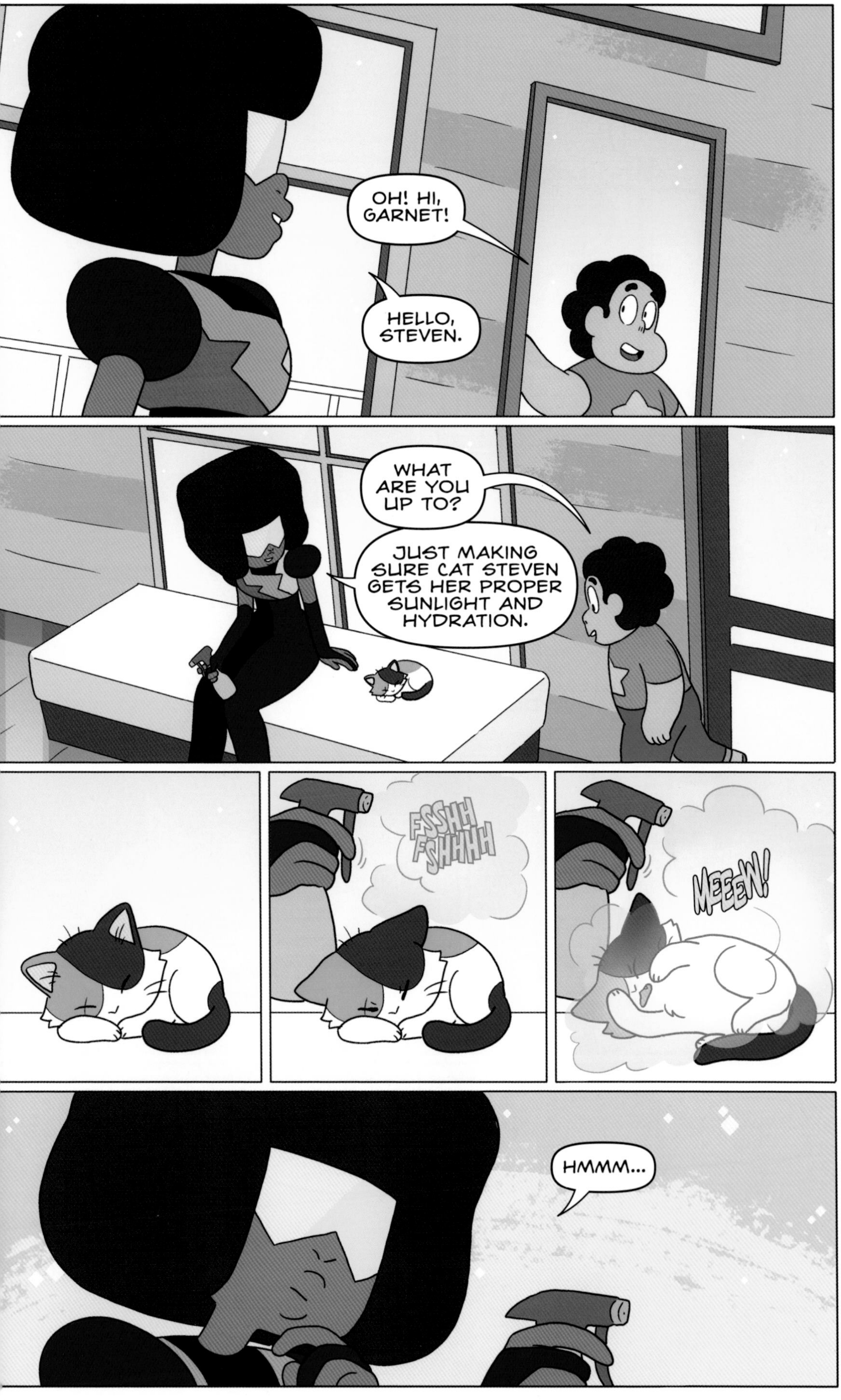
OH! HI, GARNET!
HELLO, STEVEN.
WHAT ARE YOU UP TO?
JUST MAKING SURE CAT STEVEN GETS HER PROPER SUNLIGHT AND HYDRATION.
FSSHH FSHHHH
MEEEW!
HMMM...

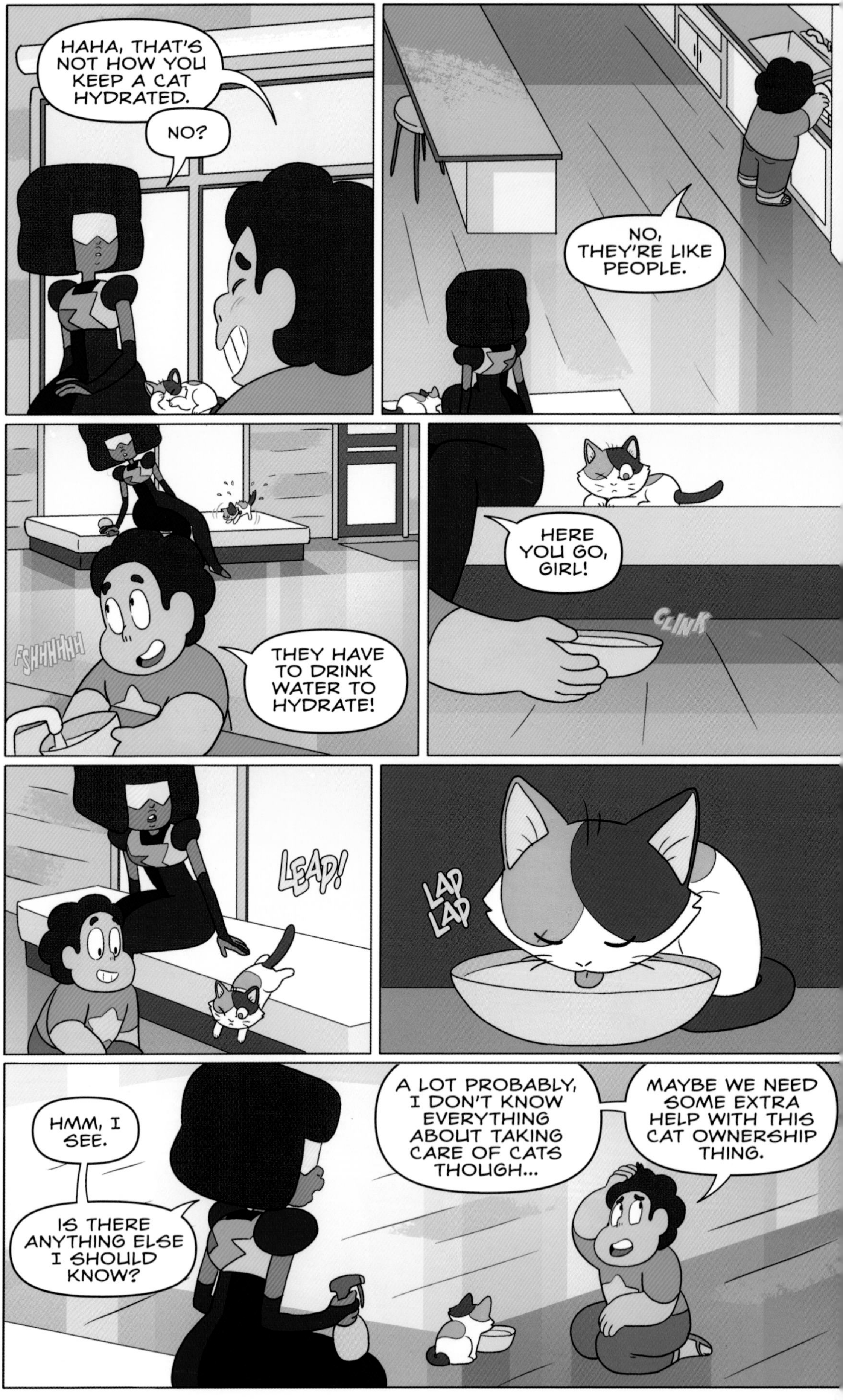
HAHA, THAT'S NOT HOW YOU KEEP A CAT HYDRATED.
NO?
NO, THEY'RE LIKE PEOPLE.
FSHHHHHH
THEY HAVE TO DRINK WATER TO HYDRATE!
HERE YOU GO, GIRL!
CLINK
LEAP!
LAP LAP
HMM, I SEE.
IS THERE ANYTHING ELSE I SHOULD KNOW?
A LOT PROBABLY, I DON'T KNOW EVERYTHING ABOUT TAKING CARE OF CATS THOUGH...
MAYBE WE NEED SOME EXTRA HELP WITH THIS CAT OWNERSHIP THING.

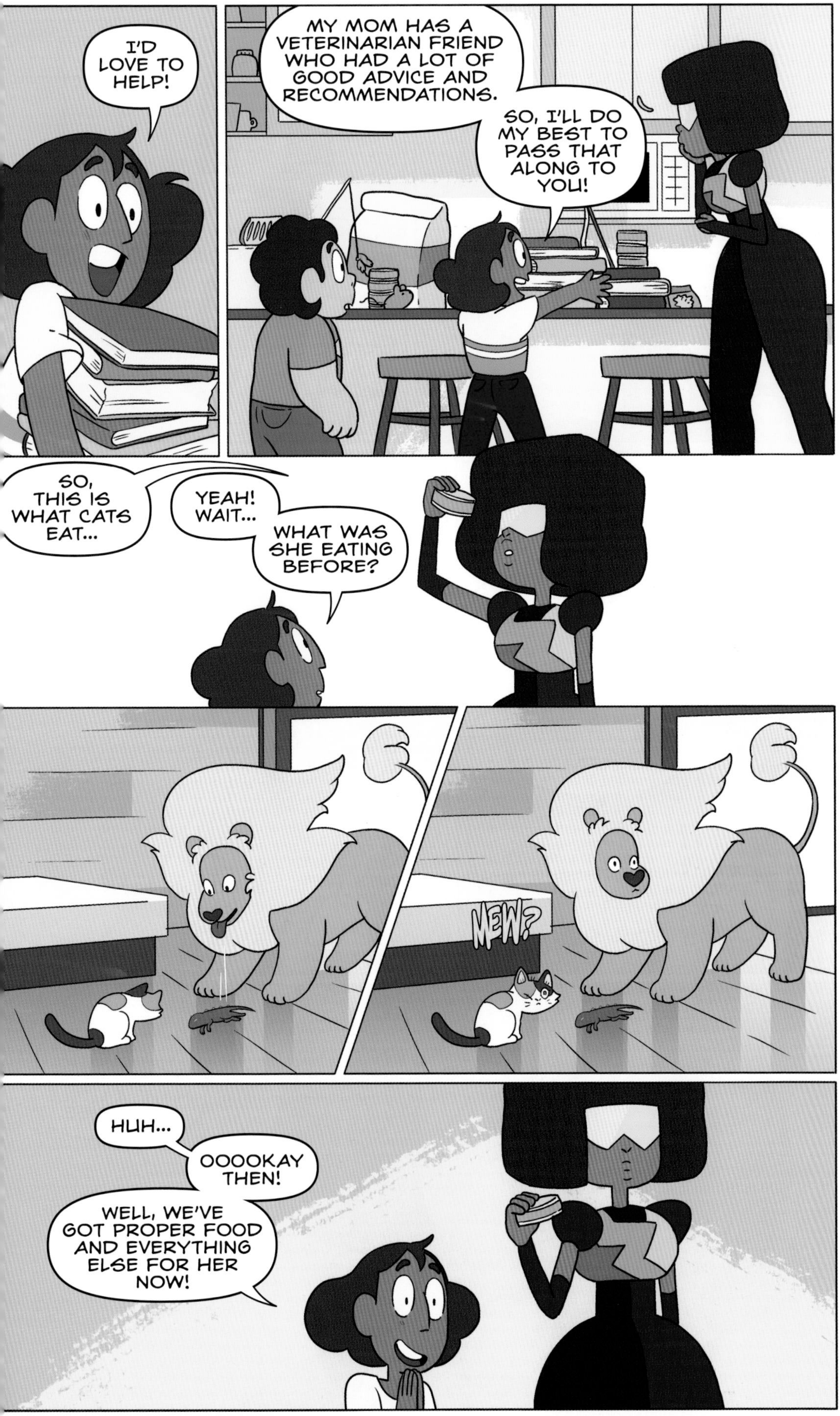
I'D LOVE TO HELP!
MY MOM HAS A VETERINARIAN FRIEND WHO HAD A LOT OF GOOD ADVICE AND RECOMMENDATIONS.
SO, I'LL DO MY BEST TO PASS THAT ALONG TO YOU!
SO, THIS IS WHAT CATS EAT...
YEAH! WAIT...
WHAT WAS SHE EATING BEFORE?
MEW?
HUH...
OOOOKAY THEN!
WELL, WE'VE GOT PROPER FOOD AND EVERYTHING ELSE FOR HER NOW!

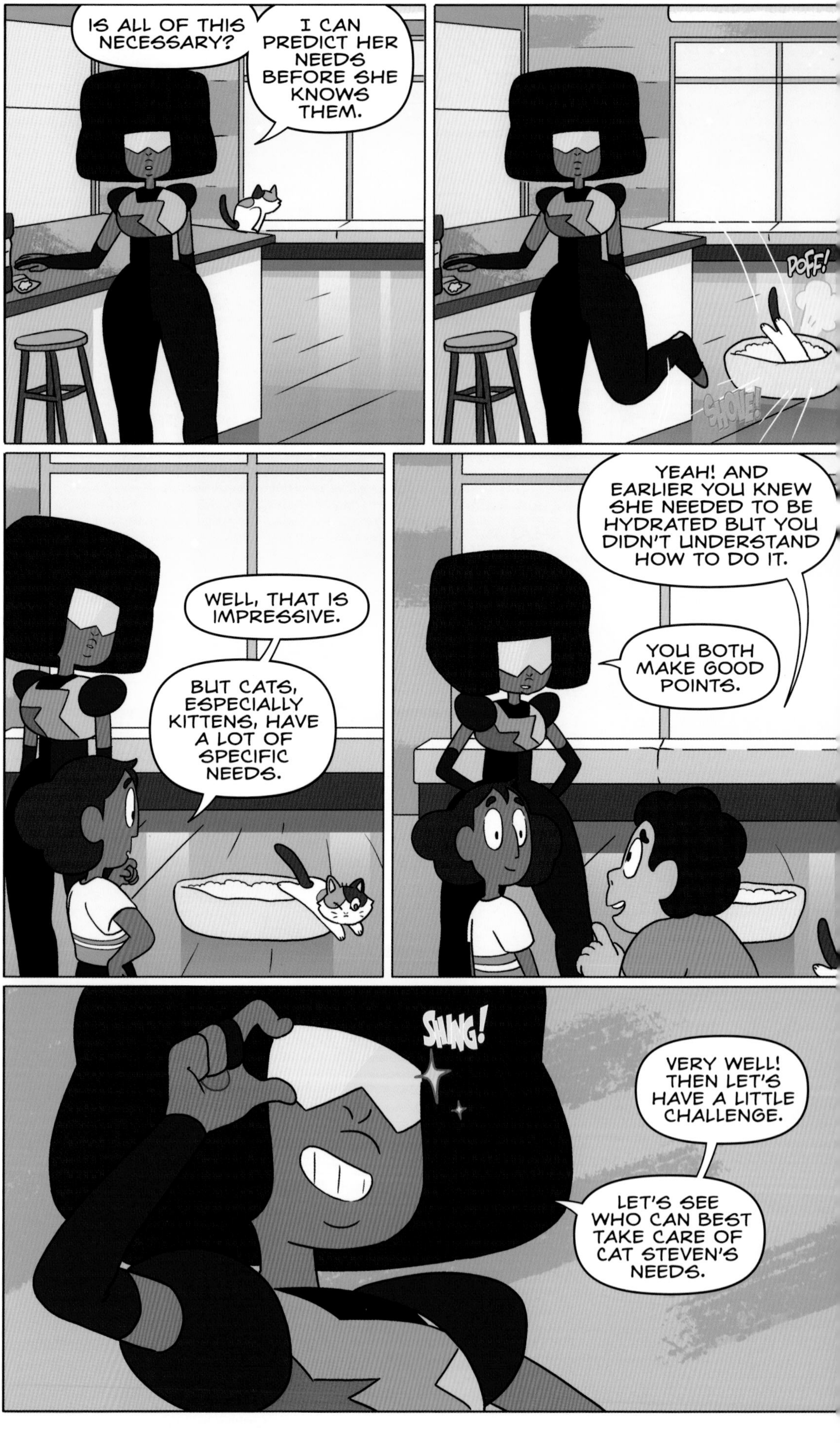
IS ALL OF THIS NECESSARY?
I CAN PREDICT HER NEEDS BEFORE SHE KNOWS THEM.
POFF!
SHOVE!
WELL, THAT IS IMPRESSIVE.
BUT CATS, ESPECIALLY KITTENS, HAVE A LOT OF SPECIFIC NEEDS.
YEAH! AND EARLIER YOU KNEW SHE NEEDED TO BE HYDRATED BUT YOU DIDN'T UNDERSTAND HOW TO DO IT.
YOU BOTH MAKE GOOD POINTS.
SHING!
VERY WELL! THEN LET'S HAVE A LITTLE CHALLENGE.
LET'S SEE WHO CAN BEST TAKE CARE OF CAT STEVEN'S NEEDS.

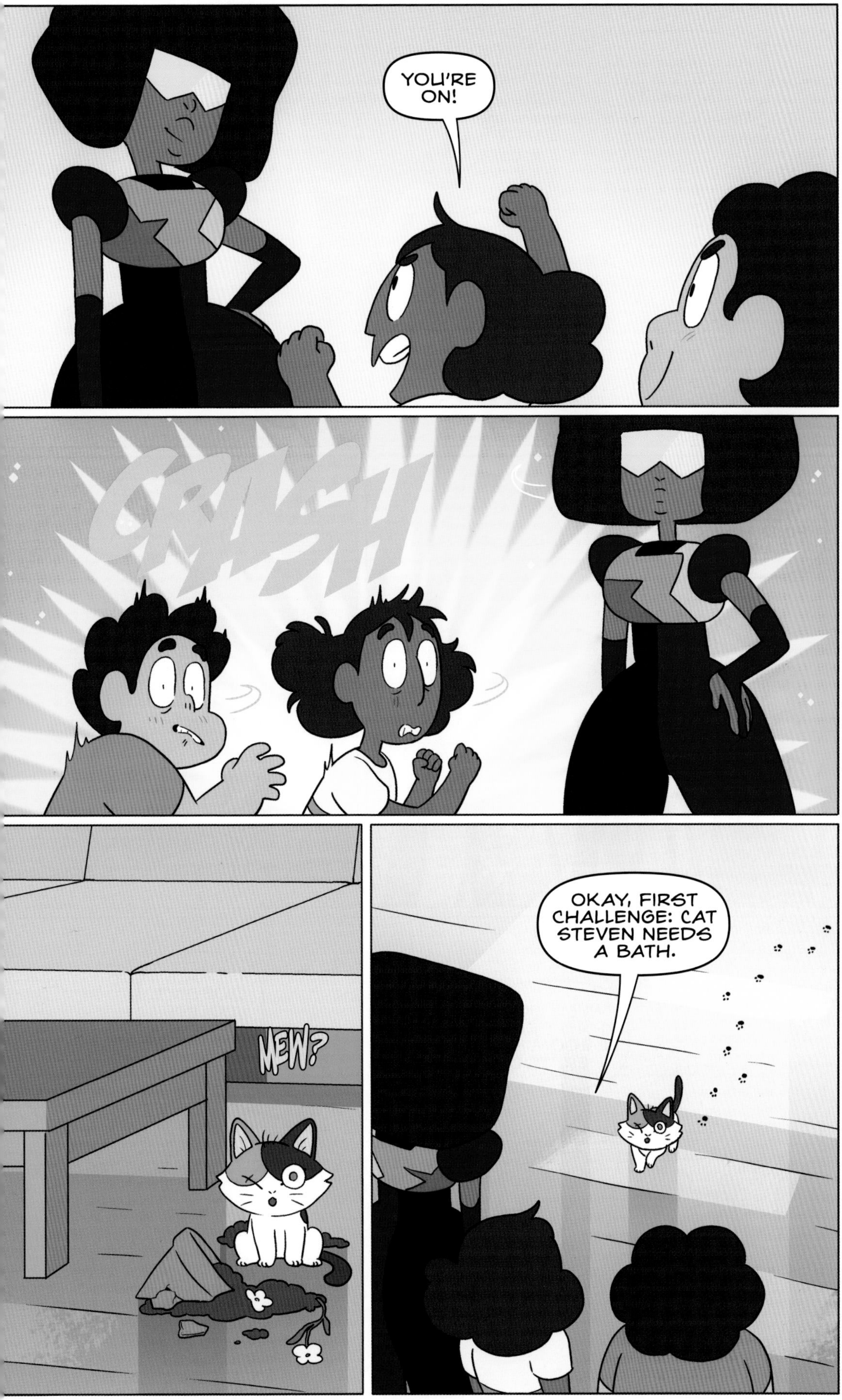
YOU'RE ON!
CRASH
MEW?
OKAY, FIRST CHALLENGE: CAT STEVEN NEEDS A BATH.

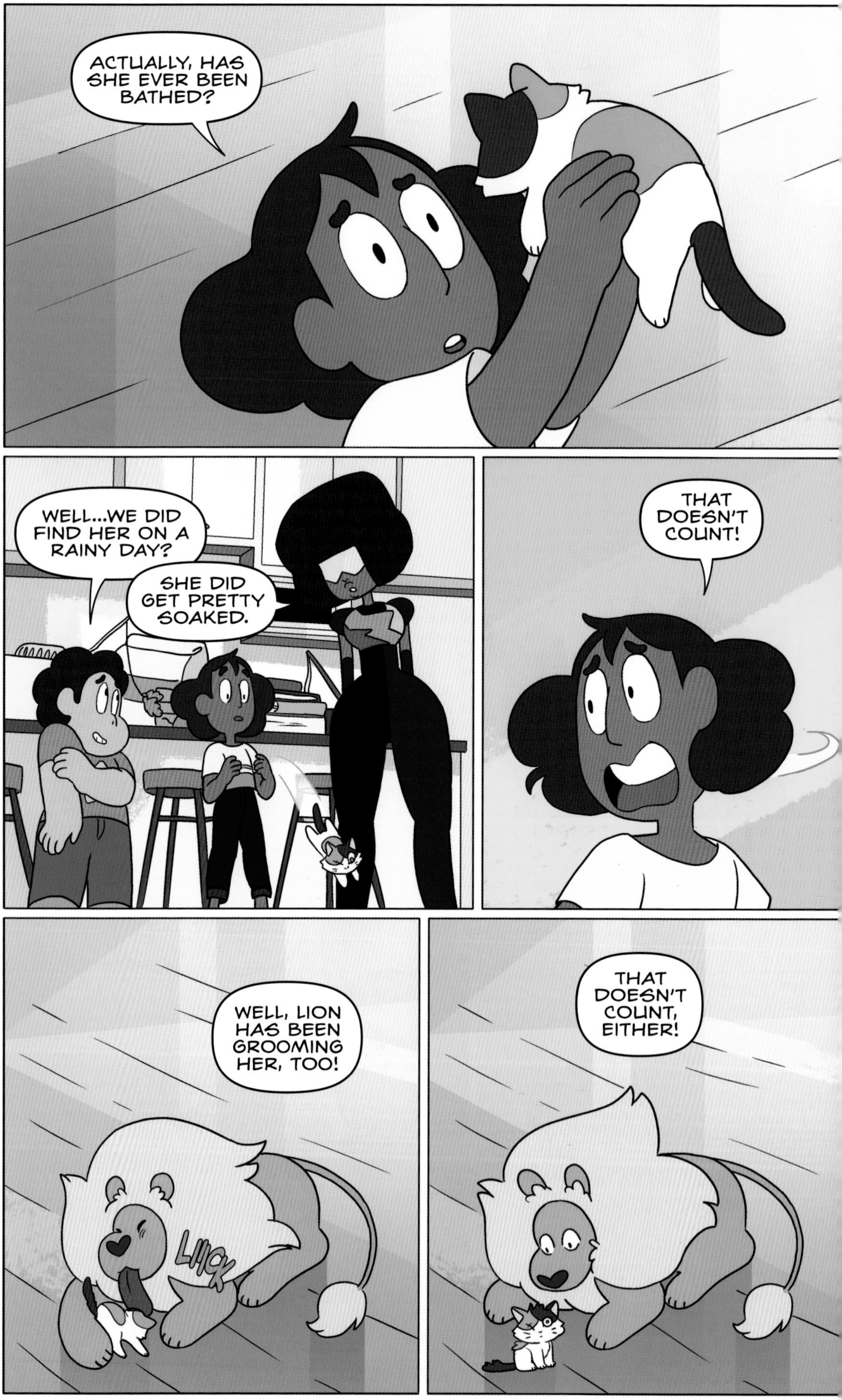
ACTUALLY, HAS SHE EVER BEEN BATHED?
WELL...WE DID FIND HER ON A RAINY DAY?
SHE DID GET PRETTY SOAKED.
THAT DOESN'T COUNT!
WELL, LION HAS BEEN GROOMING HER, TOO!
LIIICK
THAT DOESN'T COUNT, EITHER!

SO GARNET, HOW WOULD YOU CLEAN CAT STEVEN?

HMMM...

WELL, STEVEN DOES USUALLY BATHE IN THE BATHROOM.

TRUE...

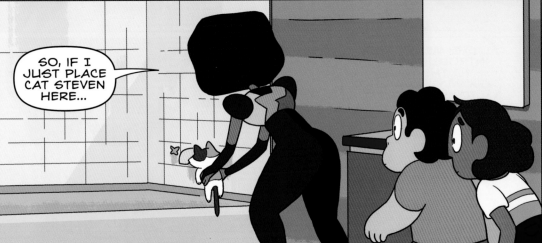

SO, IF I JUST PLACE CAT STEVEN HERE...

MEW?

AND TURN THIS ON--

STOP!!

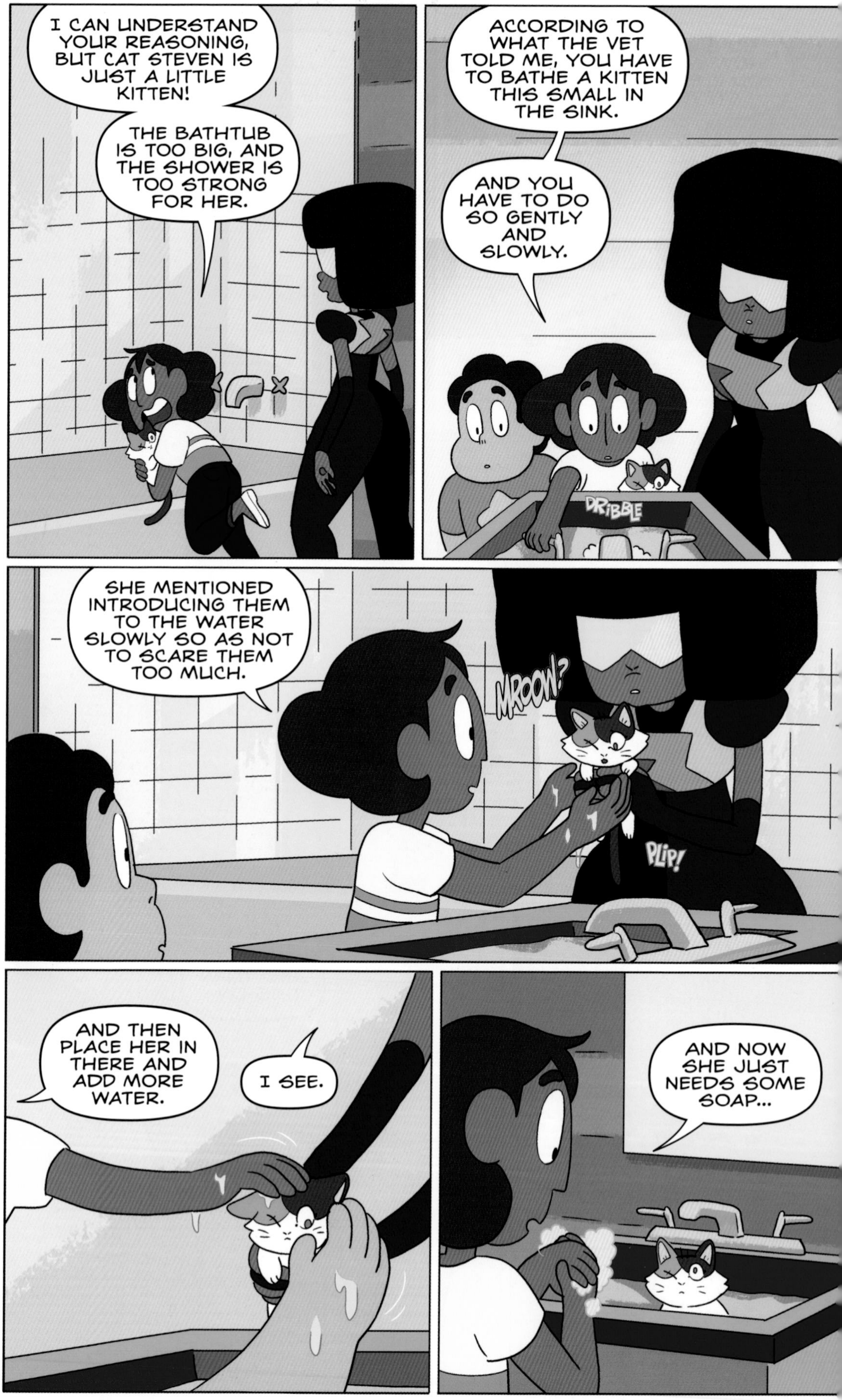
I CAN UNDERSTAND YOUR REASONING, BUT CAT STEVEN IS JUST A LITTLE KITTEN!
THE BATHTUB IS TOO BIG, AND THE SHOWER IS TOO STRONG FOR HER.
ACCORDING TO WHAT THE VET TOLD ME, YOU HAVE TO BATHE A KITTEN THIS SMALL IN THE SINK.
AND YOU HAVE TO DO SO GENTLY AND SLOWLY.
DRIBBLE
SHE MENTIONED INTRODUCING THEM TO THE WATER SLOWLY SO AS NOT TO SCARE THEM TOO MUCH.
MROOW?
PLIP!
AND THEN PLACE HER IN THERE AND ADD MORE WATER.
I SEE.
AND NOW SHE JUST NEEDS SOME SOAP...

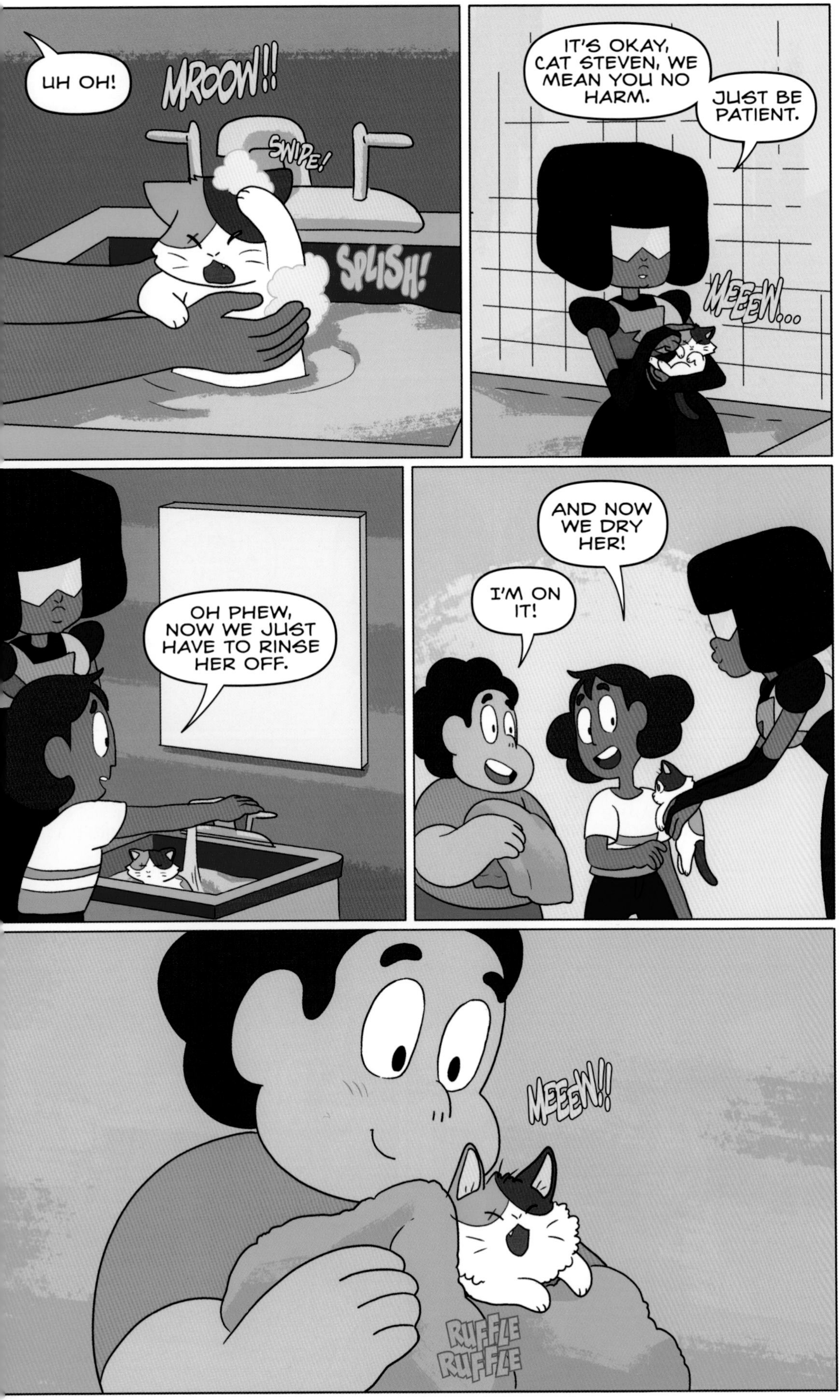
UH OH!
MROOW!!
SWIPE!
SPLISH!
IT'S OKAY, CAT STEVEN, WE MEAN YOU NO HARM.
JUST BE PATIENT.
MEEEW...
OH PHEW, NOW WE JUST HAVE TO RINSE HER OFF.
AND NOW WE DRY HER!
I'M ON IT!
MEEEW!!
RUFFLE RUFFLE

MEW...

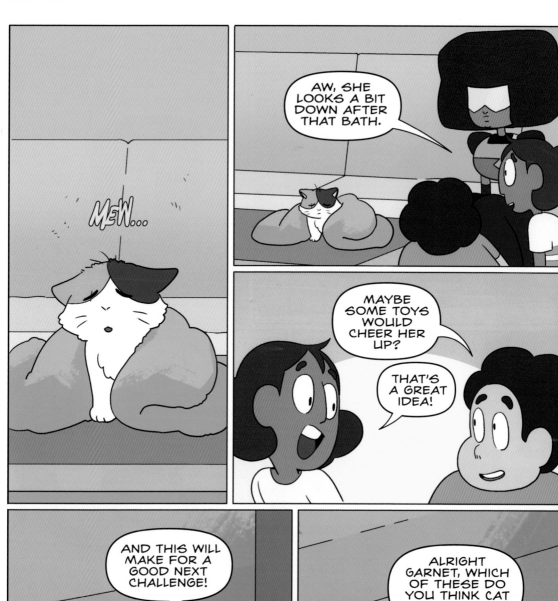

AW, SHE LOOKS A BIT DOWN AFTER THAT BATH.

MAYBE SOME TOYS WOULD CHEER HER UP?

THAT'S A GREAT IDEA!

AND THIS WILL MAKE FOR A GOOD NEXT CHALLENGE!

ALRIGHT GARNET, WHICH OF THESE DO YOU THINK CAT STEVEN WOULD LIKE?

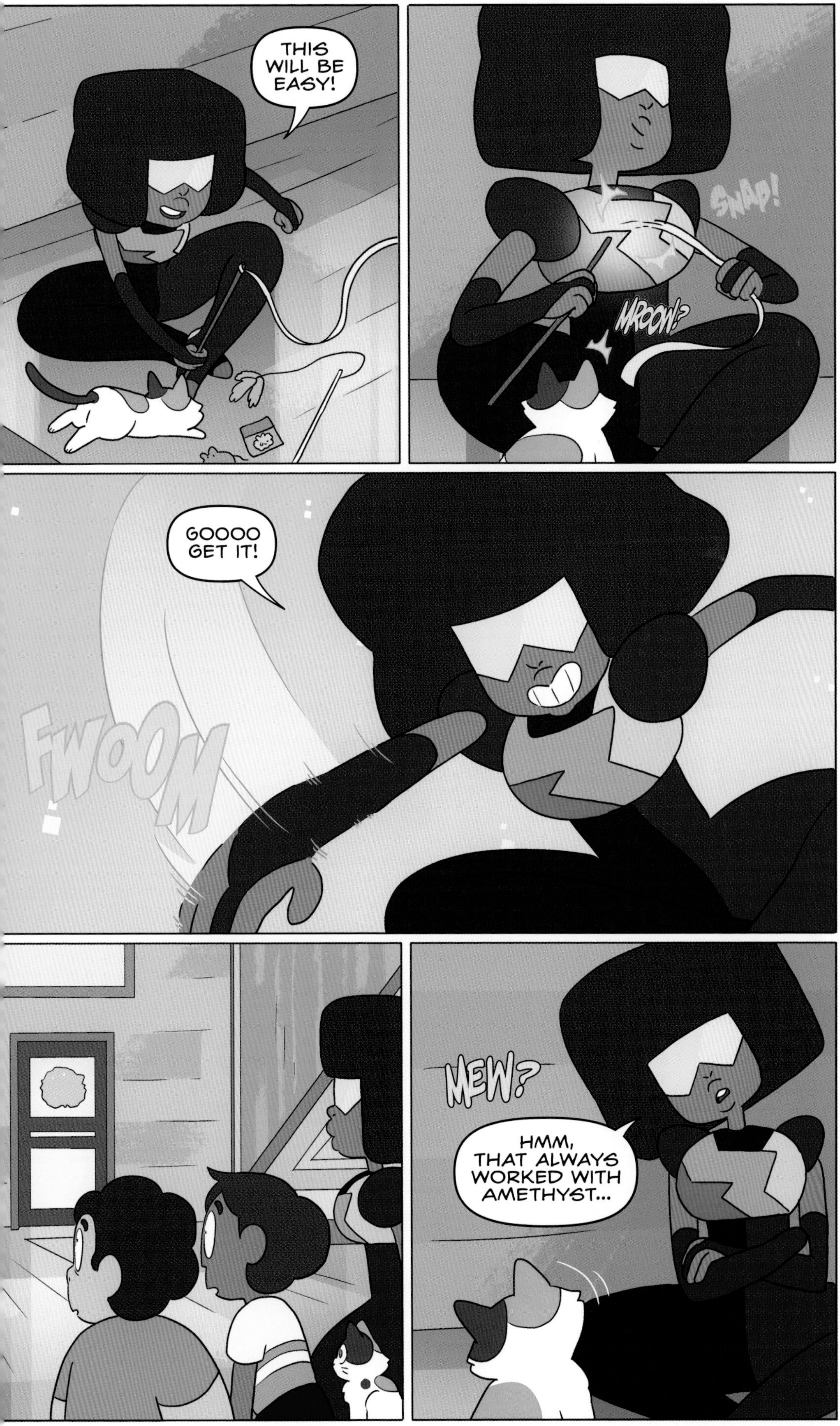
THIS WILL BE EASY!
SNAP!
MROOW!?
GOOOO GET IT!
FWOOM
MEW?
HMM, THAT ALWAYS WORKED WITH AMETHYST...

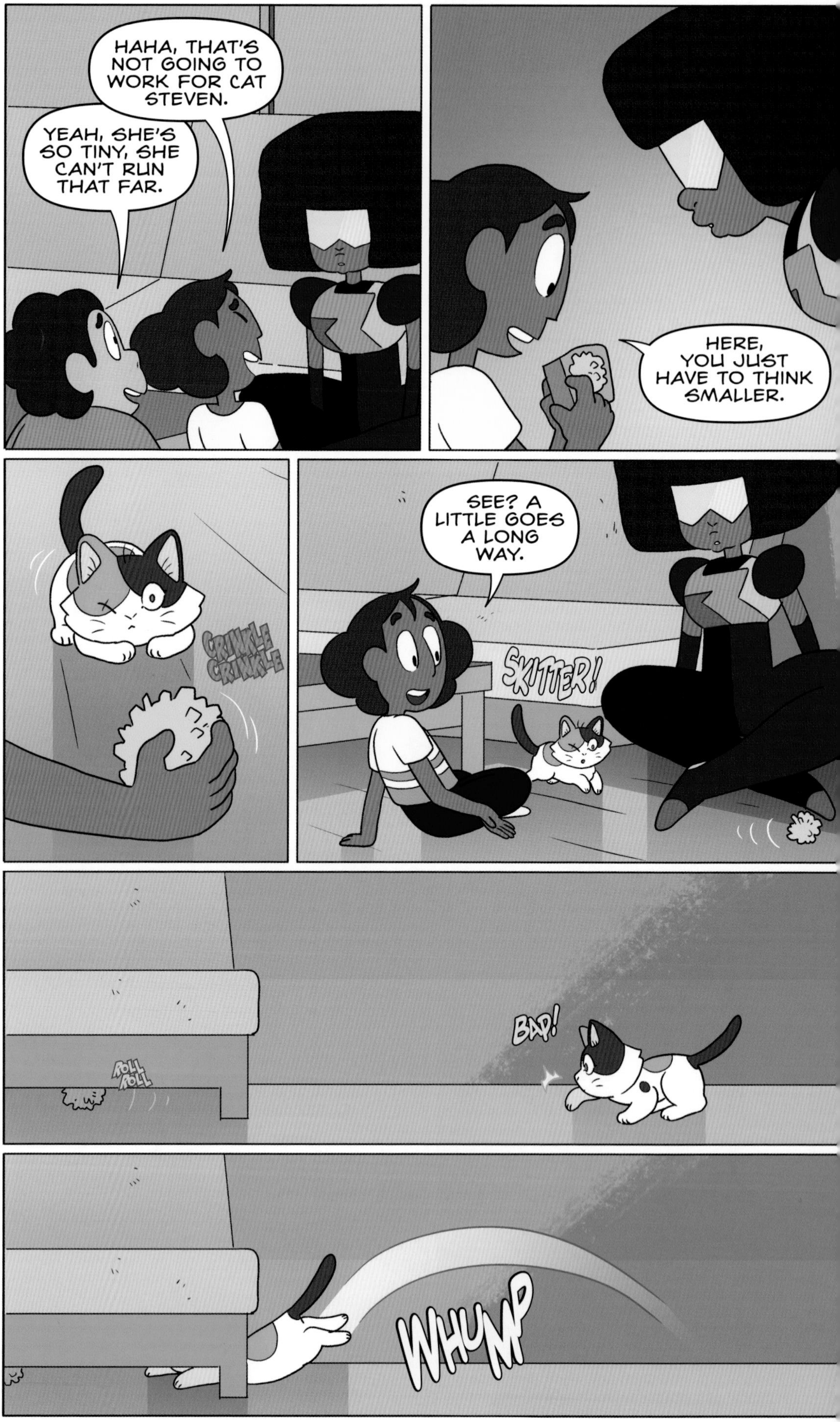
HAHA, THAT'S NOT GOING TO WORK FOR CAT STEVEN.
YEAH, SHE'S SO TINY, SHE CAN'T RUN THAT FAR.
HERE, YOU JUST HAVE TO THINK SMALLER.
CRINKLE CRINKLE
SEE? A LITTLE GOES A LONG WAY.
SKITTER!
ROLL ROLL
BAP!
WHUMP

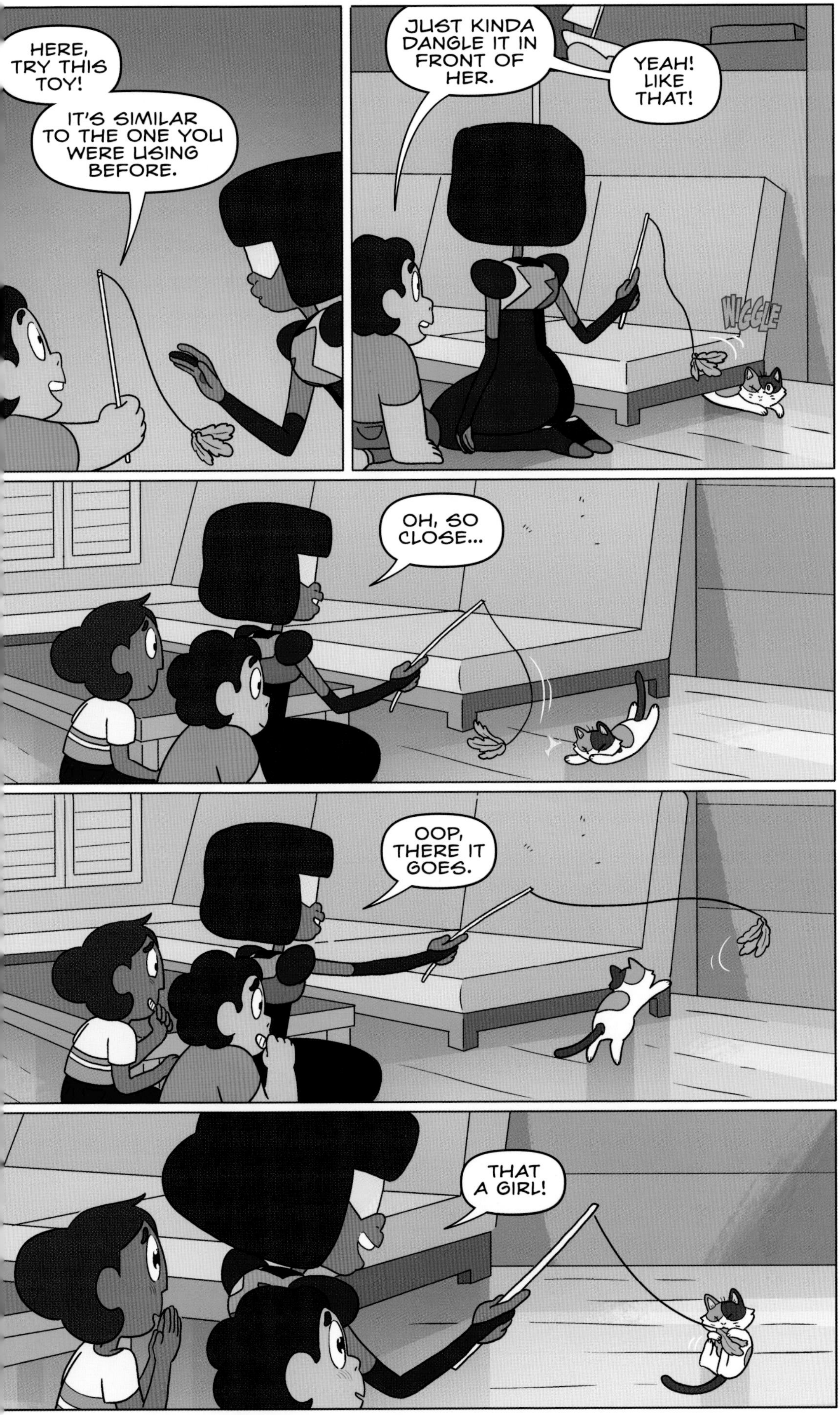
HERE, TRY THIS TOY!
IT'S SIMILAR TO THE ONE YOU WERE USING BEFORE.
JUST KINDA DANGLE IT IN FRONT OF HER.
YEAH! LIKE THAT!
WIGGLE
OH, SO CLOSE...
OOP, THERE IT GOES.
THAT A GIRL!

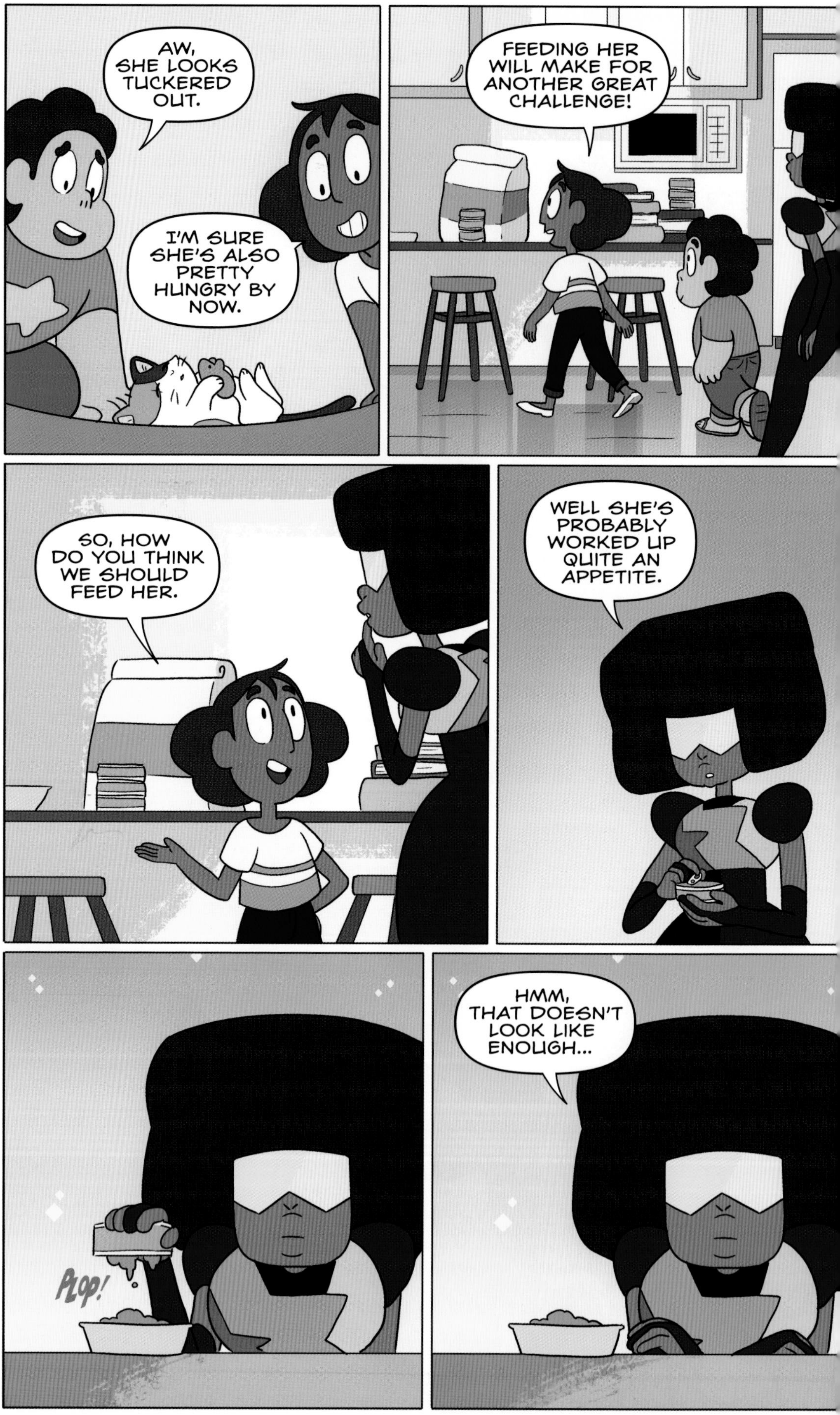
AW, SHE LOOKS TUCKERED OUT.
I'M SURE SHE'S ALSO PRETTY HUNGRY BY NOW.
FEEDING HER WILL MAKE FOR ANOTHER GREAT CHALLENGE!
SO, HOW DO YOU THINK WE SHOULD FEED HER.
WELL SHE'S PROBABLY WORKED UP QUITE AN APPETITE.
PLOP!
HMM, THAT DOESN'T LOOK LIKE ENOUGH...

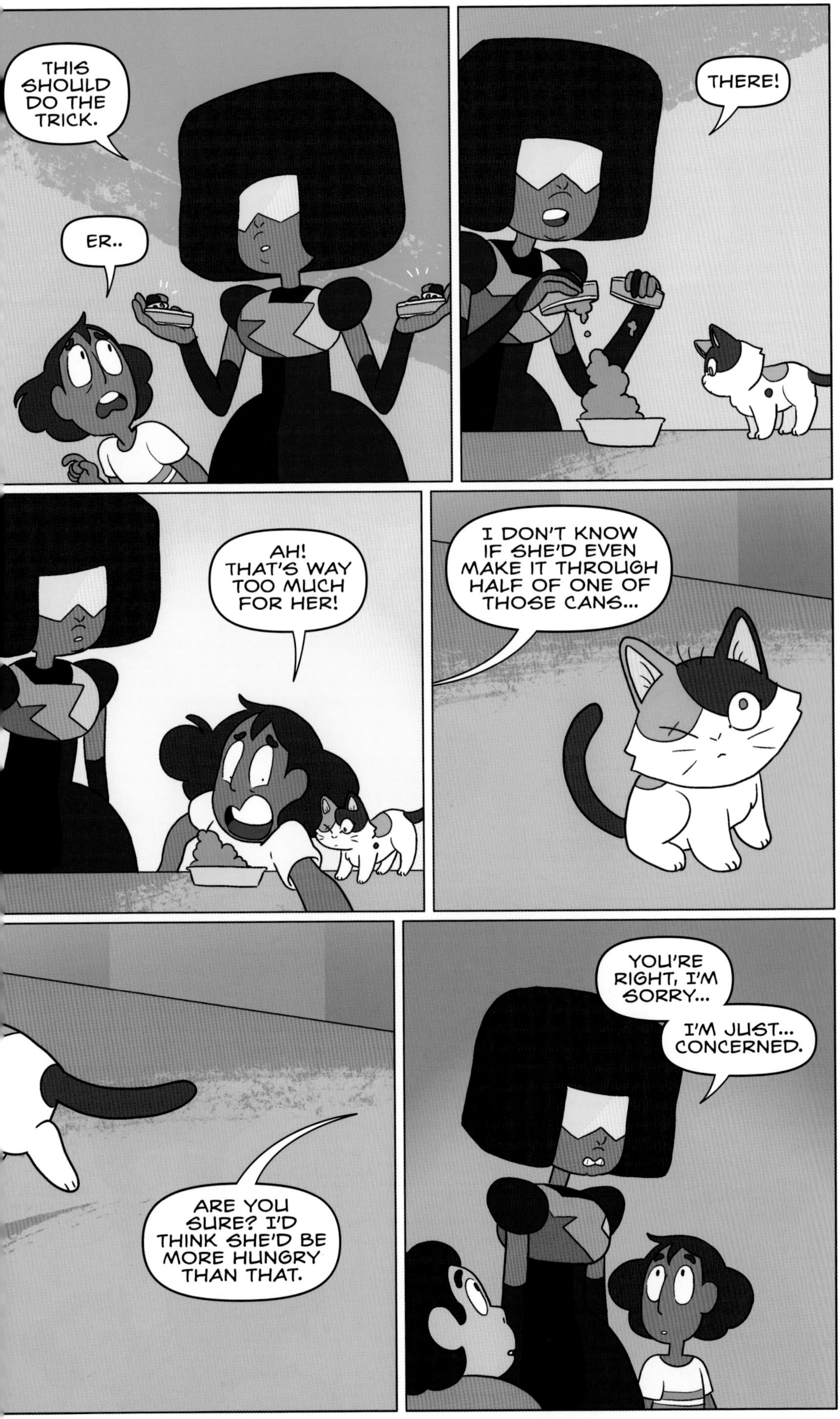
THIS SHOULD DO THE TRICK.
ER..
THERE!
AH! THAT'S WAY TOO MUCH FOR HER!
I DON'T KNOW IF SHE'D EVEN MAKE IT THROUGH HALF OF ONE OF THOSE CANS...
ARE YOU SURE? I'D THINK SHE'D BE MORE HUNGRY THAN THAT.
YOU'RE RIGHT, I'M SORRY...
I'M JUST... CONCERNED.

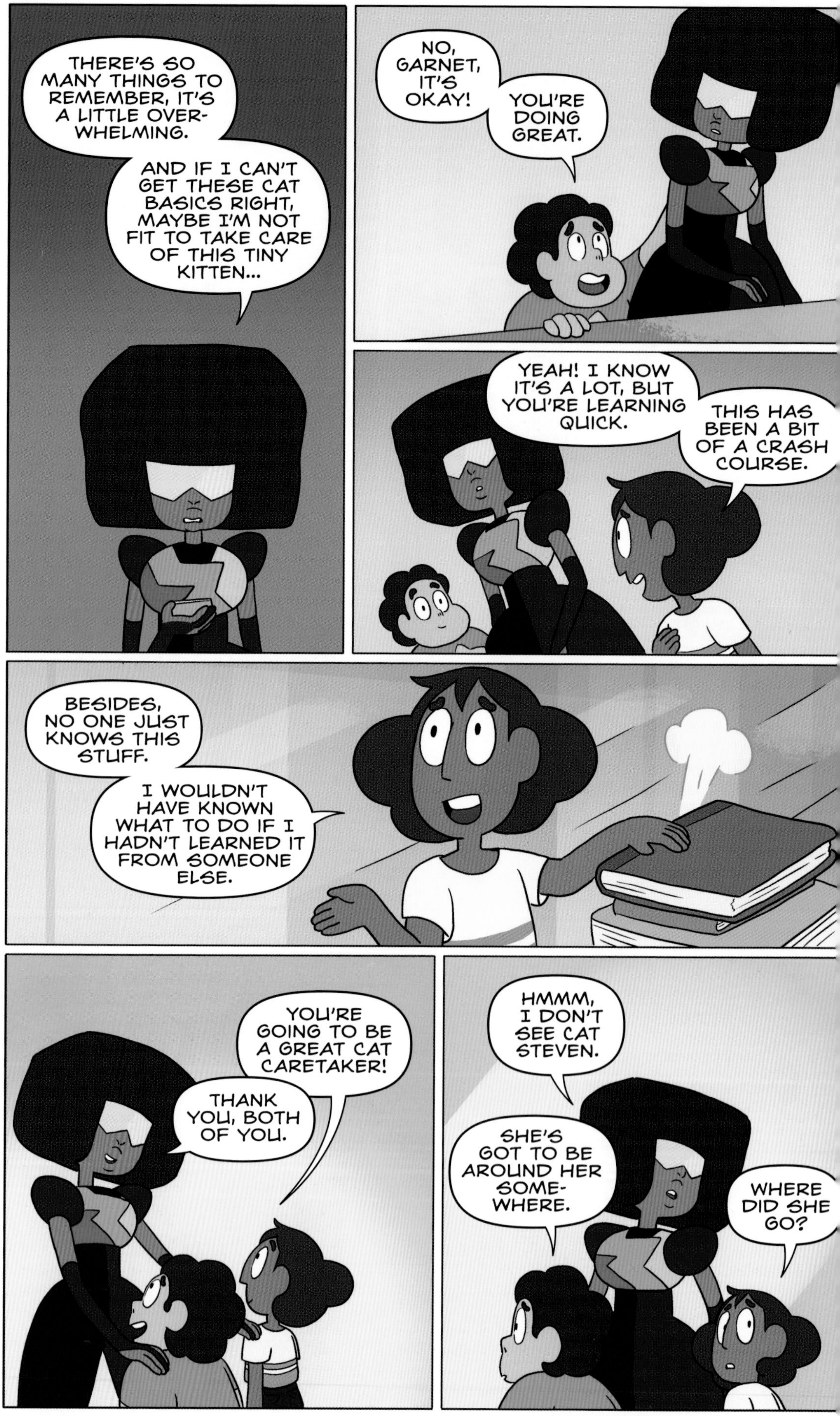
THERE'S SO MANY THINGS TO REMEMBER, IT'S A LITTLE OVER-WHELMING.
AND IF I CAN'T GET THESE CAT BASICS RIGHT, MAYBE I'M NOT FIT TO TAKE CARE OF THIS TINY KITTEN...
NO, GARNET, IT'S OKAY!
YOU'RE DOING GREAT.
YEAH! I KNOW IT'S A LOT, BUT YOU'RE LEARNING QUICK.
THIS HAS BEEN A BIT OF A CRASH COURSE.
BESIDES, NO ONE JUST KNOWS THIS STUFF.
I WOULDN'T HAVE KNOWN WHAT TO DO IF I HADN'T LEARNED IT FROM SOMEONE ELSE.
YOU'RE GOING TO BE A GREAT CAT CARETAKER!
THANK YOU, BOTH OF YOU.
HMMM, I DON'T SEE CAT STEVEN.
SHE'S GOT TO BE AROUND HER SOME-WHERE.
WHERE DID SHE GO?

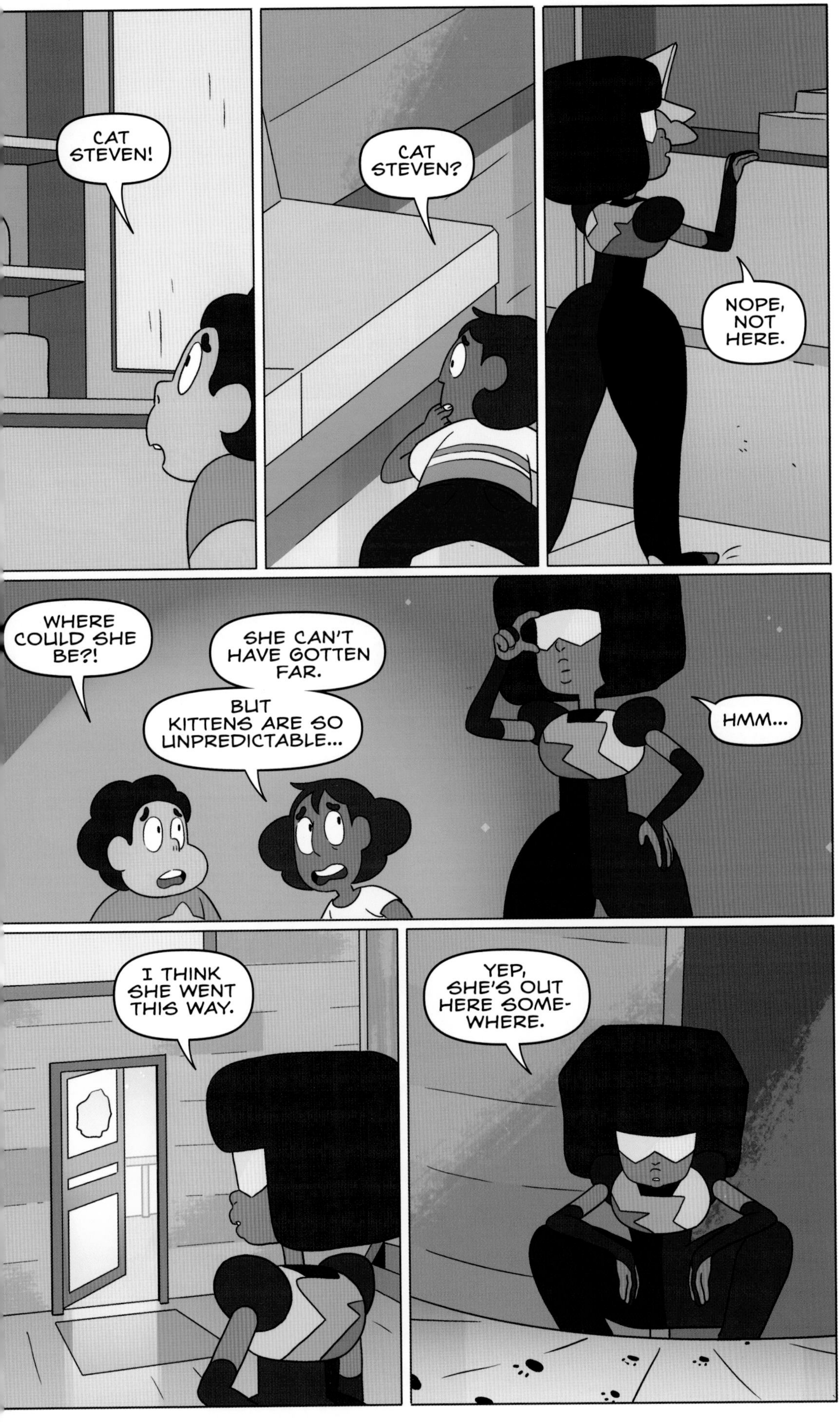
CAT STEVEN!
CAT STEVEN?
NOPE, NOT HERE.
WHERE COULD SHE BE?!
SHE CAN'T HAVE GOTTEN FAR.
BUT KITTENS ARE SO UNPREDICTABLE...
HMM...
I THINK SHE WENT THIS WAY.
YEP, SHE'S OUT HERE SOME-WHERE.

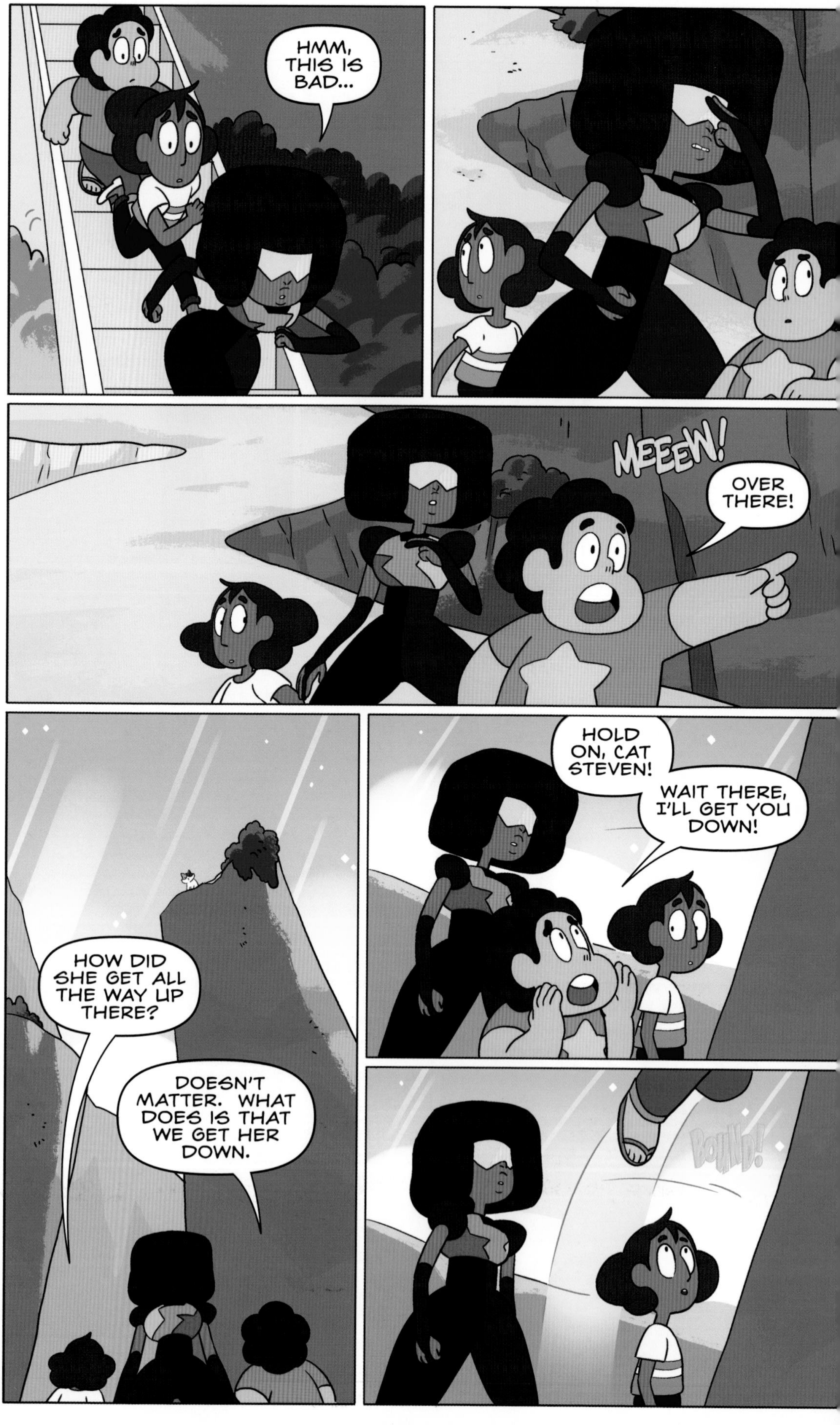
HMM, THIS IS BAD...
MEEEW!
OVER THERE!
HOW DID SHE GET ALL THE WAY UP THERE?
DOESN'T MATTER. WHAT DOES IS THAT WE GET HER DOWN.
HOLD ON, CAT STEVEN!
WAIT THERE, I'LL GET YOU DOWN!
BOUND!

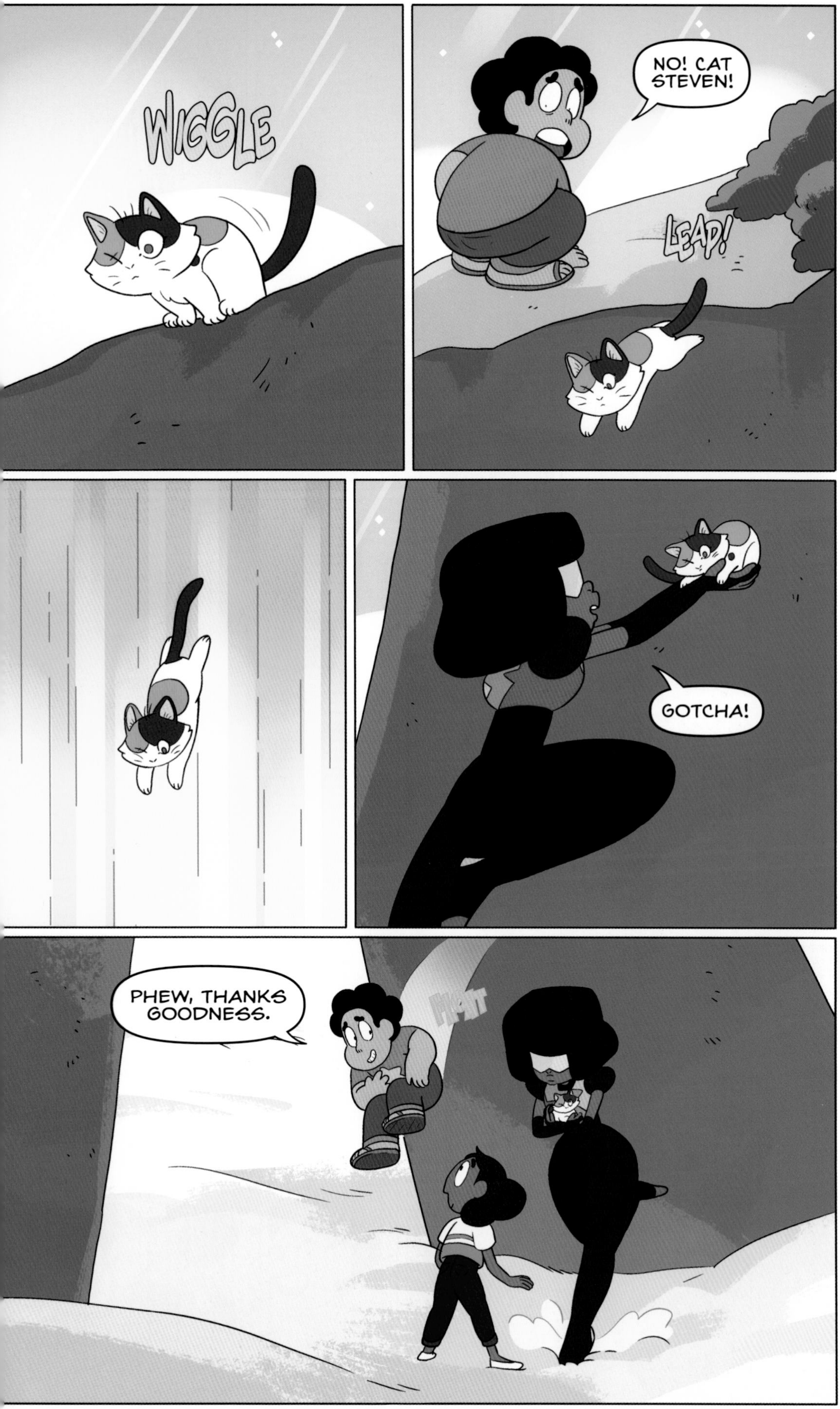
WIGGLE
NO! CAT STEVEN!
LEAP!
GOTCHA!
PHEW, THANKS GOODNESS.

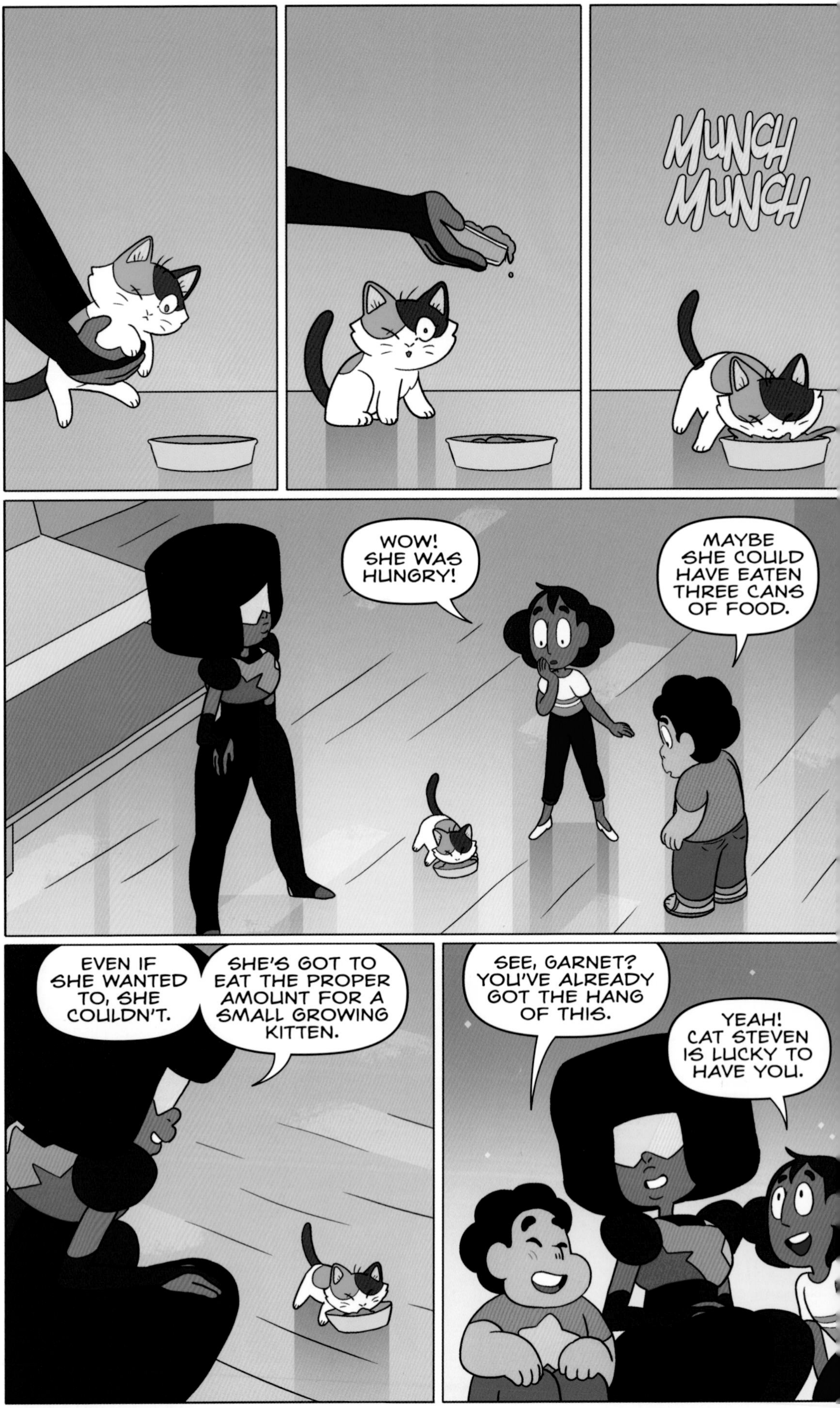
MUNCH
MUNCH
WOW! SHE WAS HUNGRY!
MAYBE SHE COULD HAVE EATEN THREE CANS OF FOOD.
EVEN IF SHE WANTED TO, SHE COULDN'T.
SHE'S GOT TO EAT THE PROPER AMOUNT FOR A SMALL GROWING KITTEN.
SEE, GARNET? YOU'VE ALREADY GOT THE HANG OF THIS.
YEAH! CAT STEVEN IS LUCKY TO HAVE YOU.

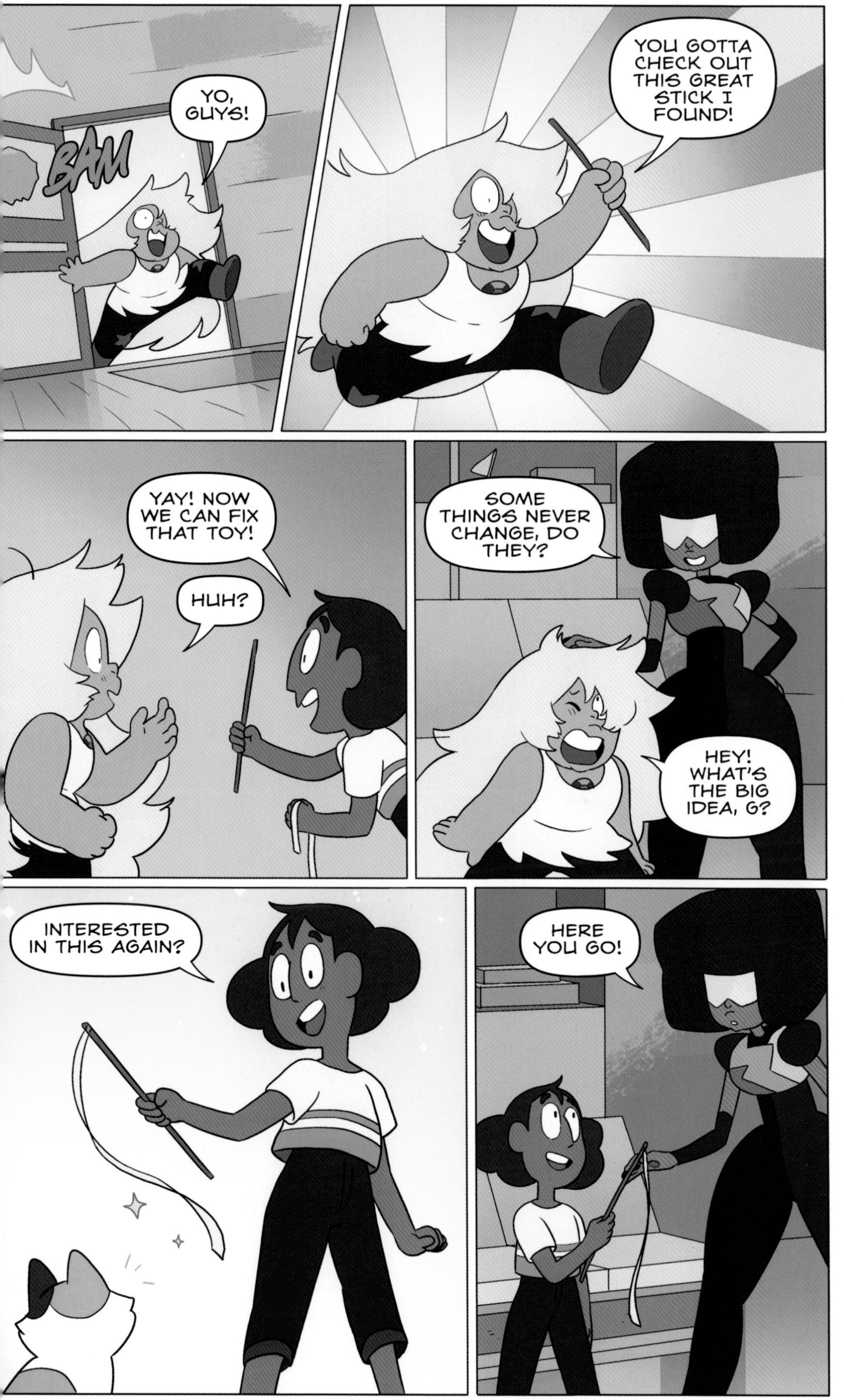
YO, GUYS!
BAM
YOU GOTTA CHECK OUT THIS GREAT STICK I FOUND!
YAY! NOW WE CAN FIX THAT TOY!
HUH?
SOME THINGS NEVER CHANGE, DO THEY?
HEY! WHAT'S THE BIG IDEA, G?
INTERESTED IN THIS AGAIN?
HERE YOU GO!

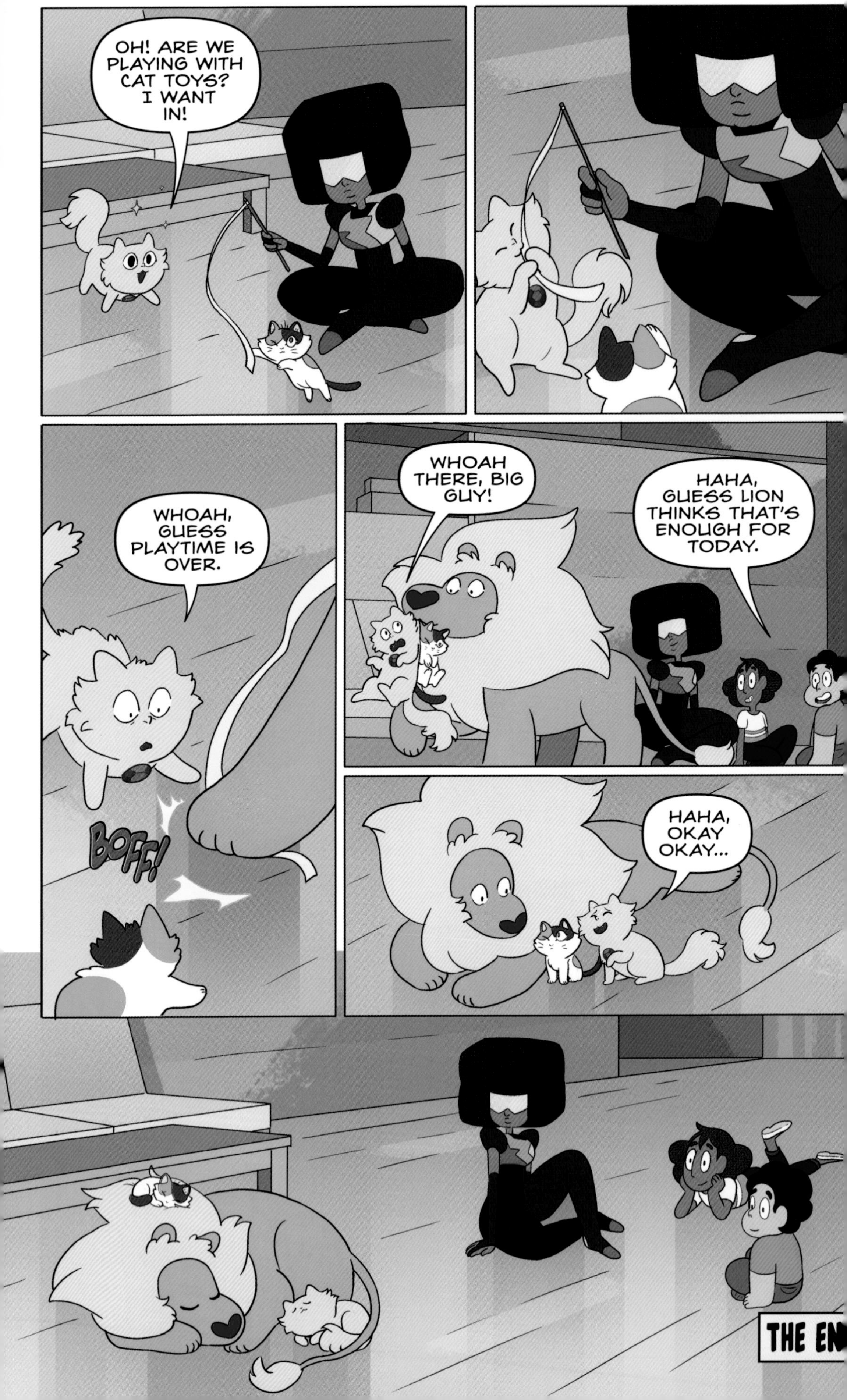
OH! ARE WE PLAYING WITH CAT TOYS? I WANT IN!
WHOAH, GUESS PLAYTIME IS OVER.
BOFF!
WHOAH THERE, BIG GUY!
HAHA, GUESS LION THINKS THAT'S ENOUGH FOR TODAY.
HAHA, OKAY OKAY...
THE EN

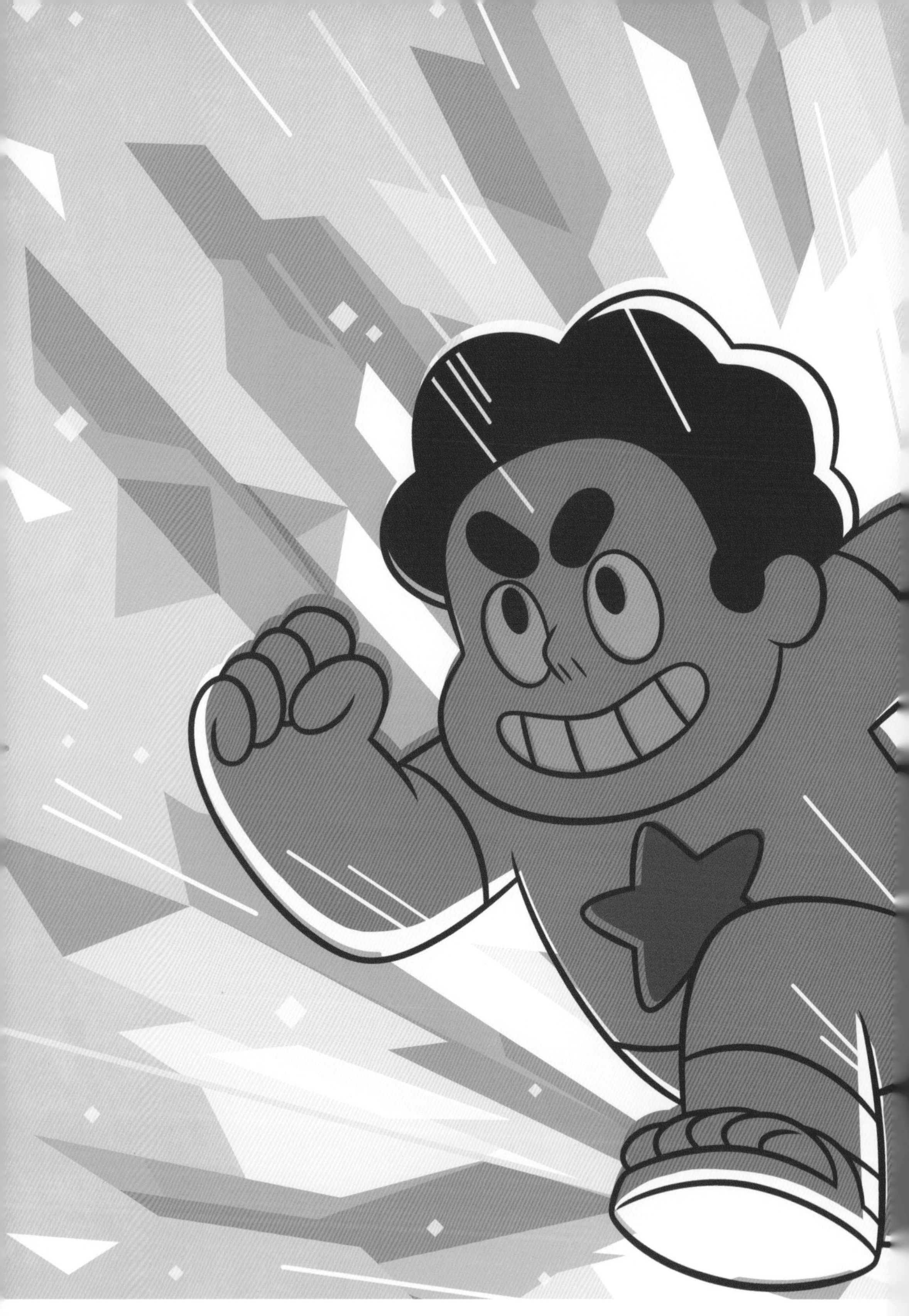

CHAPTER TWENTY-FOUR

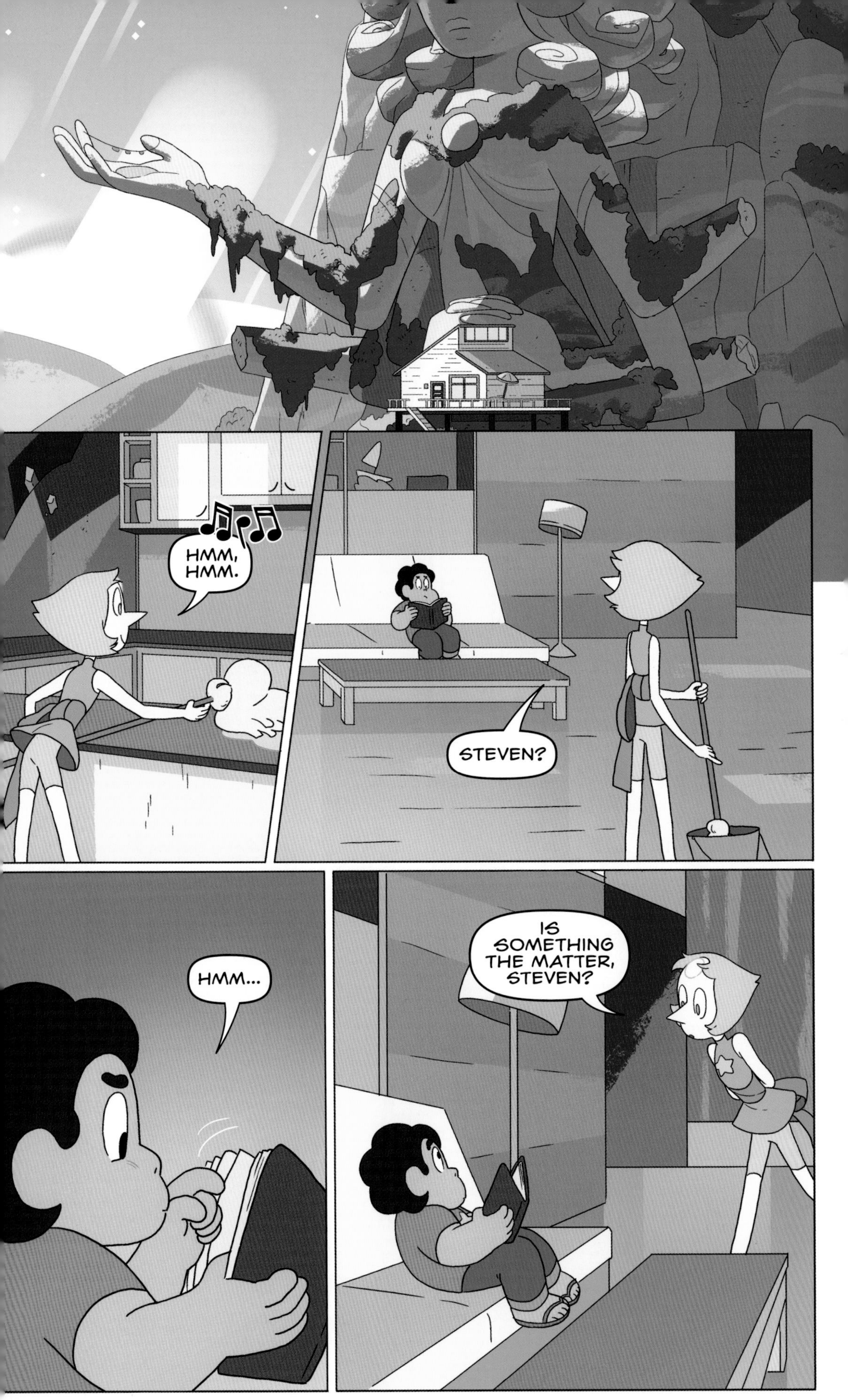
HMM, HMM.
STEVEN?
HMM...
IS SOMETHING THE MATTER, STEVEN?

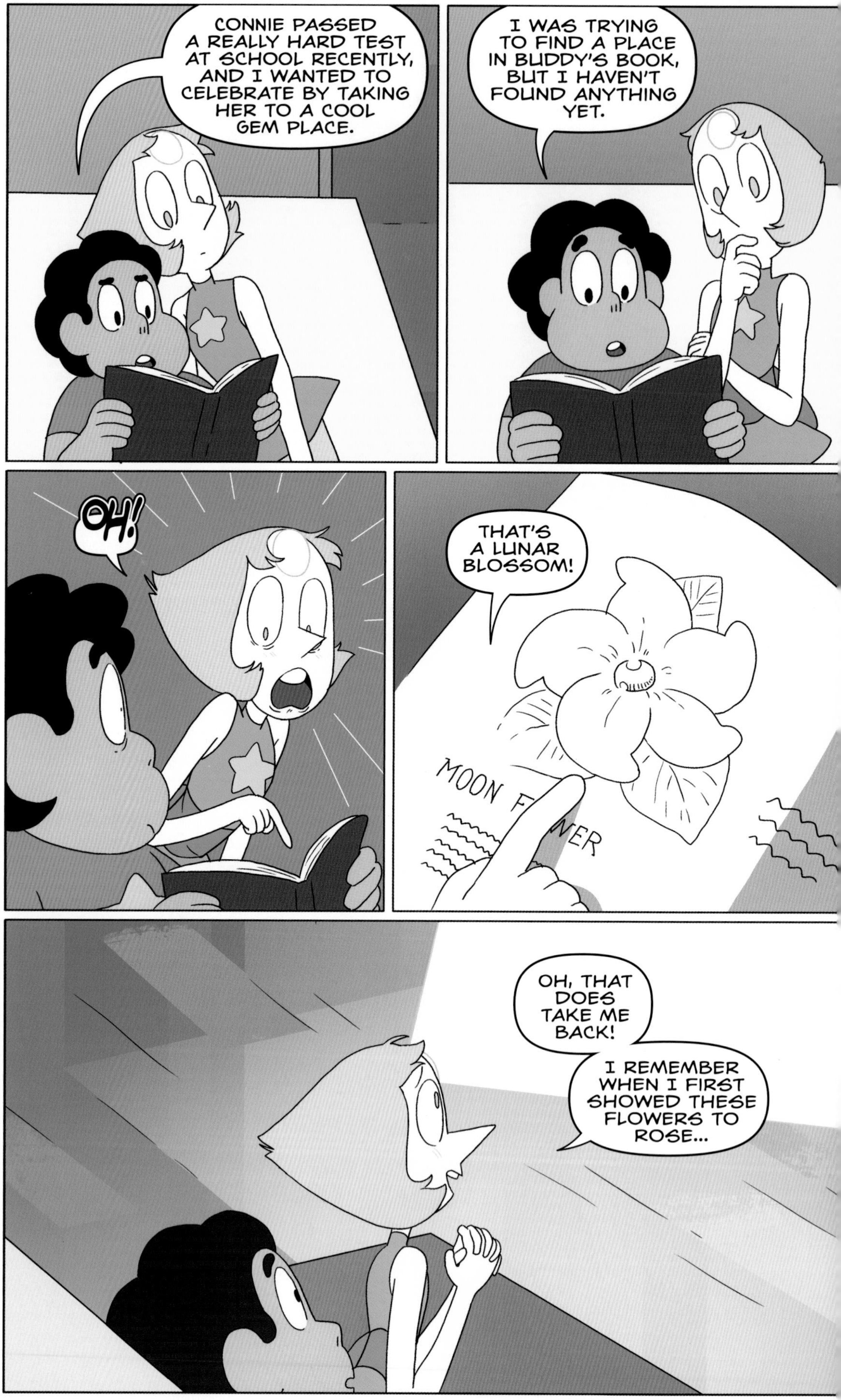
CONNIE PASSED A REALLY HARD TEST AT SCHOOL RECENTLY, AND I WANTED TO CELEBRATE BY TAKING HER TO A COOL GEM PLACE.
I WAS TRYING TO FIND A PLACE IN BUDDY'S BOOK, BUT I HAVEN'T FOUND ANYTHING YET.
OH!
THAT'S A LUNAR BLOSSOM!
MOON F
WER
OH, THAT DOES TAKE ME BACK!
I REMEMBER WHEN I FIRST SHOWED THESE FLOWERS TO ROSE...

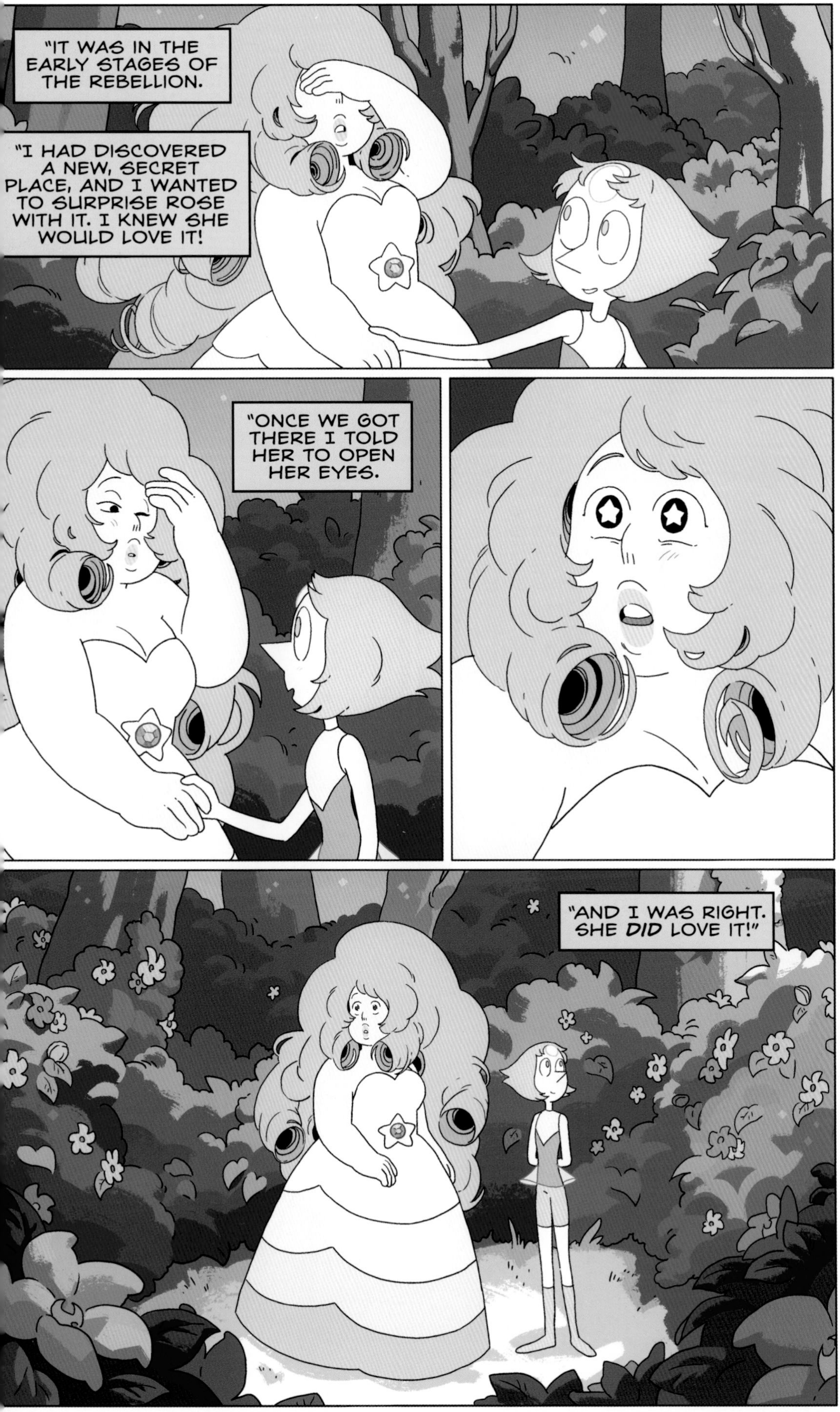
"IT WAS IN THE EARLY STAGES OF THE REBELLION.
"I HAD DISCOVERED A NEW, SECRET PLACE, AND I WANTED TO SURPRISE ROSE WITH IT. I KNEW SHE WOULD LOVE IT!
"ONCE WE GOT THERE I TOLD HER TO OPEN HER EYES.
"AND I WAS RIGHT. SHE *DID* LOVE IT!"

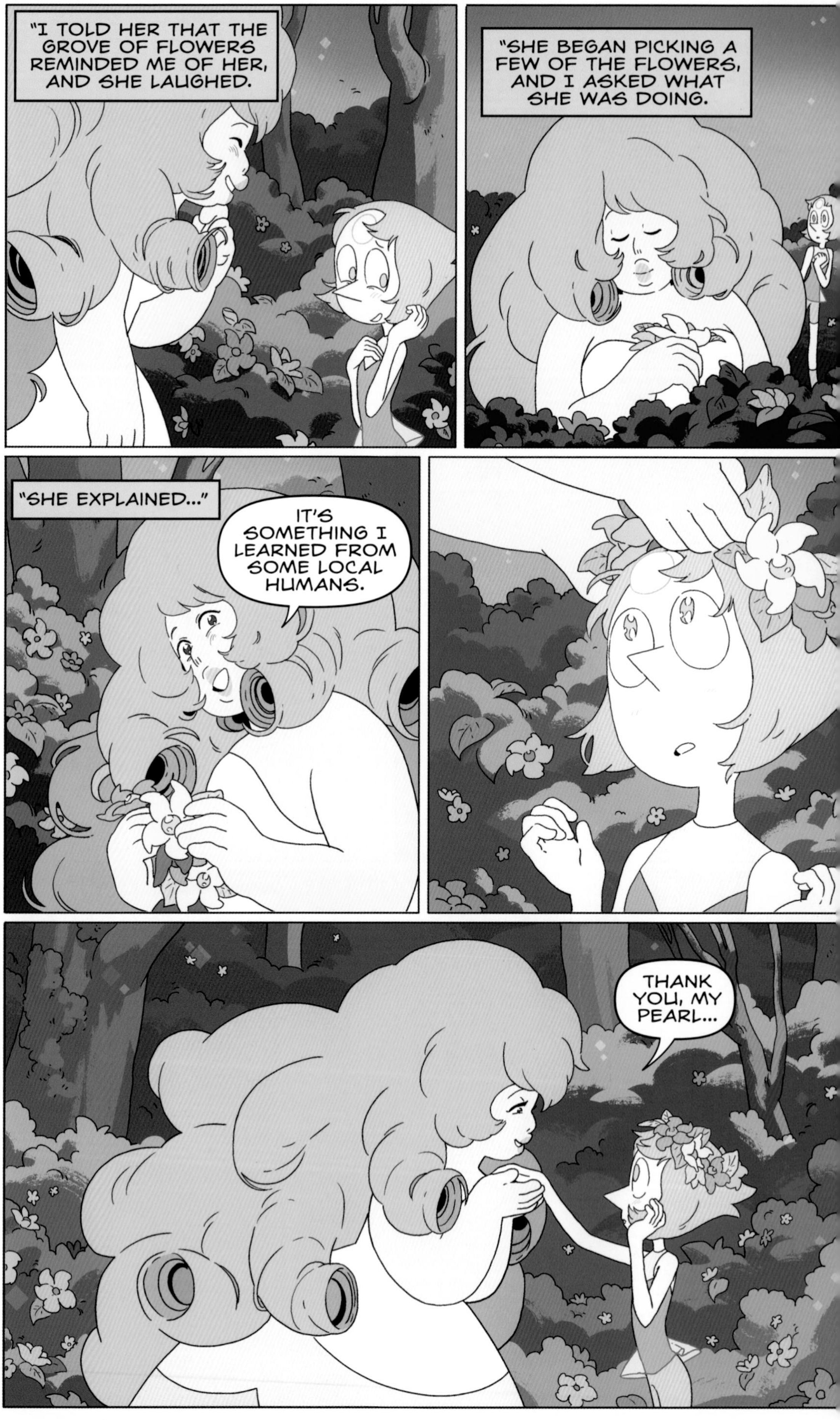
"I TOLD HER THAT THE GROVE OF FLOWERS REMINDED ME OF HER, AND SHE LAUGHED.
"SHE BEGAN PICKING A FEW OF THE FLOWERS, AND I ASKED WHAT SHE WAS DOING.
"SHE EXPLAINED..."
IT'S SOMETHING I LEARNED FROM SOME LOCAL HUMANS.
THANK YOU, MY PEARL...

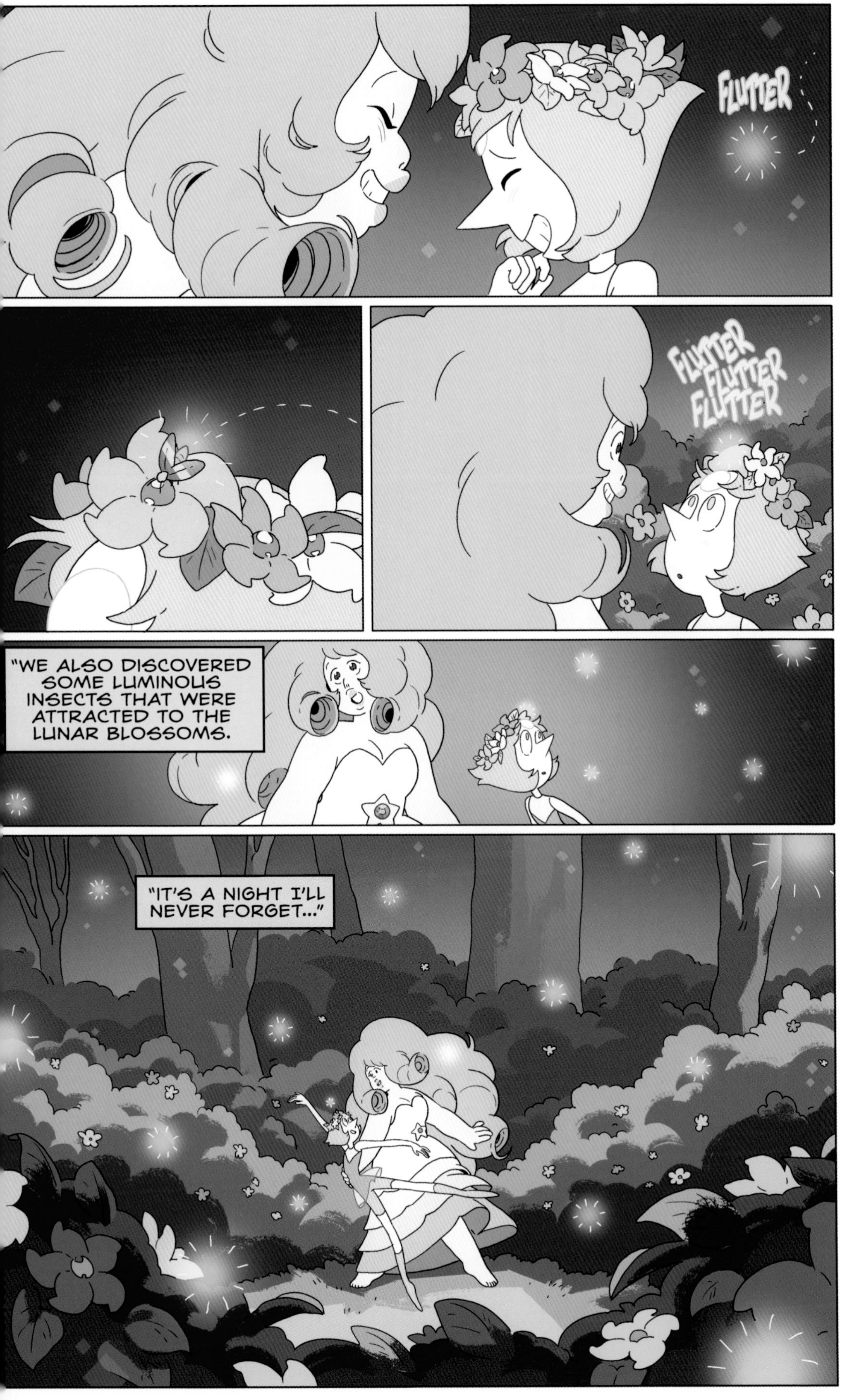
FLUTTER
FLUTTER FLUTTER FLUTTER
"WE ALSO DISCOVERED SOME LUMINOUS INSECTS THAT WERE ATTRACTED TO THE LUNAR BLOSSOMS.
"IT'S A NIGHT I'LL NEVER FORGET..."

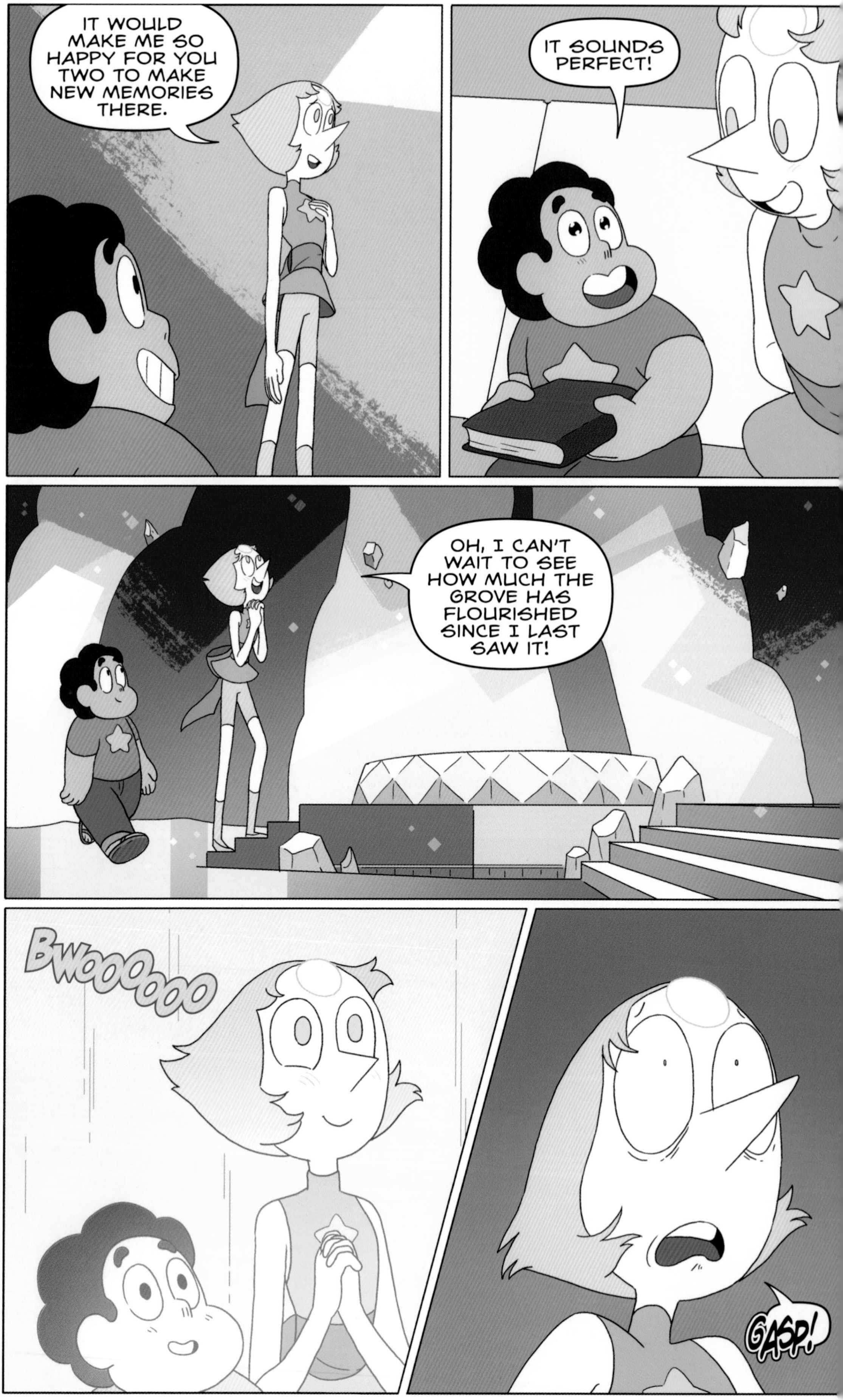
IT WOULD MAKE ME SO HAPPY FOR YOU TWO TO MAKE NEW MEMORIES THERE.
IT SOUNDS PERFECT!
OH, I CAN'T WAIT TO SEE HOW MUCH THE GROVE HAS FLOURISHED SINCE I LAST SAW IT!
BWOOOOOO
GASP!

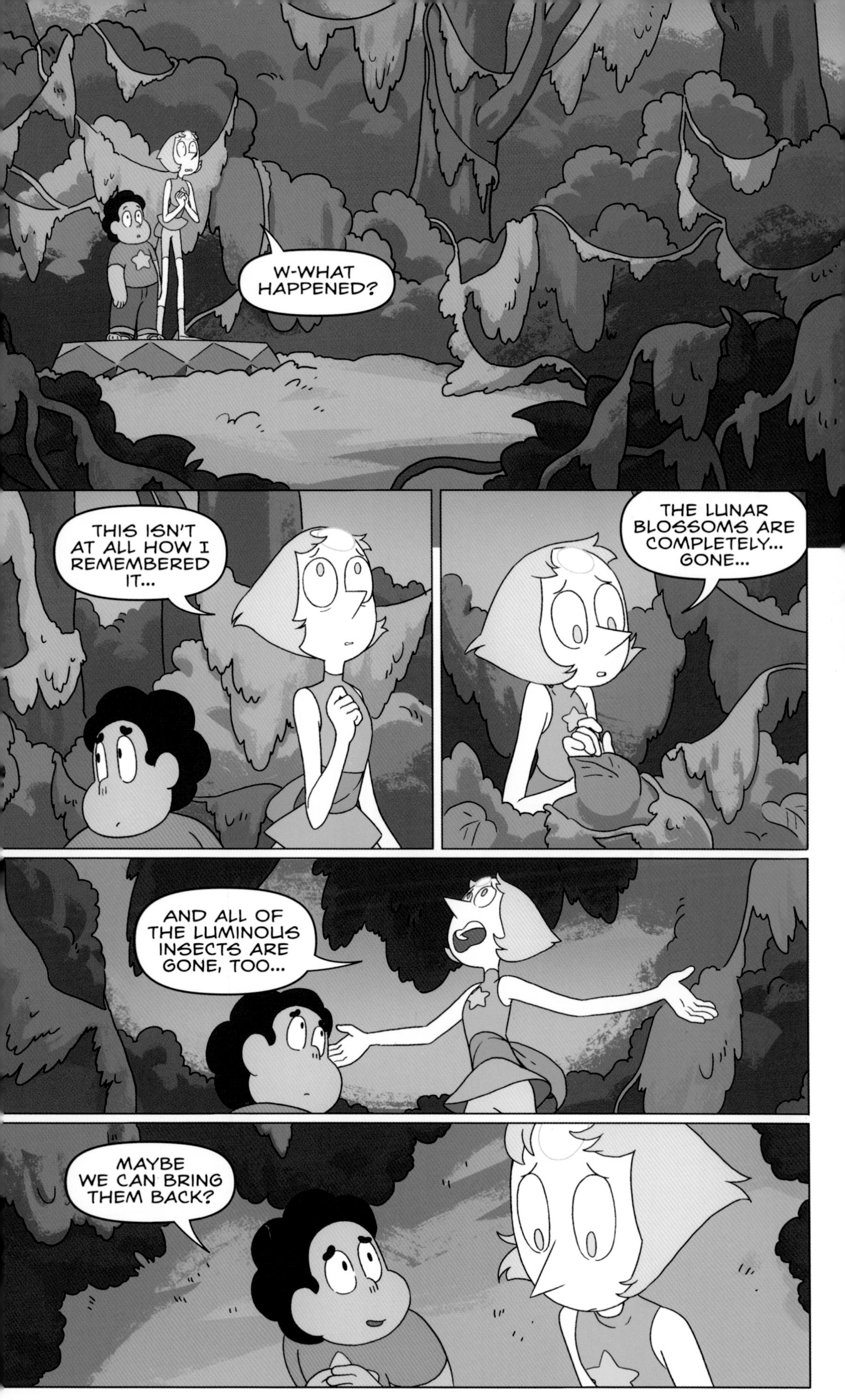
W-WHAT HAPPENED?
THIS ISN'T AT ALL HOW I REMEMBERED IT...
THE LUNAR BLOSSOMS ARE COMPLETELY... GONE...
AND ALL OF THE LUMINOUS INSECTS ARE GONE, TOO...
MAYBE WE CAN BRING THEM BACK?

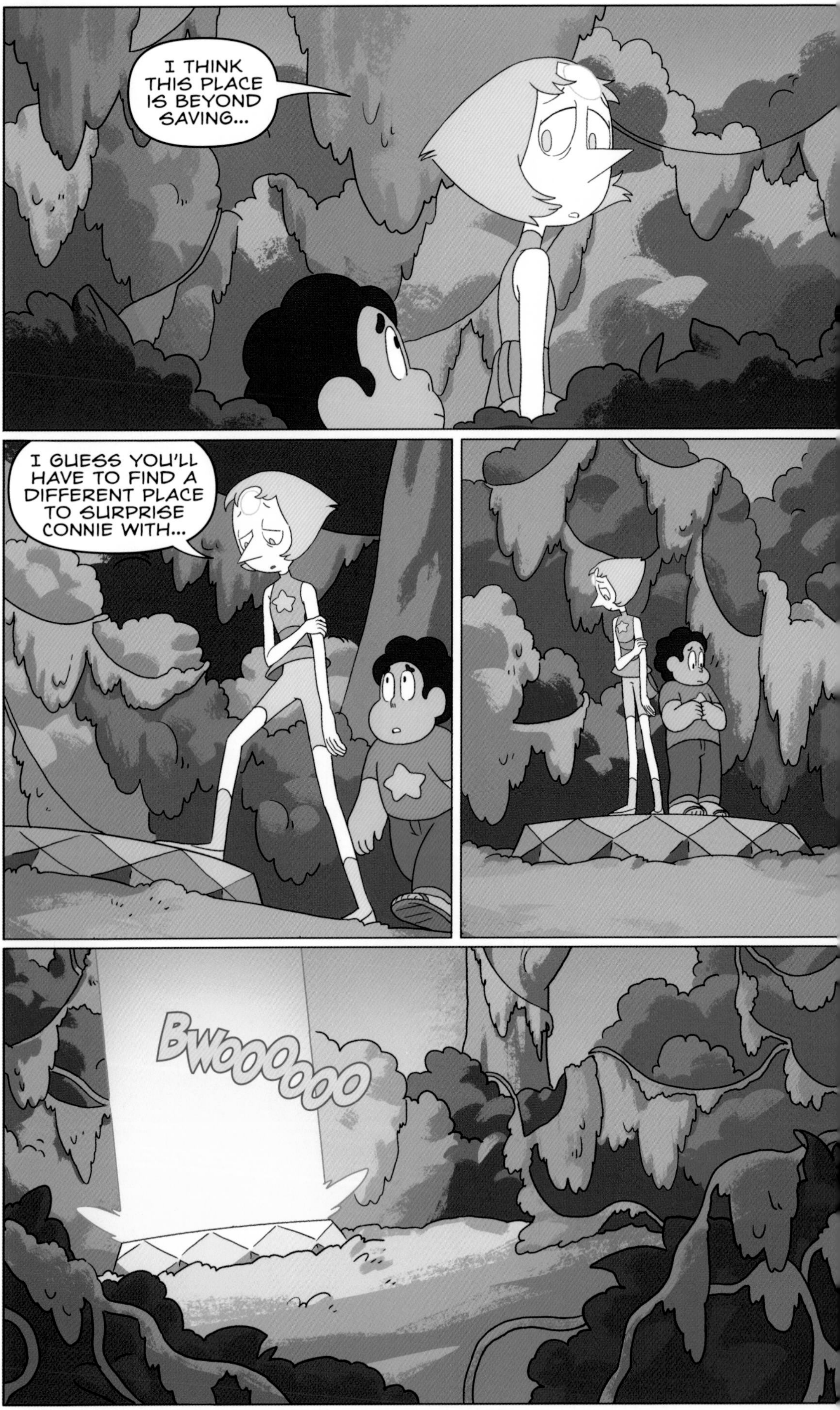
I THINK THIS PLACE IS BEYOND SAVING...
I GUESS YOU'LL HAVE TO FIND A DIFFERENT PLACE TO SURPRISE CONNIE WITH...
BWOOOOOO

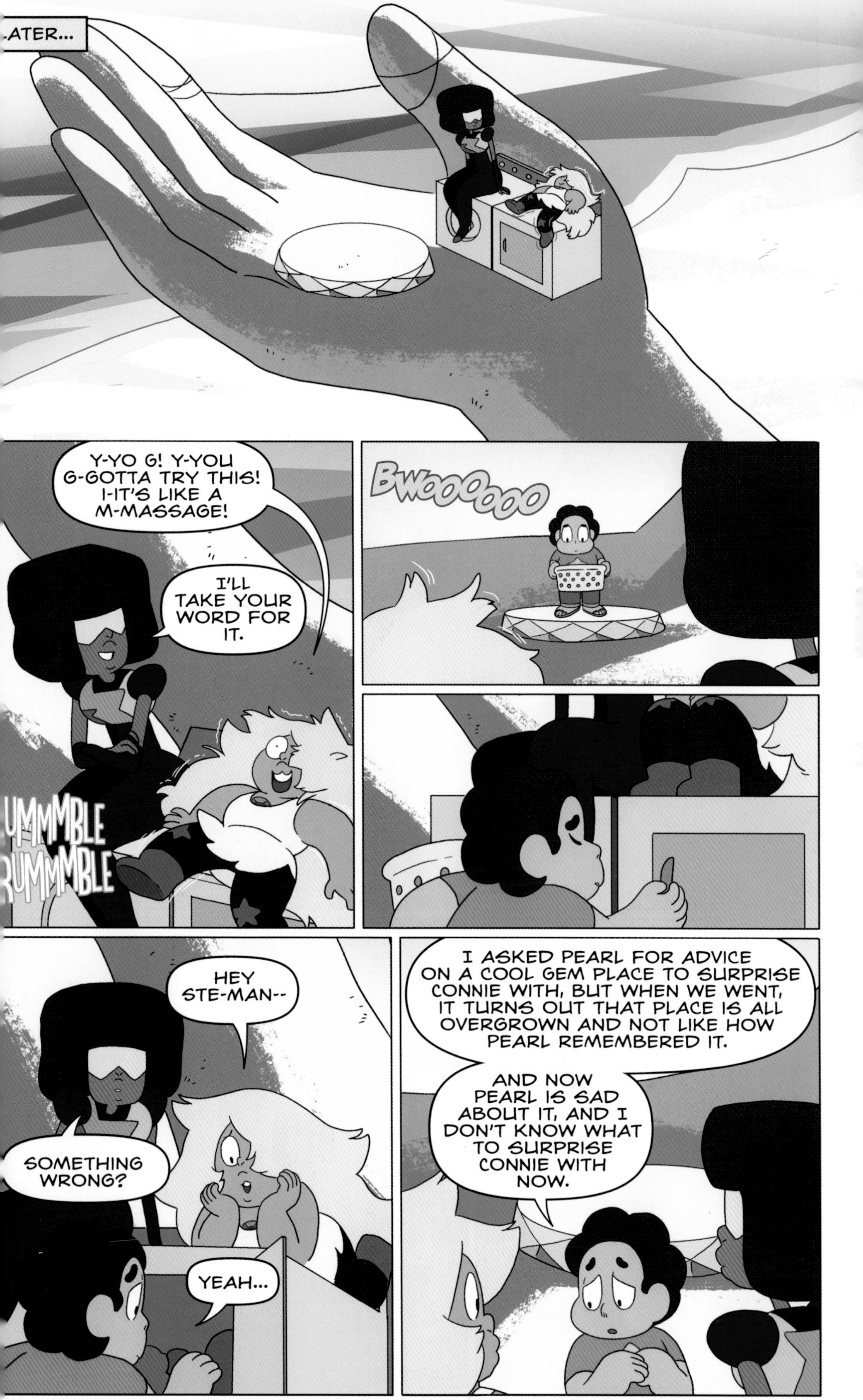
LATER...
Y-YO G! Y-YOU G-GOTTA TRY THIS! I-IT'S LIKE A M-MASSAGE!
I'LL TAKE YOUR WORD FOR IT.
UMMMBLE RUMMMBLE
BWOOOOOO
HEY STE-MAN--
SOMETHING WRONG?
YEAH...
I ASKED PEARL FOR ADVICE ON A COOL GEM PLACE TO SURPRISE CONNIE WITH, BUT WHEN WE WENT, IT TURNS OUT THAT PLACE IS ALL OVERGROWN AND NOT LIKE HOW PEARL REMEMBERED IT.
AND NOW PEARL IS SAD ABOUT IT, AND I DON'T KNOW WHAT TO SURPRISE CONNIE WITH NOW.

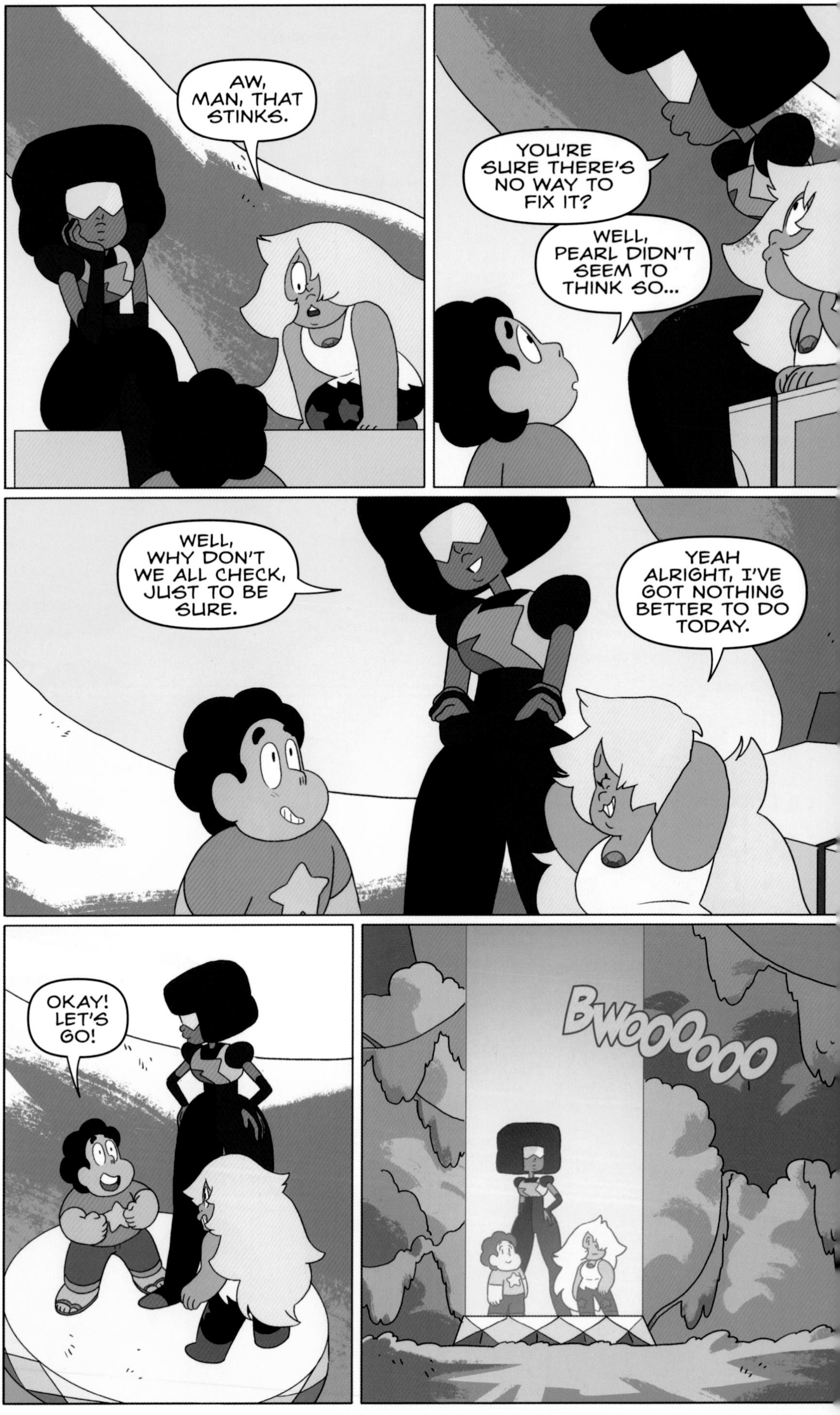
AW, MAN, THAT STINKS.
YOU'RE SURE THERE'S NO WAY TO FIX IT?
WELL, PEARL DIDN'T SEEM TO THINK SO...
WELL, WHY DON'T WE ALL CHECK, JUST TO BE SURE.
YEAH ALRIGHT, I'VE GOT NOTHING BETTER TO DO TODAY.
OKAY! LET'S GO!
BWOOOOOO

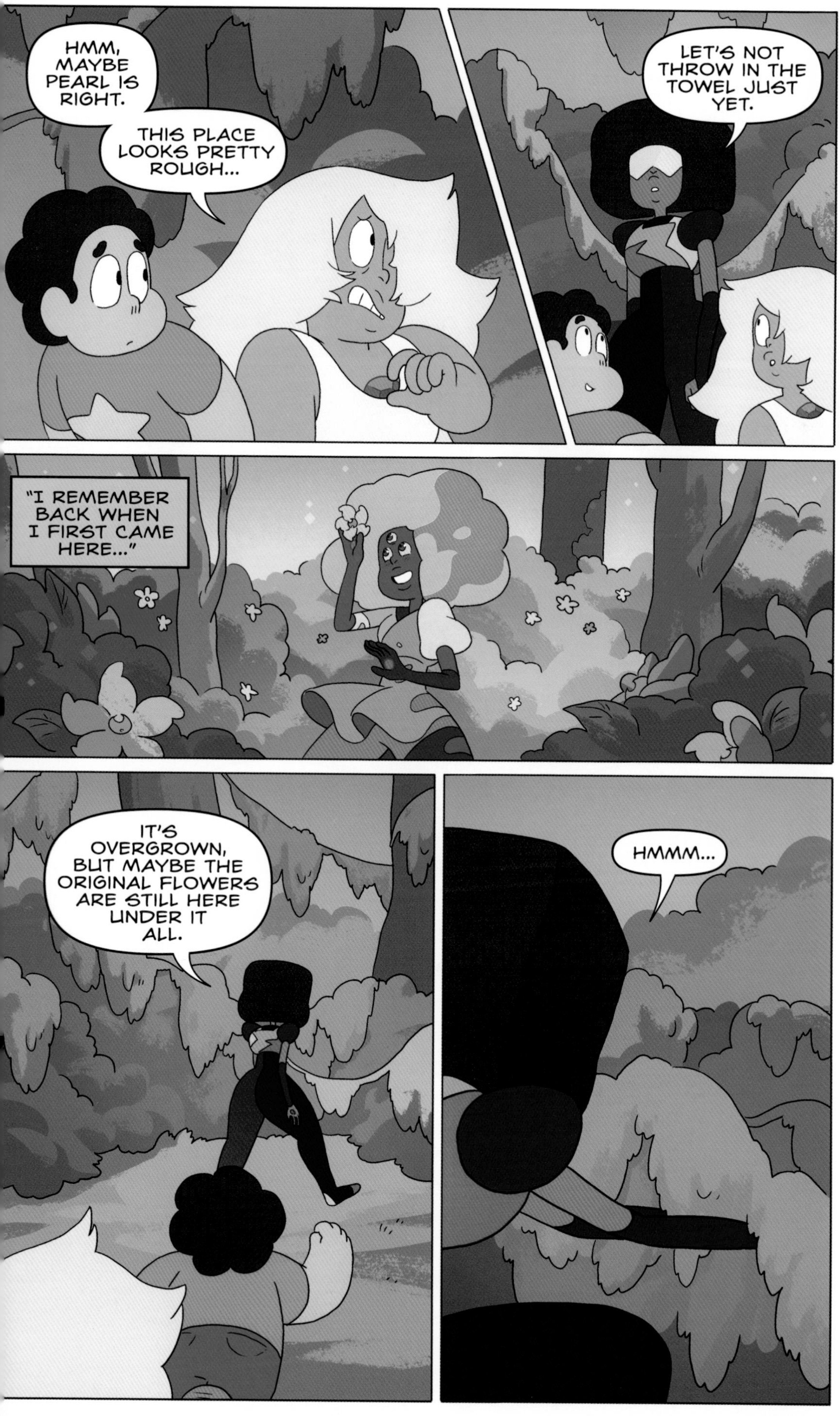

HMM, MAYBE PEARL IS RIGHT.
THIS PLACE LOOKS PRETTY ROUGH...
LET'S NOT THROW IN THE TOWEL JUST YET.
"I REMEMBER BACK WHEN I FIRST CAME HERE..."
IT'S OVERGROWN, BUT MAYBE THE ORIGINAL FLOWERS ARE STILL HERE UNDER IT ALL.
HMMM...

IT LOOKS LIKE THE FLOWERS ARE UNDER THESE VINES, BUT THEY'RE ENTANGLED IN THESE...OTHER PLANTS.

IT LOOKS LIKE AN INVASIVE PLANT THAT'S TAKEN OVER.

OOOOOH...ooo

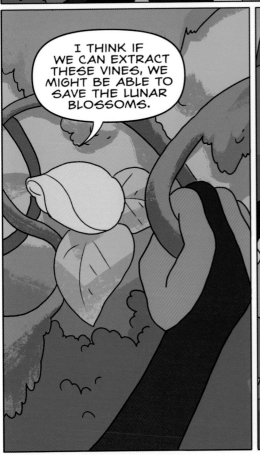

I THINK IF WE CAN EXTRACT THESE VINES, WE MIGHT BE ABLE TO SAVE THE LUNAR BLOSSOMS.

IF YOU SAY SO, G. LET'S DO THIS!

YEAH!

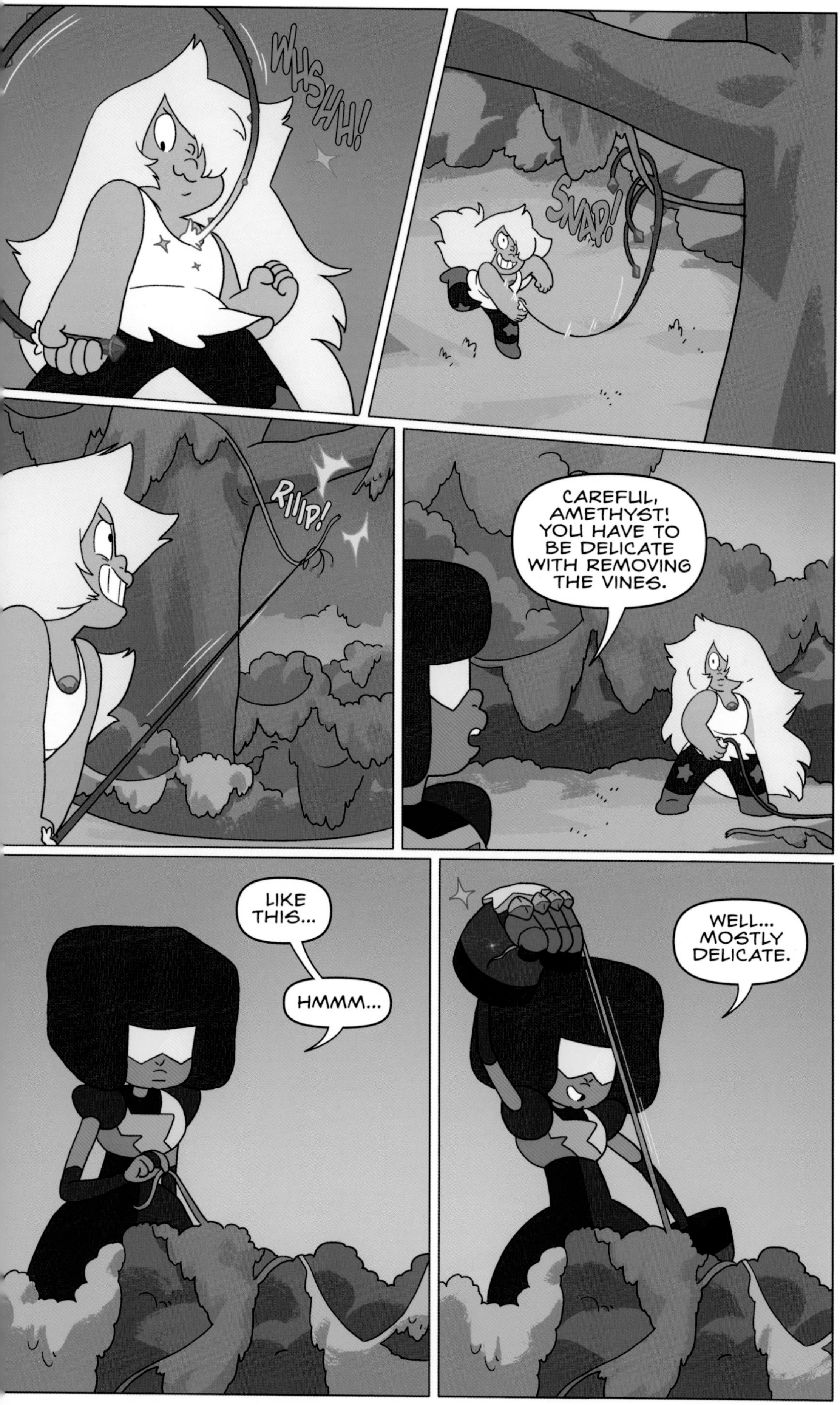
WHSHH!
SNAP!
RIIIP!
CAREFUL, AMETHYST! YOU HAVE TO BE DELICATE WITH REMOVING THE VINES.
LIKE THIS...
HMMM...
WELL... MOSTLY DELICATE.

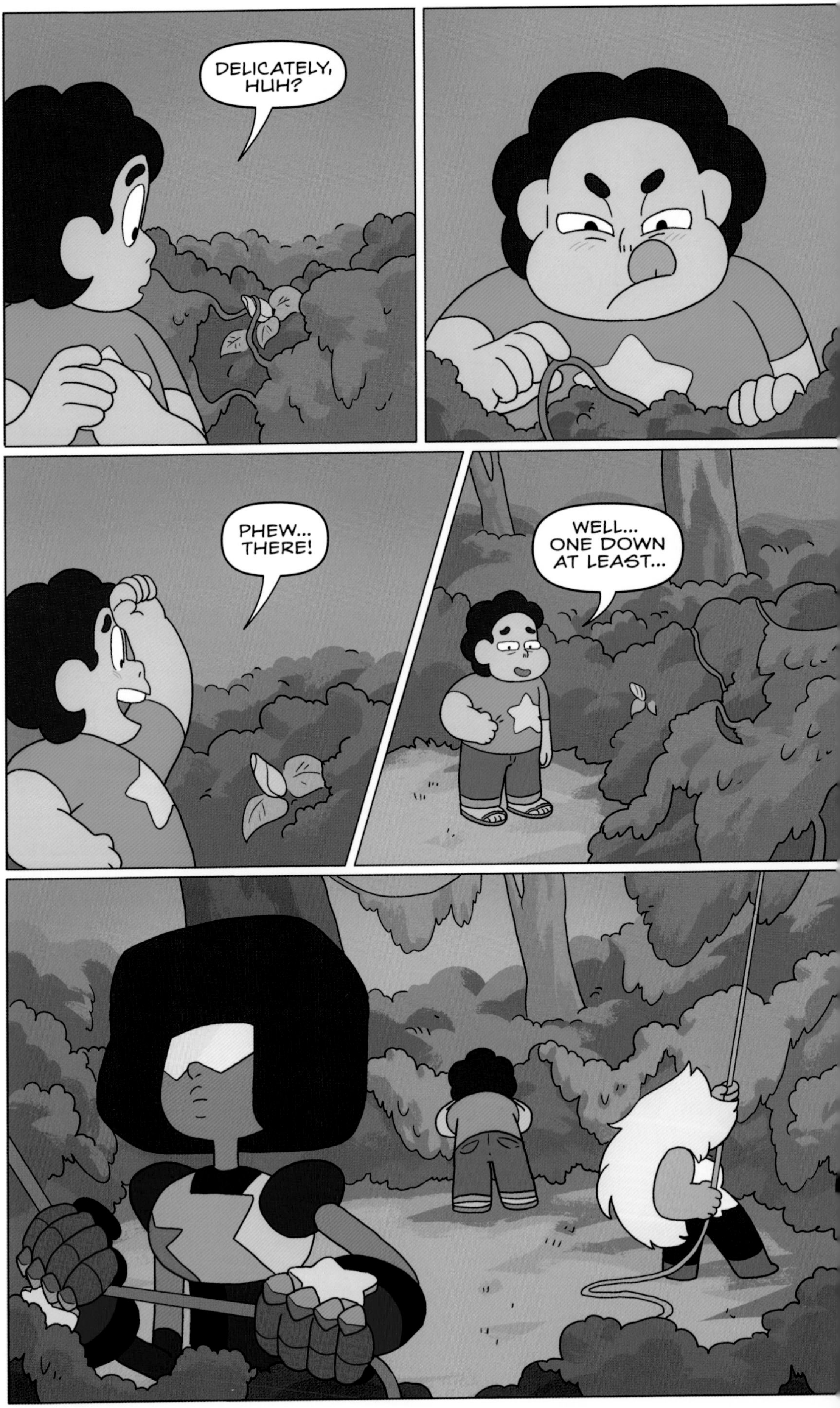
DELICATELY, HUH?
PHEW... THERE!
WELL... ONE DOWN AT LEAST...

HMM, SOMETHING STILL ISN'T RIGHT.

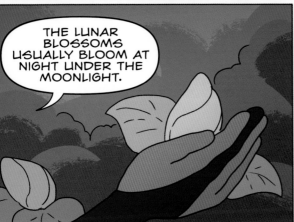

THE LUNAR BLOSSOMS USUALLY BLOOM AT NIGHT UNDER THE MOONLIGHT.

THAT'S IT! MAYBE IF WE LET SOME LIGHT IN...

WELL, IT MIGHT BE NIGHT, BUT THERE ISN'T MUCH MOONLIGHT IN HERE.

IT IS PRETTY DARK...

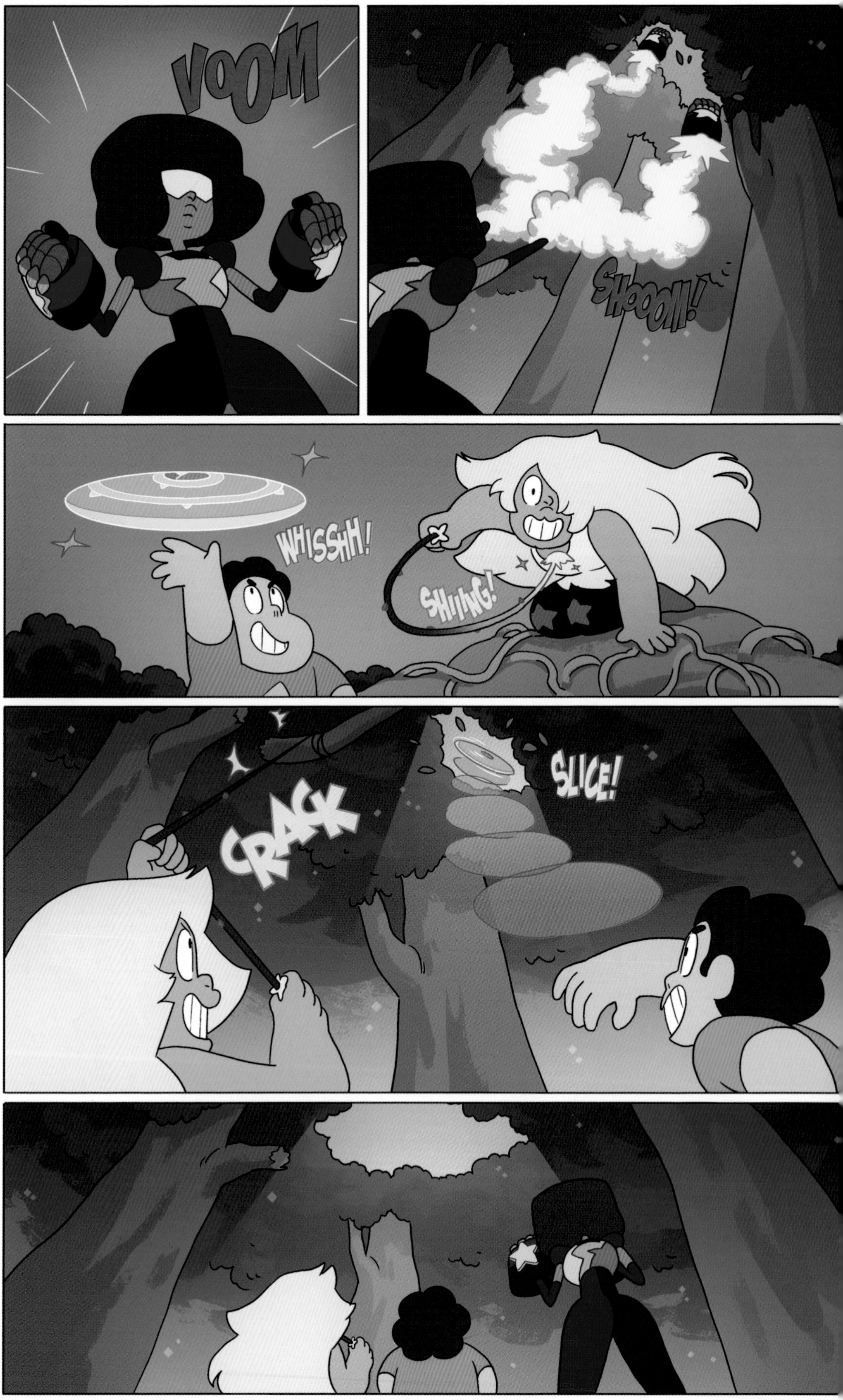
VOOM
SHOOOM!
WHISSHH!
SHIIING!
CRACK
SLICE!

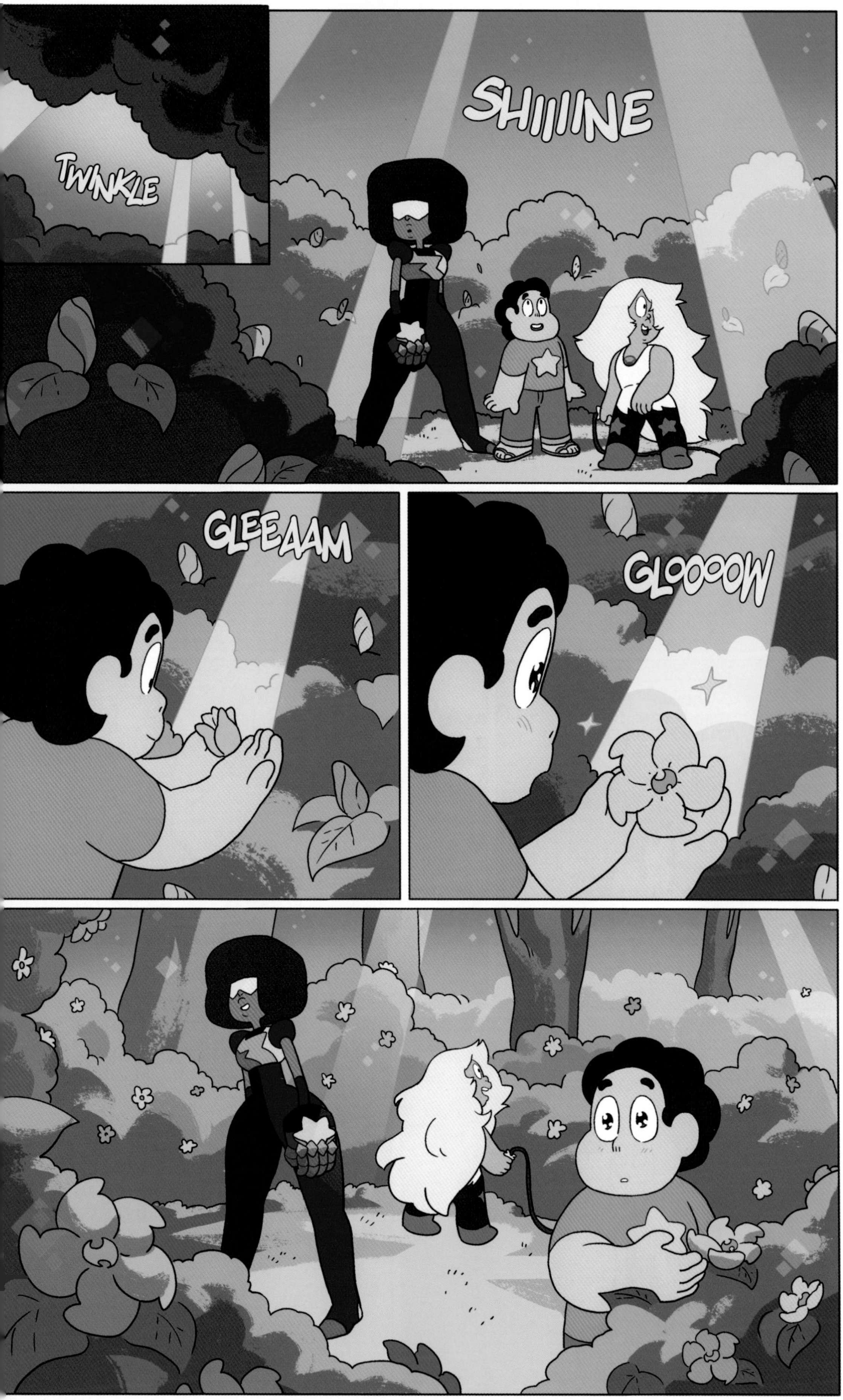

TWINKLE
SHIIIINE
GLEEAAM
GLOOOOW

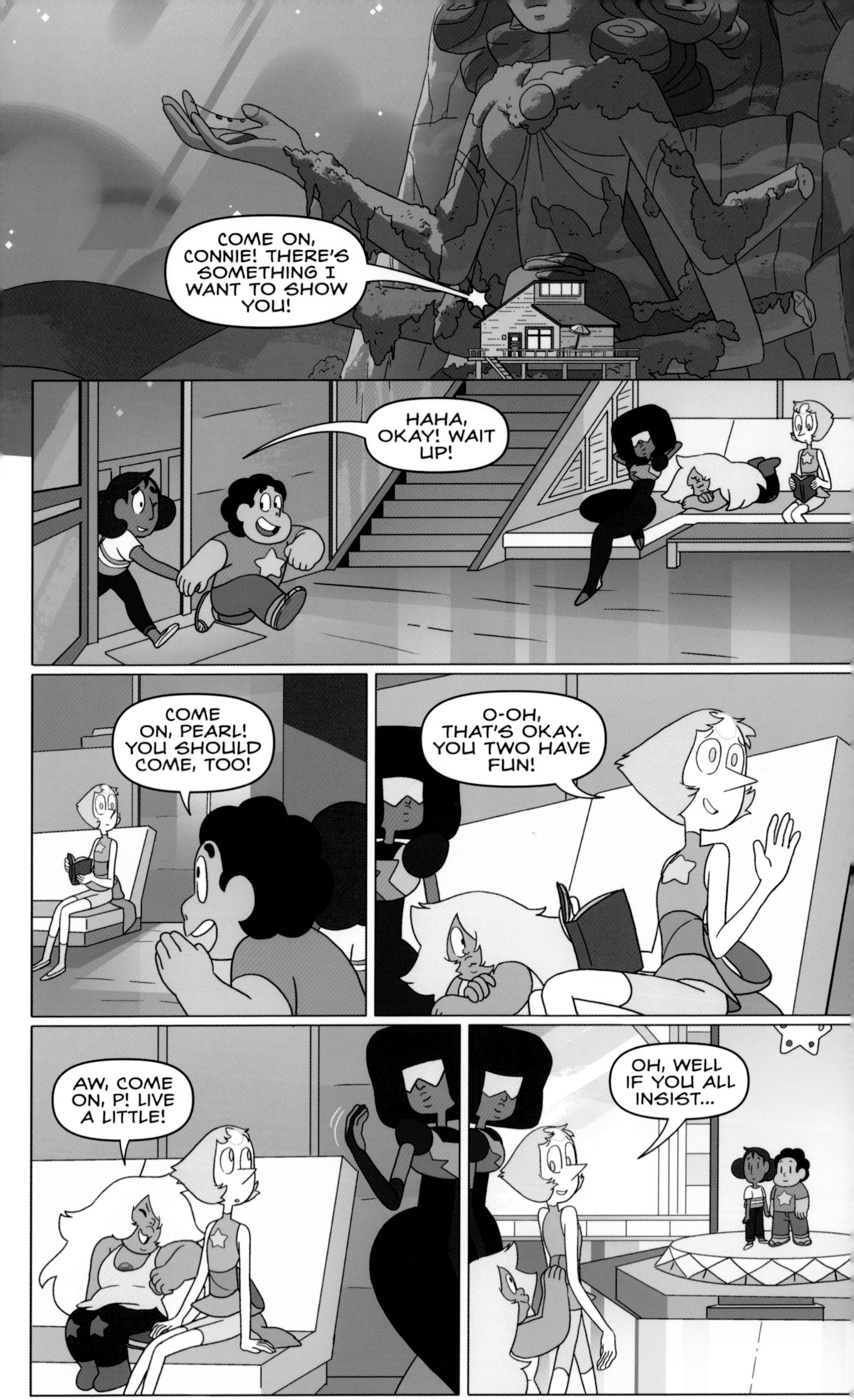
COME ON, CONNIE! THERE'S SOMETHING I WANT TO SHOW YOU!
HAHA, OKAY! WAIT UP!
COME ON, PEARL! YOU SHOULD COME, TOO!
O-OH, THAT'S OKAY. YOU TWO HAVE FUN!
AW, COME ON, P! LIVE A LITTLE!
OH, WELL IF YOU ALL INSIST...

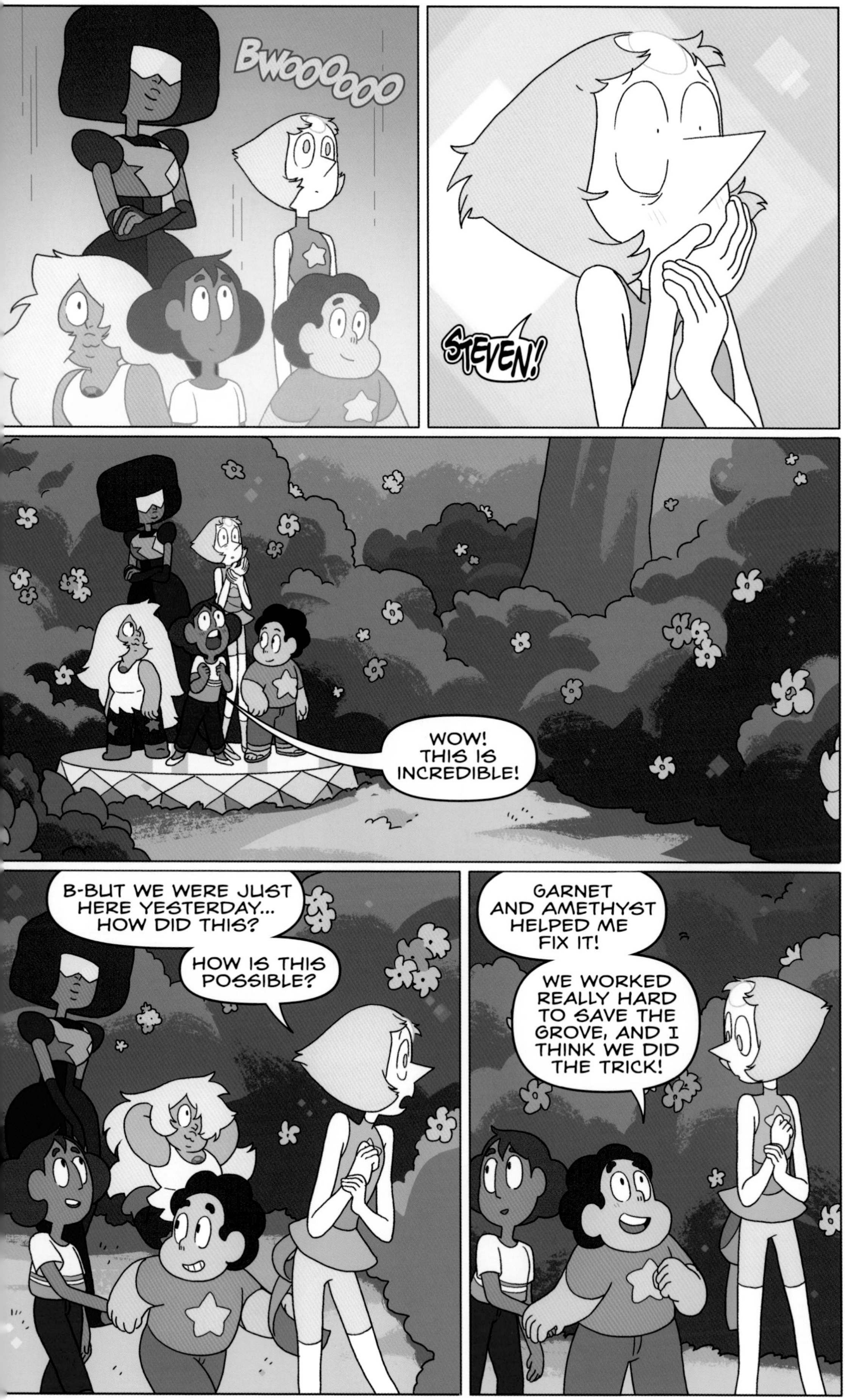
BWOOOOOO
STEVEN!
WOW! THIS IS INCREDIBLE!
B-BUT WE WERE JUST HERE YESTERDAY... HOW DID THIS?
HOW IS THIS POSSIBLE?
GARNET AND AMETHYST HELPED ME FIX IT!
WE WORKED REALLY HARD TO SAVE THE GROVE, AND I THINK WE DID THE TRICK!

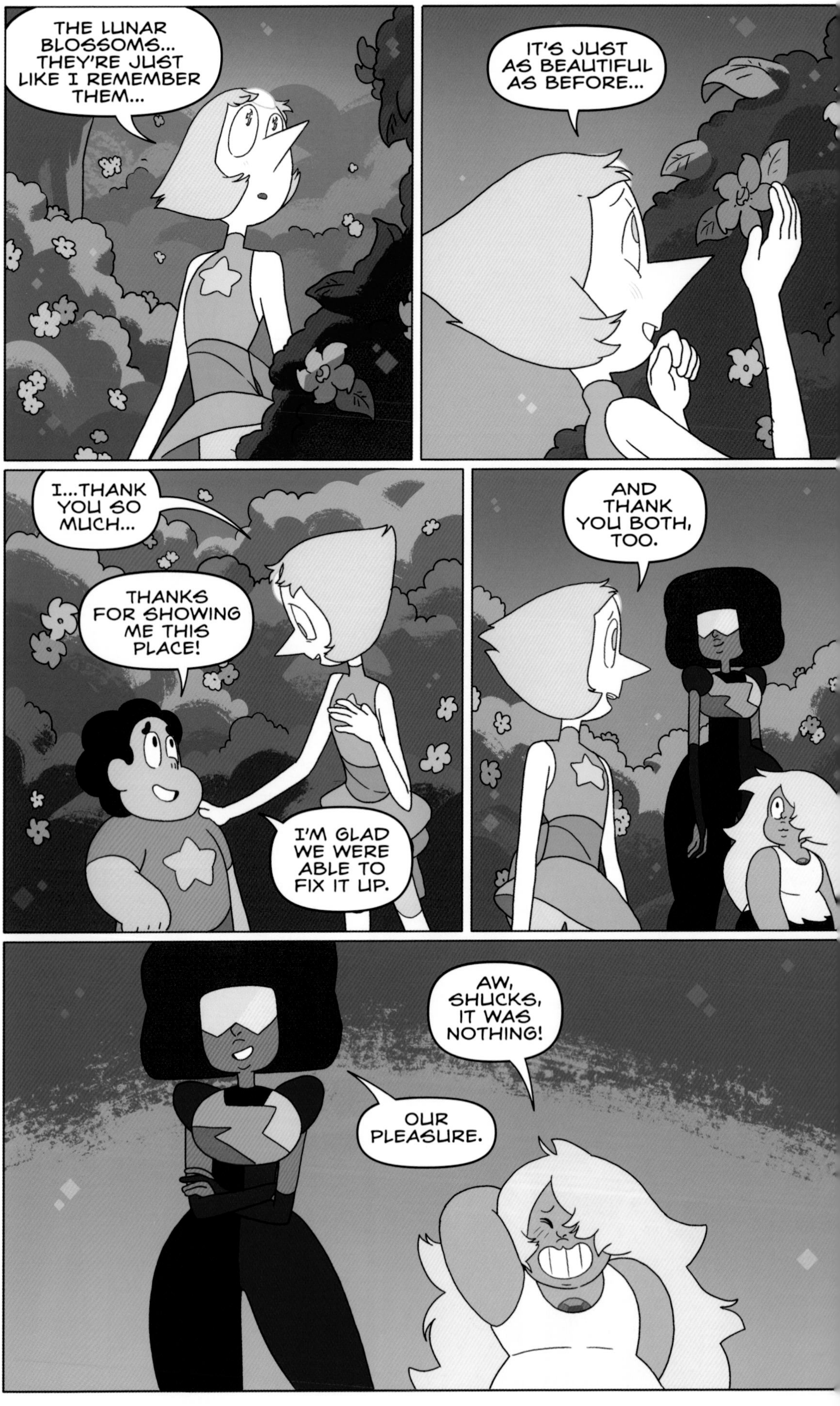
THE LUNAR BLOSSOMS... THEY'RE JUST LIKE I REMEMBER THEM...
IT'S JUST AS BEAUTIFUL AS BEFORE...
I...THANK YOU SO MUCH...
THANKS FOR SHOWING ME THIS PLACE!
I'M GLAD WE WERE ABLE TO FIX IT UP.
AND THANK YOU BOTH, TOO.
AW, SHUCKS, IT WAS NOTHING!
OUR PLEASURE.

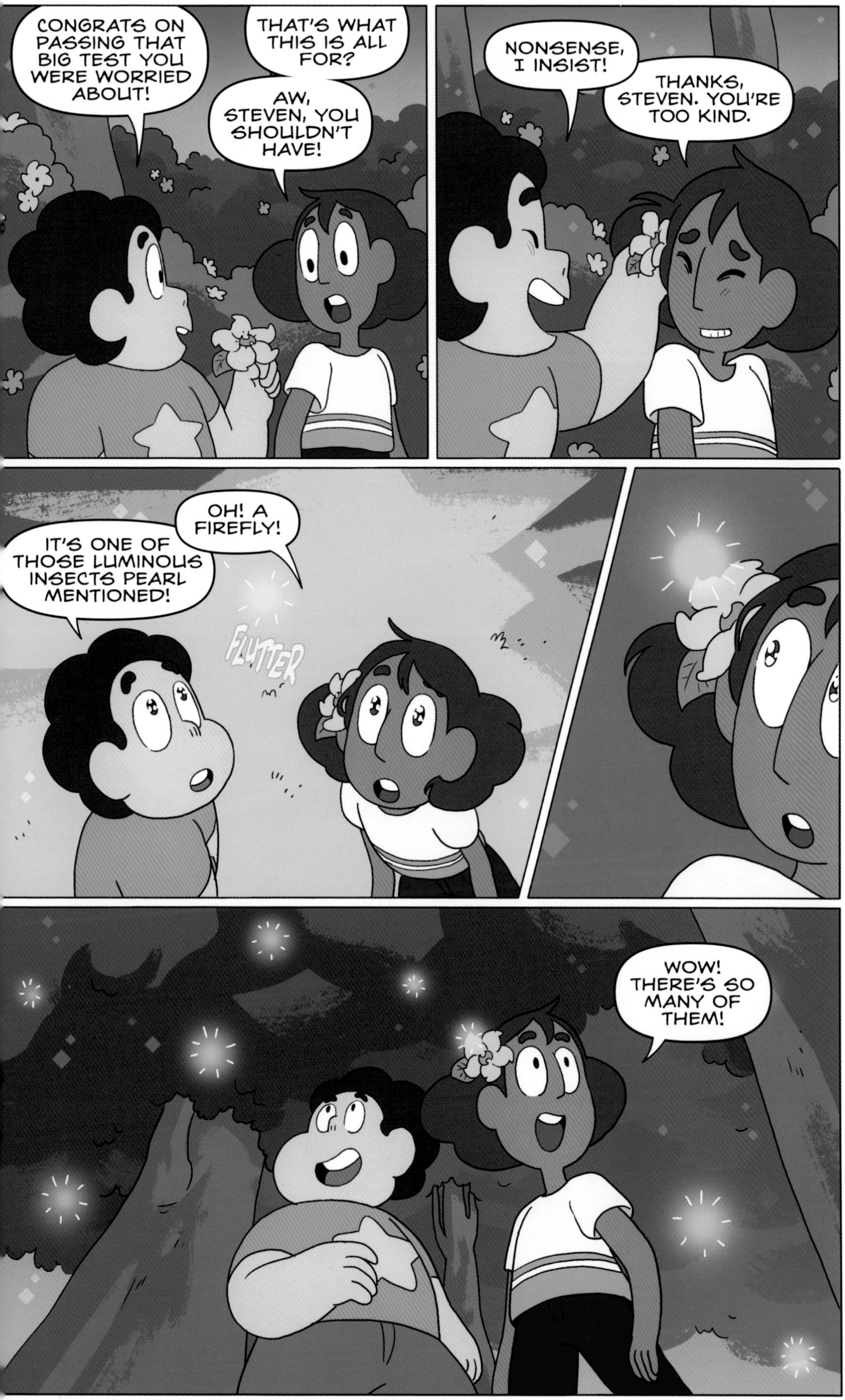
CONGRATS ON PASSING THAT BIG TEST YOU WERE WORRIED ABOUT!
THAT'S WHAT THIS IS ALL FOR?
AW, STEVEN, YOU SHOULDN'T HAVE!
NONSENSE, I INSIST!
THANKS, STEVEN. YOU'RE TOO KIND.
OH! A FIREFLY!
IT'S ONE OF THOSE LUMINOUS INSECTS PEARL MENTIONED!
FLUTTER
WOW! THERE'S SO MANY OF THEM!

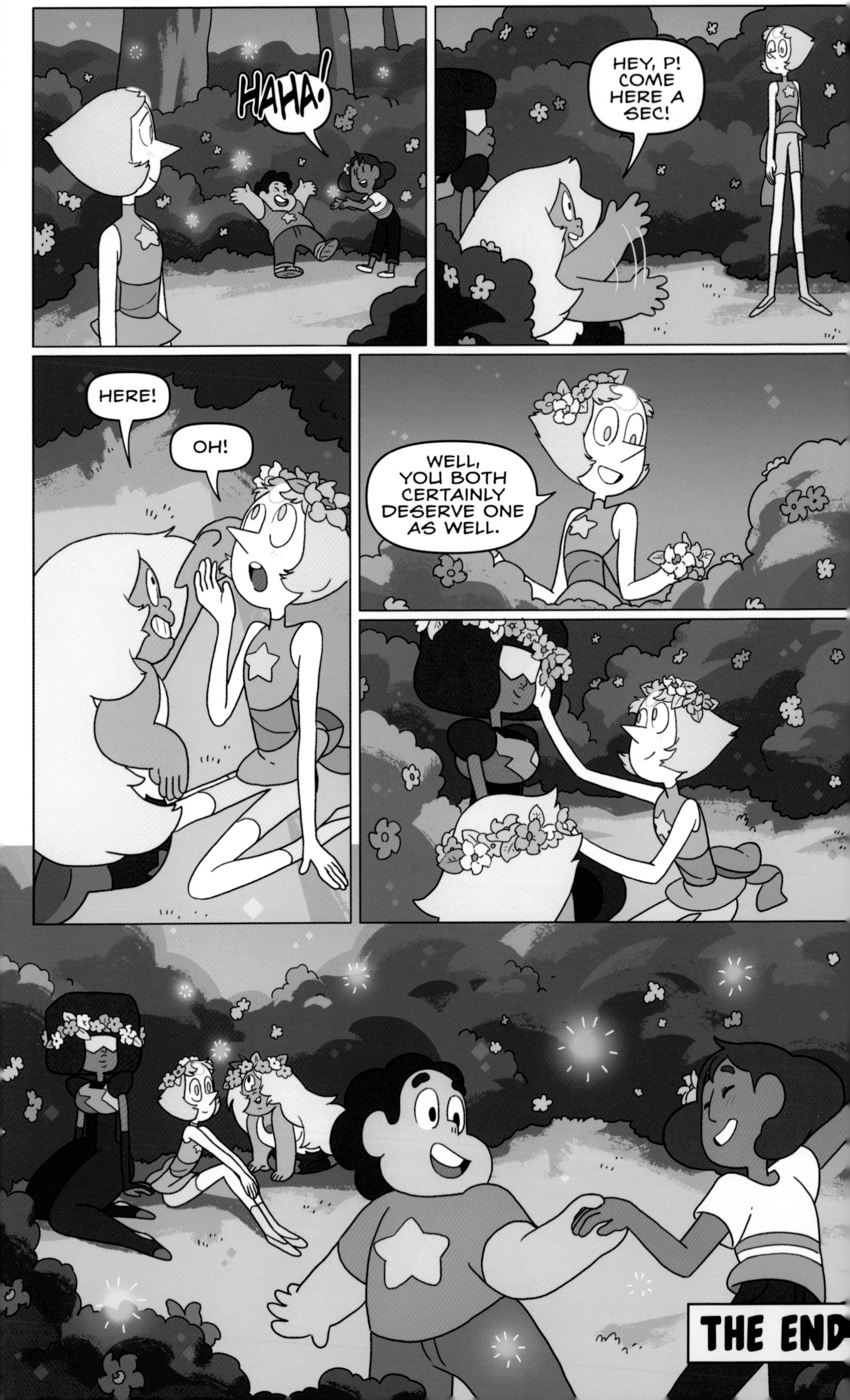
HAHA!
HEY, P! COME HERE A SEC!
HERE!
OH!
WELL, YOU BOTH CERTAINLY DESERVE ONE AS WELL.
THE END

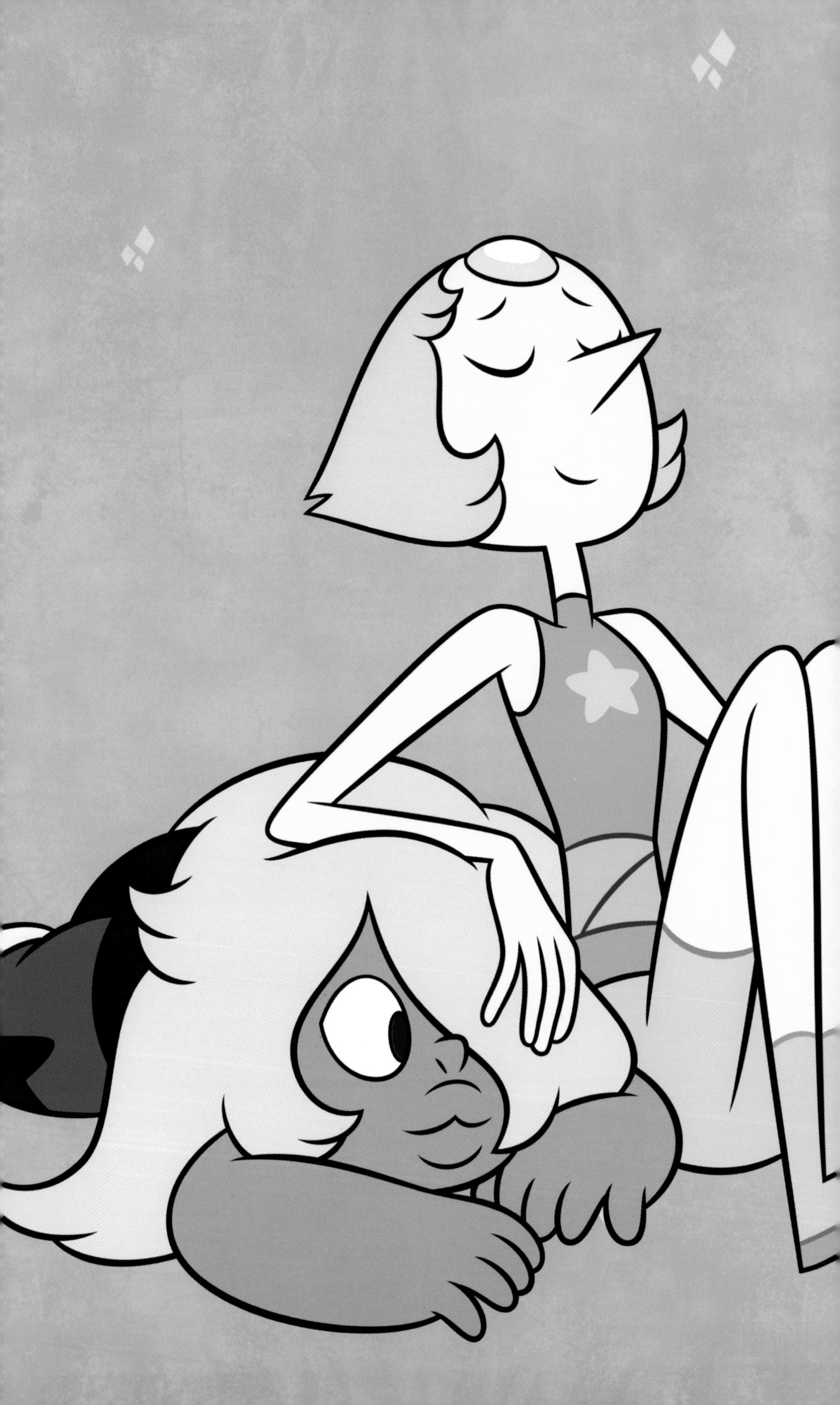

COVER GALLERY

issue twenty-one main cover
MISSY PEÑA

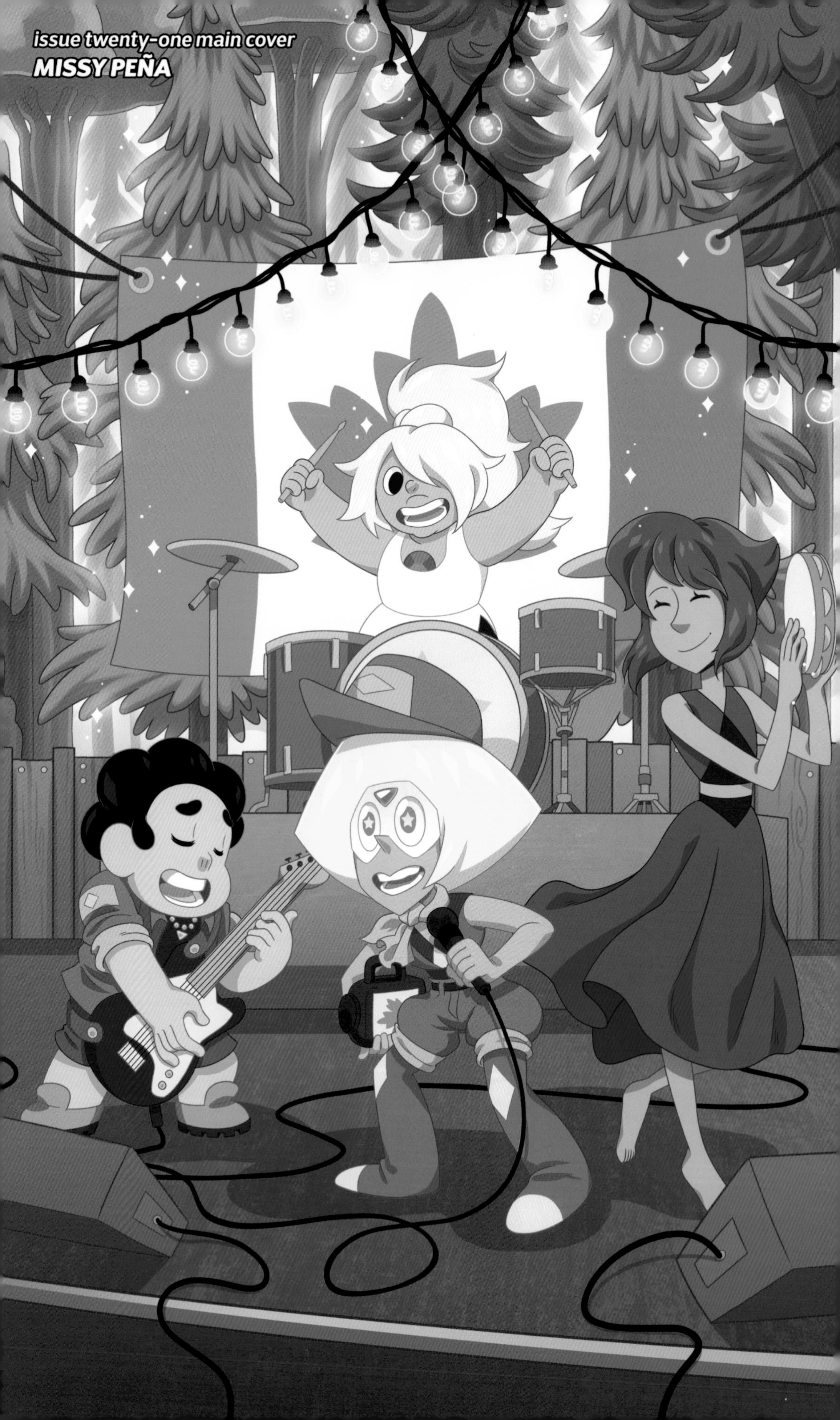

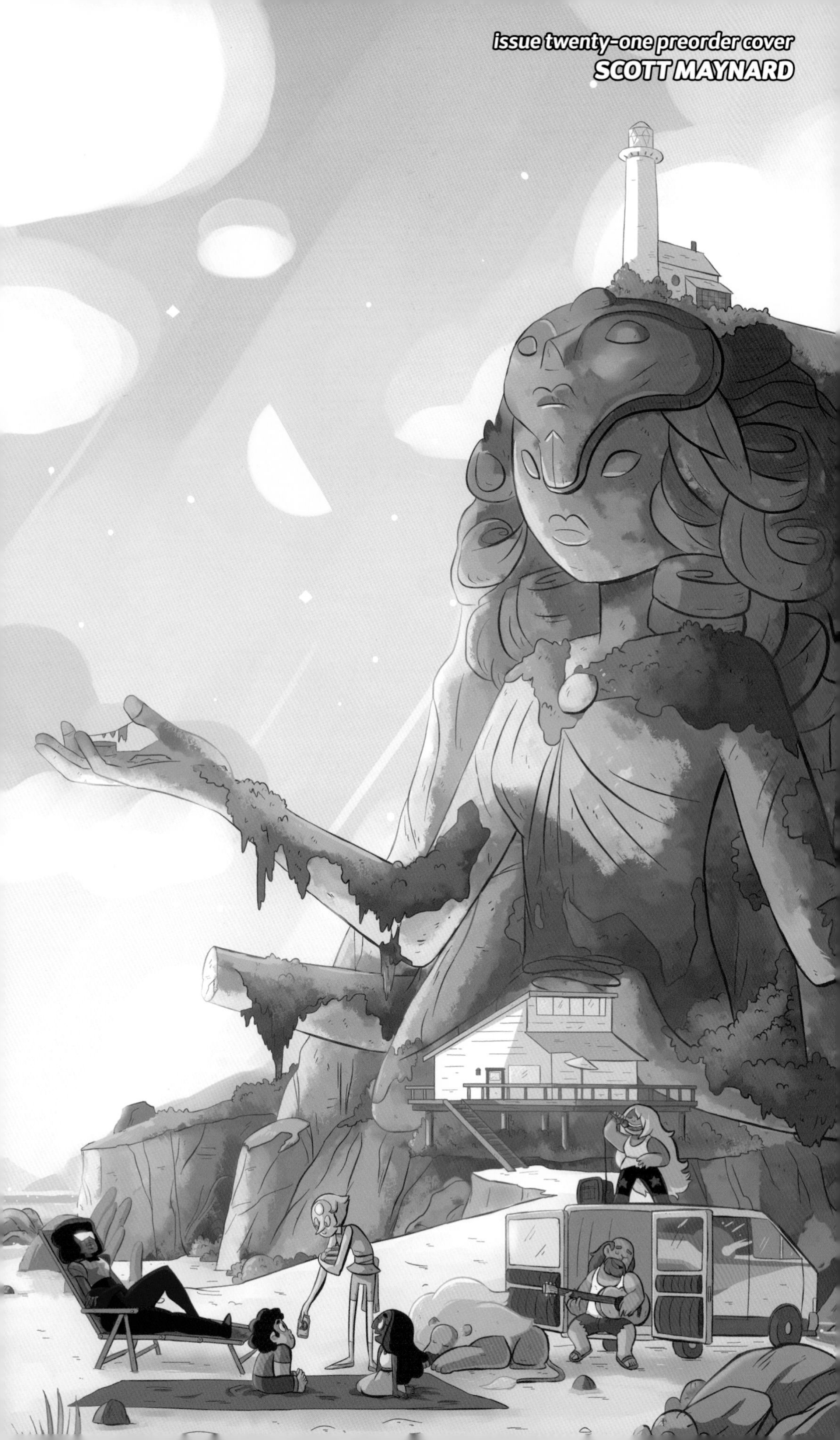

issue twenty-one preorder cover

SCOTT MAYNARD

issue twenty-two main cover
MISSY PEÑA

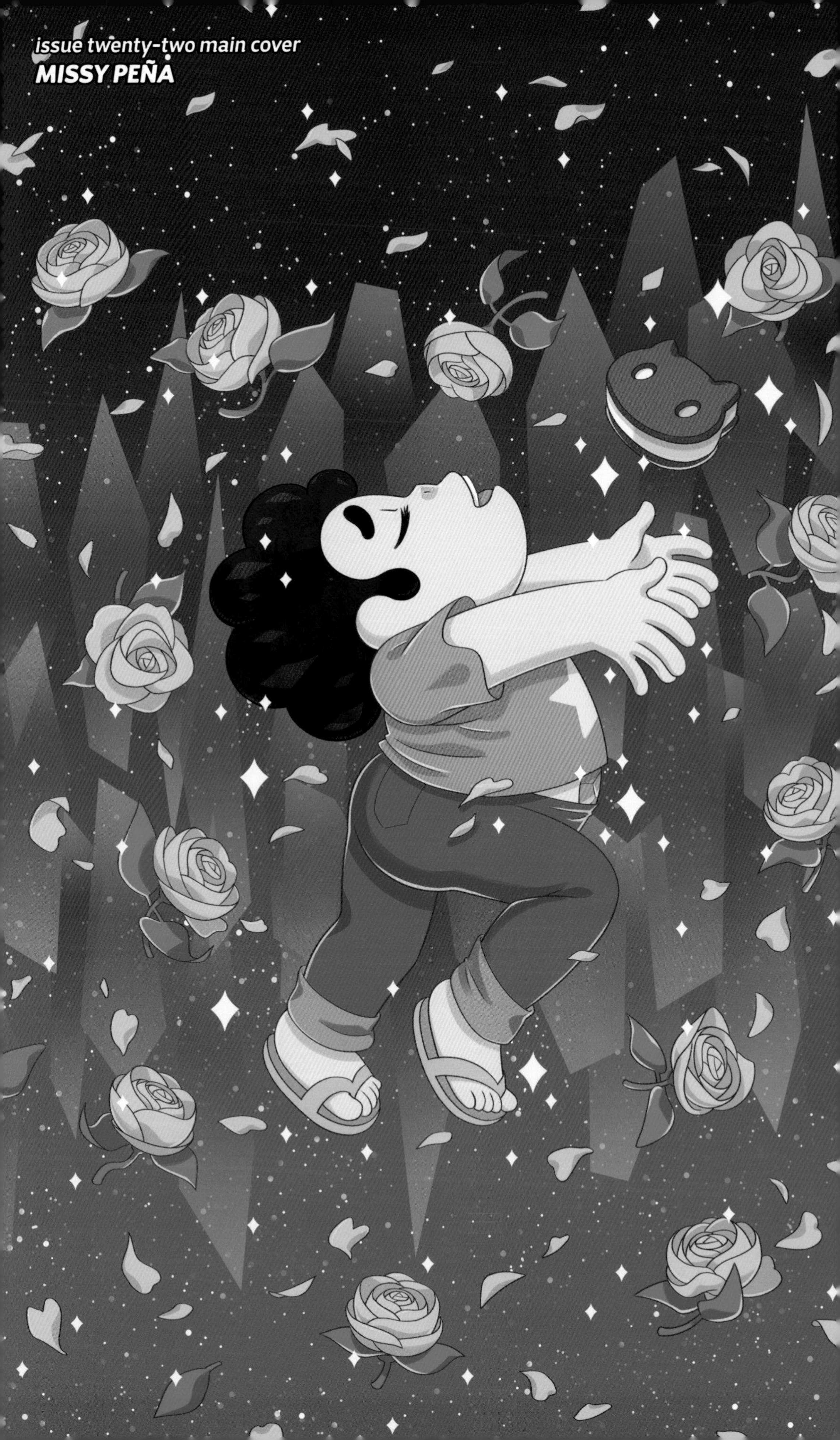

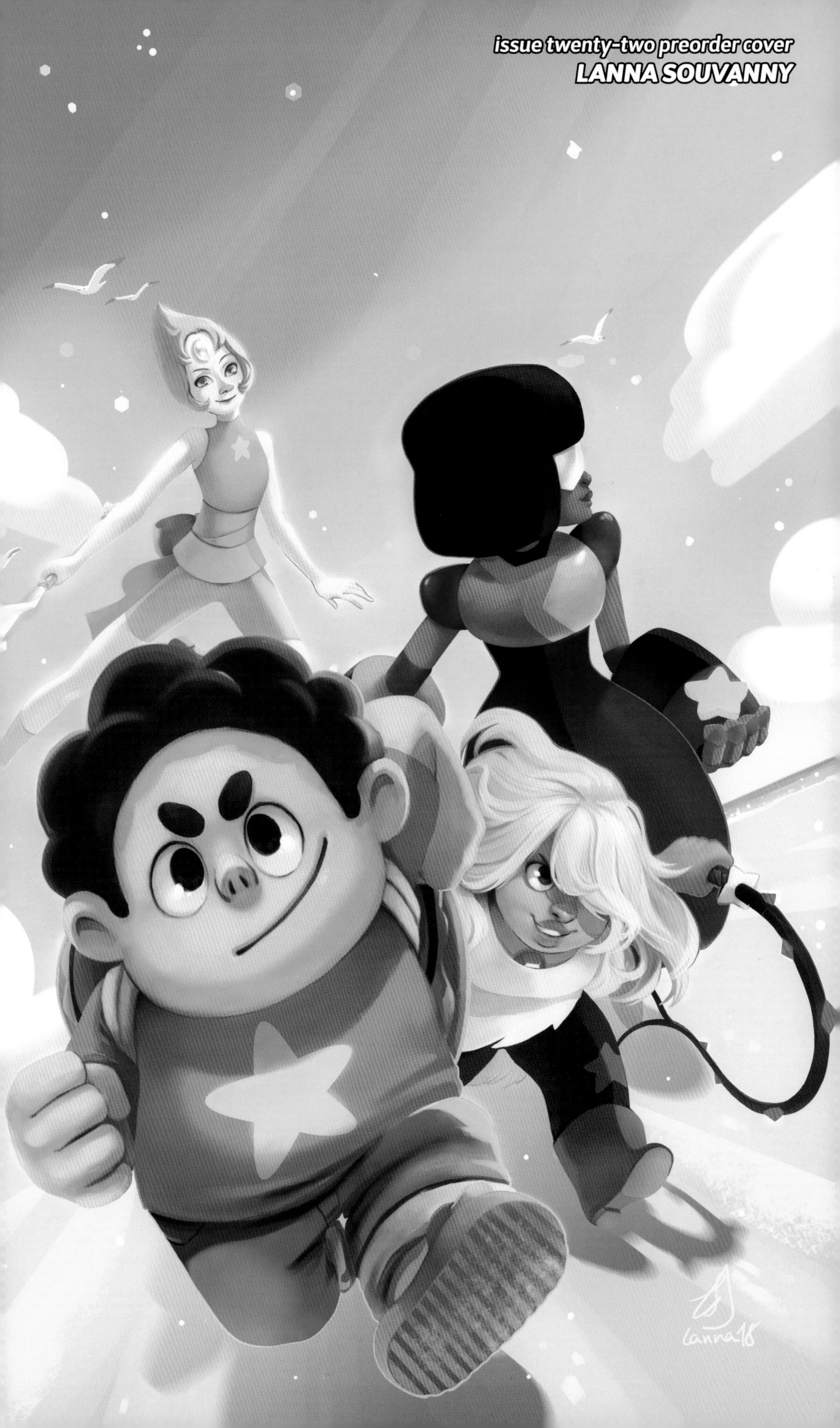
Lanna18
issue twenty-two preorder cover
LANNA SOUVANNY

issue twenty-three main cover
MISSY PEÑA

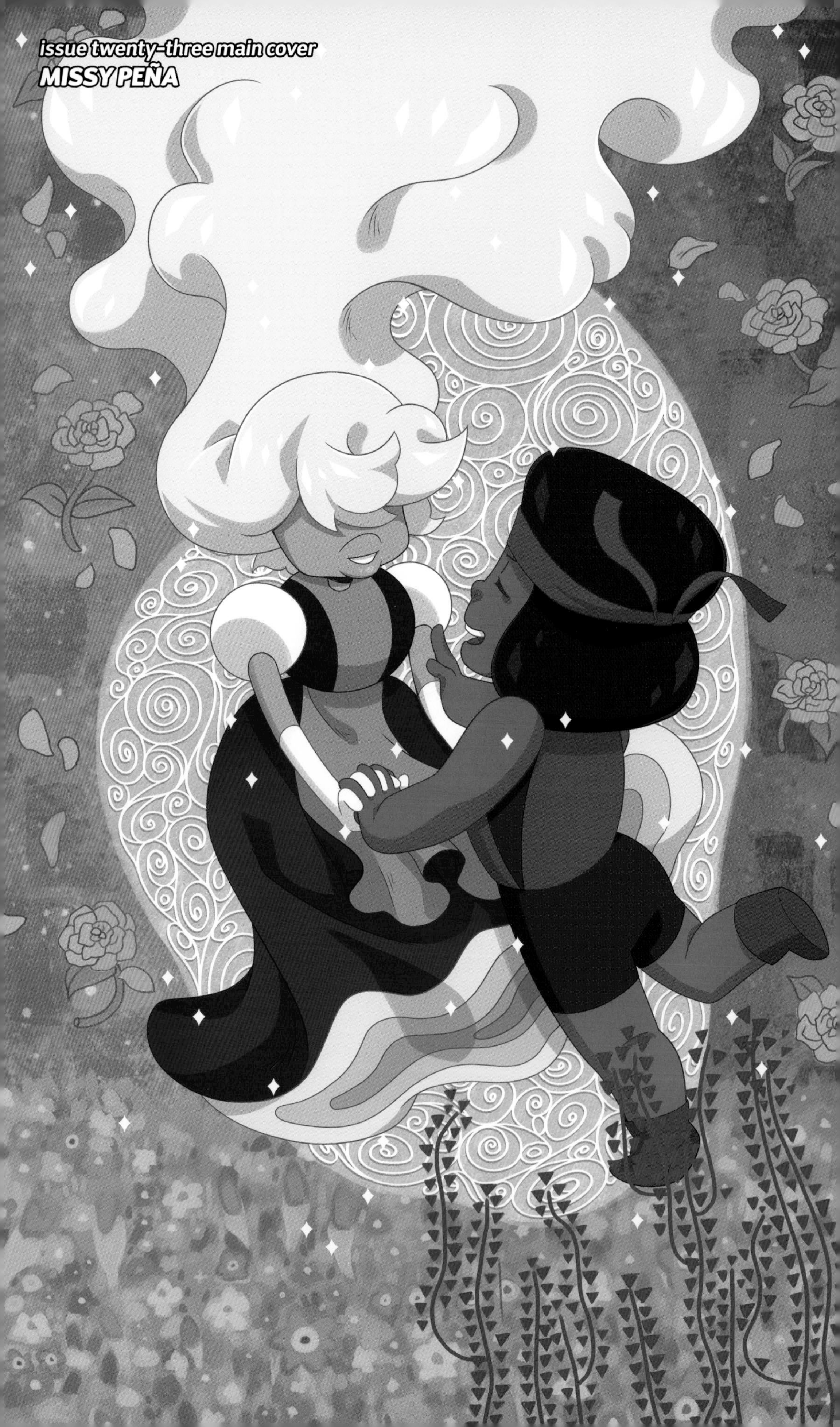

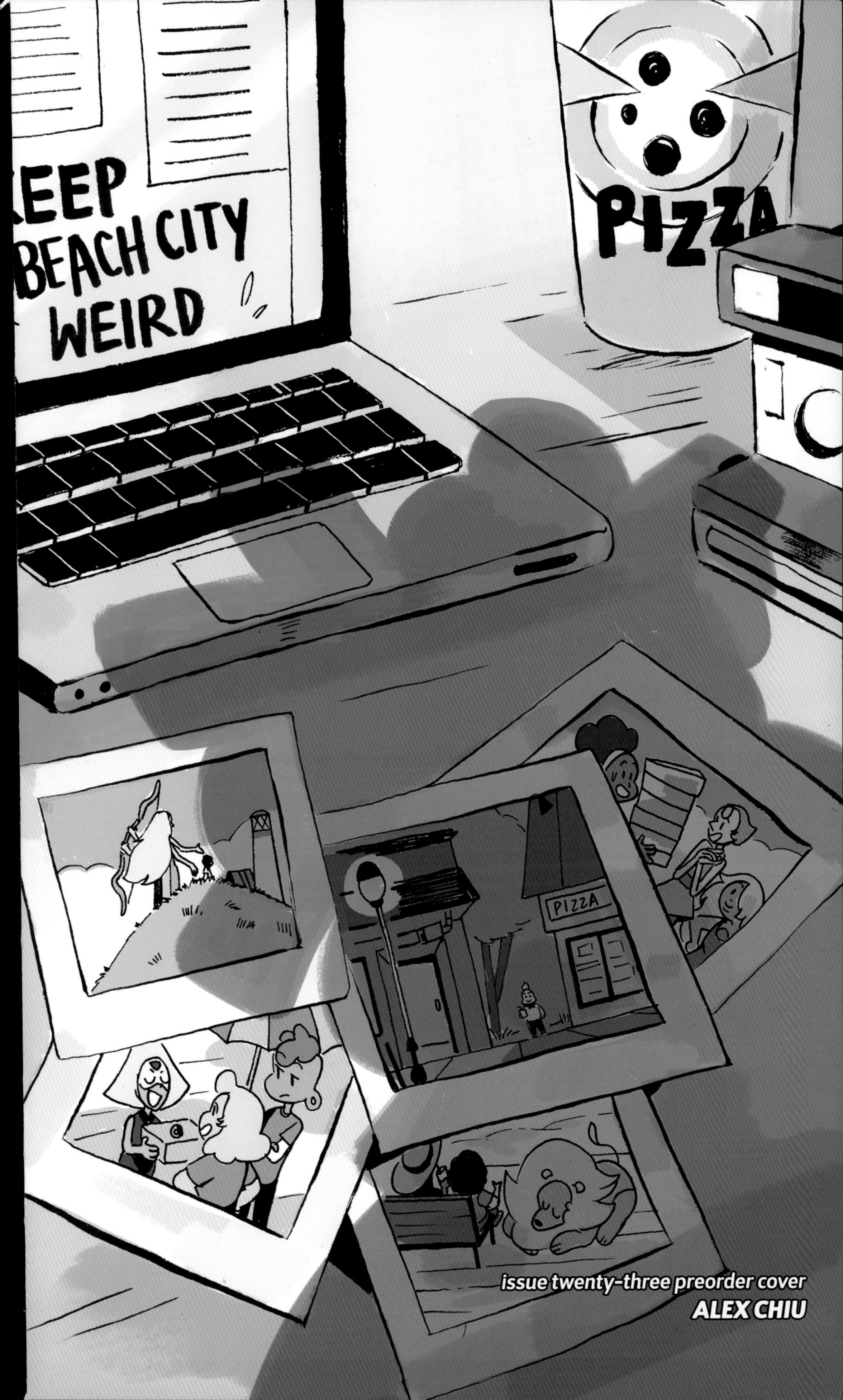

KEEP BEACH CITY WEIRD
PIZZA
PIZZA

issue twenty-three preorder cover
ALEX CHIU

issue twenty-four main cover

MISSY PEÑA

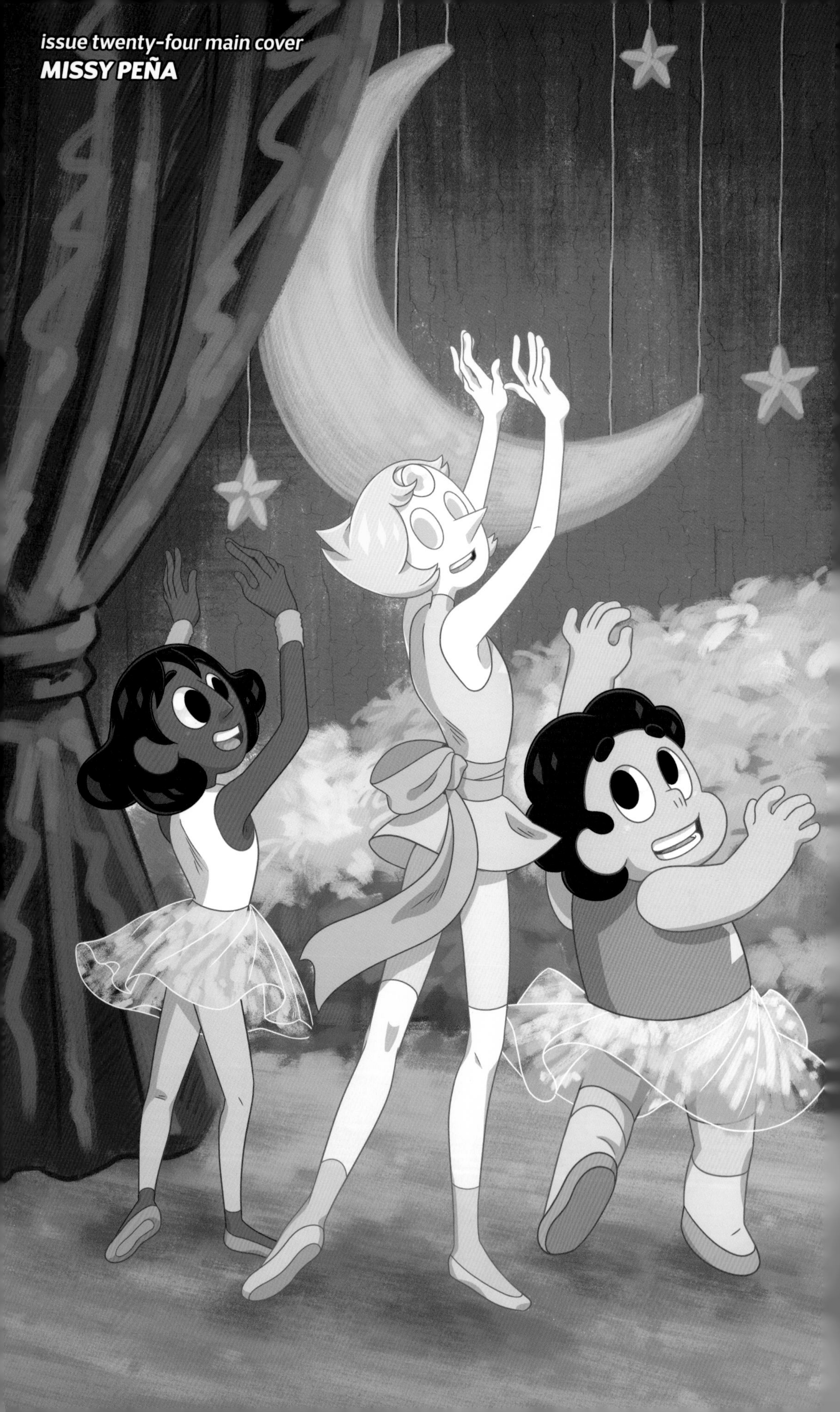

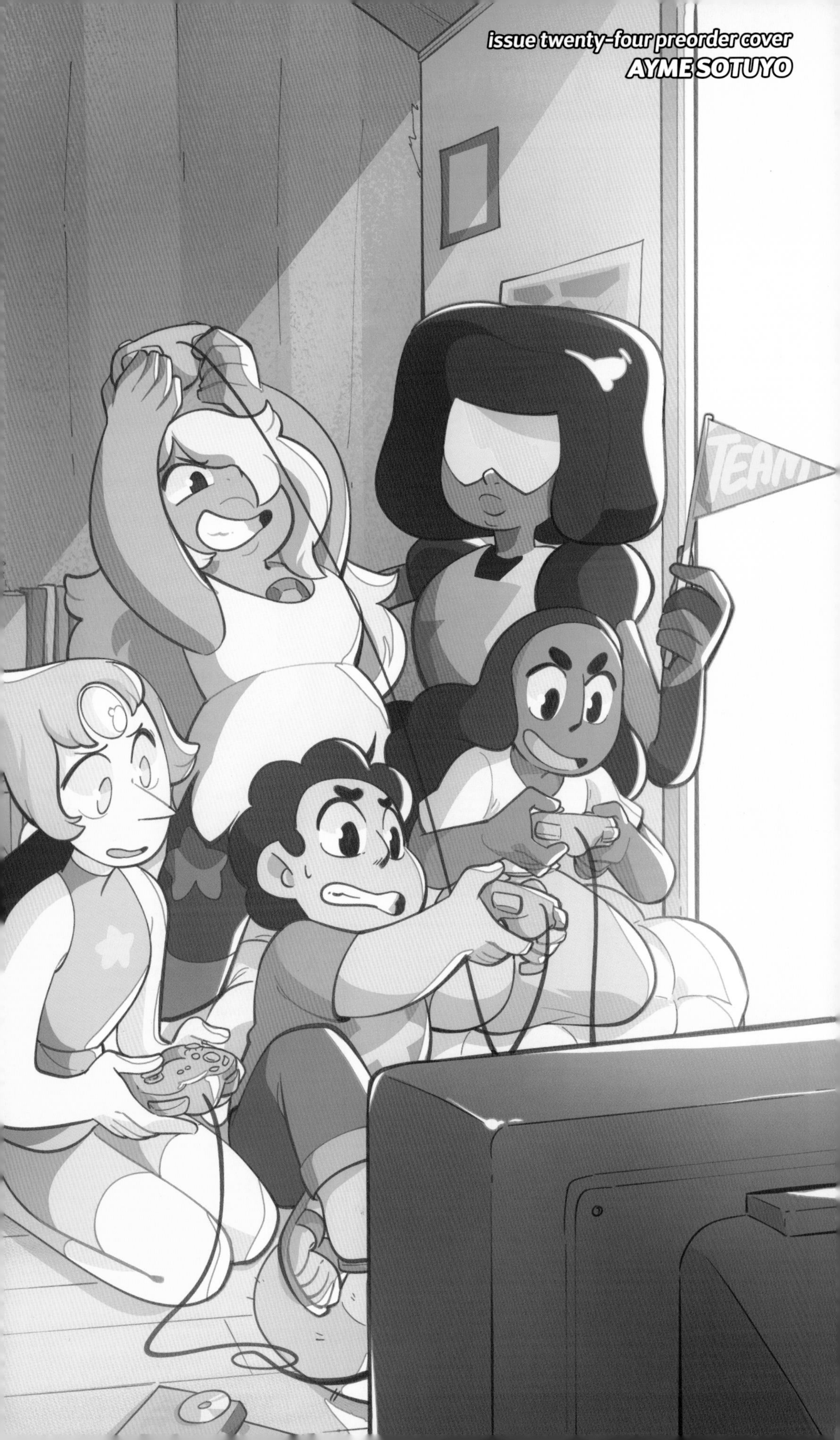
TEAM

issue twenty-four preorder cover
AYME SOTUYO

DISCOVER
EXPLOSIVE NEW WORLDS

ADVENTURE TIME

sam sykes · selina espiritu · sarah stern
BRAVE CHEF BRIANNA

KELLY THOMPSON BRIANNE DROUHARD M. VICTORIA ROBADO
MEGA PRINCESS

THE NOT-SO SECRET SOCIETY
DALEY · CRAFTS · CLARK · BRUNI

OVER THE GARDEN WALL

STEVEN UNIVERSE
VOLUME ONE

kaboom!™

AVAILABLE AT YOUR LOCAL COMICS SHOP AND BOOKSTORE

To find a comics shop in your area, visit www.comicshoplocator.com

WWW.**BOOM-STUDIOS**.COM

Adventure Time
Pendleton Ward and Others
Volume 1
ISBN: 978-1-60886-280-1 | $14.99 US
Volume 2
ISBN: 978-1-60886-323-5 | $14.99 US
Adventure Time: Islands
ISBN: 978-1-60886-972-5 | $9.99 US

The Amazing World of Gumball
Ben Bocquelet and Others
Volume 1
ISBN: 978-1-60886-488-1 | $14.99 US
Volume 2
ISBN: 978-1-60886-793-6 | $14.99 US

Brave Chef Brianna
Sam Sykes, Selina Espiritu
ISBN: 978-1-68415-050-2 | $14.99 US

Mega Princess
Kelly Thompson, Brianne Drouhard
ISBN: 978-1-68415-007-6 | $14.99 US

The Not-So Secret Society
Matthew Daley, Arlene Daley, Wook Jin Clark
ISBN: 978-1-60886-997-8 | $9.99 US

Over the Garden Wall
Patrick McHale, Jim Campbell and Others
Volume 1
ISBN: 978-1-60886-940-4 | $14.99 US
Volume 2
ISBN: 978-1-68415-006-9 | $14.99 US

Steven Universe
Rebecca Sugar and Others
Volume 1
ISBN: 978-1-60886-706-6 | $14.99 US
Volume 2
ISBN: 978-1-60886-796-7 | $14.99 US

Steven Universe & The Crystal Gems
ISBN: 978-1-60886-921-3 | $14.99 US

Steven Universe: Too Cool for School
ISBN: 978-1-60886-771-4 | $14.99 US